The Pig Goes
to Hog Heaven

The Pig Goes to Hog Heaven

Joseph Caldwell

DELPHINIUM BOOKS

HARRISON, NEW YORK • ENCINO, CALIFORNIA

Designed by Jonathan D. Lippincott

Library of Congress Cataloguing-in-Publication Data available on request.

ISBN 978-1-883285-45-6

11   12   RRD   10   9   8   7   6   5   4   3   2

To
My Mother
Whose all-purpose expletive
—in wonder or in wrath—
was
"Glory be to Saint Patrick!"

Author's Note

The reader should assume that the native Irish characters in this tale, when speaking among themselves, are speaking Irish, the first language of those living in County Kerry, Ireland, where the action takes place. What is offered here are American equivalents. When someone ignorant of the language is present, the characters resort to English.

"All's well that ends well."

—William Shakespeare
famous Irish playwright

The Pig Goes
to Hog Heaven

1

A aron McCloud, a reasonably young American writer as yet undistracted by fame or fortune, had come to Ireland, to County Kerry, to the shores of the Western Sea, to bewail the refusal of an inordinately plain woman to cooperate in his determination that he become the object of her undying love. However, through the inexplicable offices of a wayward and willful pig, he had, before his anguish had found meaningful expression, fallen in love with—and subsequently married—an inordinately beautiful auburn-haired Kerry swineherd, Lolly McKeever. Then, to further remove him from his American routine, Lolly, possibly through an osmosis derived from the age-old supposition that in marriage the two become as one, decided to become a writer, leaving Aaron to slop her pigs.

This he had done, not without satisfaction. Swine-herding, he discovered, had more similarities than he had suspected to the writing of a novel: an unremitting commitment, an unrelenting discipline, an uncertain outcome, and, ultimately, the unpredictable prospects when the time for marketing arrived.

For Aaron the swineherd, that day had come to pass. And it proved to be quite possibly the greatest triumph of his life. Riding now in the emptied truck, his adored wife driving at his side through the narrow roads of County Kerry, he had no means to suppress the euphoria surging through him. The sale of the pigs, fed and fattened under his tuition, had brought in profits well beyond even his wife's encouraging expectations.

His writing, two novels completed in his thirty-two years, had not gone unnoted, but they came nowhere near the remuneration the slaughterhouse had just forked over. In truth, this was the result he had obsessively longed for. A few semi-favorable reviews and an obscure prize were all well and good, but to have one's labors—either as a writer or as a swineherd—given such an extravagant evaluation provoked in him a retroactive satisfaction for all the pig-filled days and nights when failure was a constant threat, fidelity its own reward, and marketing possibilities the source of an unbearable apprehension.

To intensify his euphoria, there had arrived that very morning an e-mail from a Dublin literary agent—the same woman who had steered Aaron's Irish aunt Kitty, also a novelist, to heights of renown, a pinnacle Aaron, in his more delusional moments, had presumed to be reserved for himself. That his wife would ascend in the same direction as his aunt was a thought he'd done his faltering best to avoid, but the fear, thank God, proved unfounded. The agent, to Aaron's intermittently shame-filled relief, had been somewhat impolitic.

"Lolly McKeever," the e-mail began. (Lolly had submitted the manuscript under her birth name, not wanting to be confused with Kitty McCloud.) "I have read with some interest the novel you so kindly sent, and which will be returned to you shortly through the post. It is beyond doubt the most regressive tale about Ireland, about the Irish, written by a citizen of this country within the previous century or, quite possibly, within more than several centuries past. A haunted castle? Whatever were you thinking? And the ghosts, we are asked to believe, are actually present, not even justifying their appearance as the objects of a fevered brain. Soon you will be writing about leprechauns and little people and pots of gold and Hags and Seers and kingdoms hidden under the earth. Forgive me—or, rather, don't forgive me—because it must be said: You've disgraced your native land and all the people in it. And your attitude toward the Anglo-Ascendancy? Cannot the past be relegated to the past? Are we expected to have our righteous wrath aroused by misdeeds committed so many years ago? Have we not advanced beyond the eternal cries against wrongs inflicted upon our ancestors long departed? Please allow me to offer some explanation for your misguided efforts. I have been informed that your husband, Aaron McCloud, nephew of the estimable Kitty McCloud, is an American and reputed to be a writer. It is my surmise that he, not you, wrote this abomination. No one native-born in Erin could possibly be so ignorant of what Ireland is and who the Irish are. Only an American of Irish descent—still wallowing in complaints long since exhausted—would dare to insult current Irish sophistication by claiming that ghosts roam the land and are seen and accepted by adults educated in Irish schools and reared in modern Irish ways. Only an American, whose people abandoned Ireland in distant times, would promote a sense of outrage against the English to whom we are now reconciled except for some sullen Catholics in the north. The British, after all, have become our most active trading partner and a ready market for Irish exports. I do hope this exoneration, this naming of your American husband, is, for your sake, applicable. Allow me, in charity, to assume so.

"One thing more: I suggest that your husband renounce all literary pretensions and, with your assistance and at your insistence, invite you—a born Irishwoman with, no doubt, tales of her own to tell—to take his place at the computer while he becomes, for once and forever, a keeper of pigs. I most strongly propose it. The future of Irish letters demands it. Most sincerely, Fiona O'Toole."

During her time as a writer, Lolly, if she had not lost all her mirth, had been deprived of a goodly portion of her characteristic enjoyment of calamity. Uncertainty and doubt, as well as fears for her self-sufficiency, were emotions so new to her that she lacked the equipment to control, if not conquer, them. Only when, with cheerful impatience, she had been schooling Aaron in the joys of slopping pigs did she again become herself, a reversion now completed, thanks to Ms. O'Toole's brutality.

Rather than dismiss the woman's words as the blind and ignorant rant of an obvious incompetent—a reaction Aaron himself had had to resort to on more than one occasion—Lolly had, with raucous delight, required her husband to repeat out loud choice passages that intensified her hilarity and heightened the pitch of her laughter. She was, however, disappointed that Ms. O'Toole had failed to properly disdain the plot's resolution: to be rid of the ghosts, blow up the castle. This absurd denouement had been suggested by Kitty and her husband, Kieran, when Lolly had appealed to them for some way to bring the entire debacle to an acceptable conclusion And the absurdity increased when they further suggested that gunpowder was already planted in the flagstones of the castle's great hall. Lolly was embarrassed by this want of invention, but, innocent that she was, she did as she was told. Why had the agent not remarked on this obvious failure of the imagination?

But when Lolly had said to Aaron, "Read again the part about it must have been you who wrote it. That part."

"I think once is enough, thank you."

As the drive continued, he felt even more acutely an unease that had earlier intruded on his present satisfactions. With the delivery of the pigs that had so greatly benefited from his ministrations, and with the unmourned novel's ruthless demise, he and Lolly would now return to their previous callings, he to his computer, she to her pigs. Why he failed to feel all that eager to get on with his career was a subject he preferred not to examine. He would concentrate, as much as possible, on the day's triumph, with an unarticulated promise that, if necessary, he would allow the source of his unease to reveal itself at a time of its own choosing—which, if he were lucky, would be never.

Intentional or not, their present seating in the cab of the truck symbolized the day's reversion: On the way to market, with the pigs on board, Aaron had driven. Now, as they moved along the road with their lightened load, Lolly was driving.

They had gone some distance when Aaron realized they were not headed for home, where the surviving pigs would be protesting the delay in their scheduled feeding. He had become aware that the truck was coming not just close to where the cliffs fronted the sea, but to the site where Aaron's Aunt Kitty's house once had stood. The altered landscape was now marked by a wave-battered cove; the house itself, as well as the garden, pasture, and an empty grave, had long been drawn down and swallowed by an adamant sea.

"Where are we going?" he asked.

"You'll see when we get there."

"You're going to where the house used to be. I can tell."

"If you can tell, what need is there for me to do the same?"

"But why do you want to go there?"

"Isn't it obvious? It's because I want to."

"There's nothing there. Just the cliff and the sea and not even the land where the house used to be."

"If there's nothing there, why object?"

"I'm not objecting. I'm just curious."

"Maybe I have no reason."

"You always have a reason."

"There's a first time for everything."

When her husband failed to challenge her further, Lolly decided to apply a mild goad. "I don't have to tell you everything. Can't I have reasons of my own?"

"Okay. Okay."

They were getting closer to the sea. Aaron sat up straighter in the passenger seat and examined his wife's face in the rearview mirror. She was as exquisite as ever. As he watched, she reached up and smoothed an eyebrow that had no need of attention. She puckered then relaxed her lips. They were, as they had always been, full and luscious. Surely he was the most fortunate of men. He returned his gaze to the road ahead. This was the woman who loved him. Him. Aaron McCloud. Rather than ask outright for some verification of her affections, he said, "Is it because that's where we realized we were in love? Is that why?"

Lolly answered with a noncommittal no.

"Is it because you want to see if anything of the house has washed back onto shore?"

"I'm not telling."

"Then don't."

"I won't."

"Fine with me."

"Fine with me, too."

"All right then."

With as much indifference as he could summon, Aaron glanced out the side window. They were on a narrow road that would intersect with the one that ran closer to the edge of the cliffs, the old boundary of the McCloud property that had boasted a house of stone, two stories high, with well-appointed rooms, some of their windows looking out over a stretch of meadow that ended at the precipice that dropped to the sea below. Nothing was left now, the meadow having been eroded bit by bit over the years, and the house itself ultimately delivered in one great gulp into the sea—after which Lolly McKeever and Aaron McCloud, Kieran Sweeney and Kitty McCloud, had all admitted to their love. It was as if, now free of the house and all its complicated history, they were able to see into their hearts and find there a surprising and inevitable ardor that would sustain their lives for all time to come. Or so they hoped. Or so they expected.

It should be mentioned that it wasn't just the remnants of the meadow and the fine stone house that had been claimed by the waves. Nor was it only the chattel accumulated by more than several generations of McClouds. In the house at the time of the havoc wreaked by the roiling waters and the insistent winds was a laid-out skeleton, handsomely clothed, resting in a coffin of fine boards and embroidered cushions.

The bones of Declan Tovey, master thatcher and celebrated seducer, who was murdered and then buried with the tools of his trade in the garden of Aaron's aunt, had been unearthed by the rootings of a pig.

The murder had never been solved, the identity of the murderer complicated by the last-minute confessions of no fewer than three of those attending the irreverent Irish wake of the unfortunate Mr. Tovey: Lolly McKeever, Aaron's Aunt Kitty, and Kitty's new husband, Kieran Sweeney. One by one each had claimed credit for the thatcher's despatch, complete with motive and method. Aaron himself, the fourth participant in the burial rites, suspected but couldn't verify that each in turn might be protecting one of the others, making it impossible to identify the one true malefactor among them.

(The authorities, of course, were not allowed to get involved. The crime concerned Lolly, Kitty, and Kieran, and no one else. Also, who would go to the gardaí and implicate one of their own? Although years had passed since the days of Irish oppression, the word *informer* still retained a stench sufficient to gag even the most vengeful proponent of that most elusive ideal of all: justice.)

It should be remembered as well that part of the attraction that fulfilled itself in the marriage of Lolly and Aaron, then of Kitty and Kieran, was the possibility that one might be marrying a murderer, bringing to the conjugal couch an implicit forgiveness along with a hint of courage that one would place oneself in so perilous a situation for the rest of one's life. To sleep night after night next to a possible killer is hardly conducive to deepest repose, but since all marriage commitments are founded on risk, on the unknowable, on the brave surrender to uncertainty, why would something so touchingly rash as a killer's confession be considered an impediment? Did love not conquer all? Did it not consist, in part, of an attraction to mystery and its corollary, danger? And so each had found in the other an increase of interest in that very element that might have discouraged someone less willing—or less able—to accept a wider range of possibility, a deeper complexity, in one's choice of an everlasting mate. Declan Tovey, dead, had achieved the impossible: the joining of two of the least likely couples imaginable, Leda and the swan and Titania and the ass included.

As the truck lumbered along, Aaron could see, off to his left, evidence of the changes that were altering the countryside in recent years. Prosperity had shocked all Ireland into rejuvenation. Whole villages were springing up, with "holiday houses" meant to lure not only intruders from abroad, but also Irish urban dwellers denied, until now, the means to mingle among the agreeable company that the truer Irish County Kerry could so readily provide.

Bereft of their poverty, the Irish now had to adjust to changes just as challenging as the coming of freedom, if not more so. That they deserved both freedom and prosperity and had dearly earned them was beyond question; still, it was change. Aaron could hardly mourn his people's loss of hardship. He couldn't wait to see them adjust. He reveled in the awakening. Lolly, of course, might worry that it could make even more archaic her pig farming. Would the avalanche burying the past doom her show of independence, which had planted its standard in the muck and mire of her beloved farm, the stubborn flag uprooted as if it were a mere sapling, highly qualified for extinction? Aaron devoutly hoped it would not.

•

A settlement of the aforementioned "holiday houses" was behind them after a turn in the road. Up ahead, however, an equally unnerving spectacle confronted them. On the far side of a field to the left, an aggregate of equipment was arrayed along the road that bordered what had been part of the McCloud property. Tarred gravel was being spewed onto a widened roadbed, and an elephantine steamroller advanced slowly, almost solemnly, behind, the newly paved portion reaching almost into the ditch that ran between the meadow and the road. Aaron's first thought was that, surely if God still loved Ireland, the equipment would be tipped into the ditch before more desecrations could complete themselves. But then a native sympathy intervened, and he quickly wished no evil upon those earning their daily bread (and beef and stout and fish and vegetables and fruit and tarts and french fries) by the sweat of their swarthy brows. These men had jobs. If anyone were to complain, it wouldn't be Aaron McCloud.

This did not prevent him from saying to his wife, "We have to go back," his relief at the necessity badly disguised. "We can't turn onto the road where they're working."

"Nonsense. We'll just get out and walk across the field, then up to the edge of the cliffs."

"There's a ditch just to our left."

"Why would a ditch stop us?"

"It's a very wide ditch. And there's water at the bottom."

"If we get wet," Lolly said, "we'll get dry"—an age-old assurance central to Irish survival. She stopped the truck, opened the door, swung her legs around, and let herself out onto the road. To give emphasis to what she'd said, she slammed the door shut, went around to the front of the truck, and started down into the ditch. "Uuh. Nice and mucky. You're going to love it."

Aaron was out of the truck. "I won't love it."

"That's all right. It'll love you, and that should be enough." She slogged through the muddy bottom and climbed the opposite bank. The swineherd boots she had never relinquished during her novel-writing days were coated with a thick black ooze, suggesting that oil might be lurking not far beneath the sacred soil of Kerry. After stepping into the field, she called out, "Look at the lovely gorse. Come smell it." She snapped off the prickly sprig and held it up to her nose. "Come," she said, holding out the flowering shrub. "Rewards await."

Determined not to soil, much less wet his loafers, Aaron decided to jump the ditch. It was a successful leap, but the earth on the far side was unappreciative of his athleticism, and no sooner had he landed than the sodden incline sent first his right foot, then his left, down into the muck he had so foolishly tried to avoid. To further punish his refusal to accept the ditch on its own terms, his entire torso was sent down the embankment, the dirt adhering to his shirt, his pants, his hands, and the tip of his nose. When he raised his head, his wife, ignoring his predicament, simply reached down, placed the gorse under his muddied nose, and said, "Smell. Lovely."

"Aren't you going to help me up?"

"Oh, do you need help? *I* didn't need help." She smiled the smile of the preeminently pleased. "But of course if you need me . . ." Aaron reached out his hand. "Oh. Filthy. Filthy. Brush it against your pants. You certainly don't expect me to muddy myself. Hardly a fitting reward for the help I'm about to give. That's right. Take hold, but don't pull me down with you. One disgraced member of the family is more than enough."

Firmly she took his hand and yanked him, not without agreeable aggression, into the thicket of gorse lining the ditch. "There you are, you stupid lump. Do I get to clean you when we get home? Umm. Delicious."

"We should have turned back."

"Too late now. We don't want your mishap to be in vain."

"How do we cross that road when we get to it? It's wet tar."

"In your condition, what's a bit of tar?"

"They won't let us."

"Who needs to be let?"

"Everyone does. By the men working there."

"Everyone does not include us. Come along."

On they walked through the gorse and the heather, the smell of the tar almost overwhelming the scent of the sea. Nor could the growls and grinds of the road-building equipment completely drown, so to speak, the sound of the waves bashing themselves against the cliffs. Wife and husband came to a fence and climbed over. They passed some sheep that *baa*ed at them, expressing their disdain for anyone passing through who failed to offer them a sack or two of feed. They continued on. There was a narrow wooden gate at the next fence, adorned with a sign that warned BEWARE OF THE BULL, meant to intimidate trespassers unfamiliar with a commonly known absurdity. Aaron passed through without hesitation, rubbing the tip of his nose, expecting to wipe away the residue deposited by the ditch. He succeeded in transferring the remaining mud onto his upper lip. He spit. Then spit again.

When they got to where the McCloud house had been,

a convenient bend in the road shielded them from the sight of the workmen. They crossed the road. The tar glued some of the gravel onto the soles of Aaron's pampered loafers and Lolly's experienced boots. As they were clambering over a final fieldstone wall, Aaron gallantly offered his stained hand to Lolly, helped her up, then stopped to survey the fields, the stones, the widened road, and the horizon to the west, where the sea became indistinguishable from the sky. To honor her husband's pause, Lolly, too, paused and took in the world around them.

Facing the sea, Aaron said quietly, "Is it because you want to see the grave where Declan Tovey was buried and where we were going to bury him back again before the sea came and took him?"

This was not an idle question. With Lolly, Kitty and Kieran out in the yard, Aaron was, except for the skeleton, alone in the house when the winds had had their way with it, tilting, sliding, sinking the house into the welcoming waves. That Aaron was saved by divine intervention had never been doubted. He had managed to escape the house through a hole a pig had forced in the mesh door that led from the kitchen to the garden, where that very same pig had unearthed the skeleton. Then, as if that weren't miracle enough, a wayward canoe, first thought to be a shark, had nudged his panicked body, and he was given just enough strength and skill to raise himself over the side, when the waves promptly heaved him toward the shore and onto the beach.

Lolly, Kitty, and Kieran had watched from the top of the cliff, at first despairing, then disbelieving, then hopeful, then astonished—an astonishment that ultimately advanced to jubilation. With Aaron's nearly drowned body safely ashore, the heavenly presence lingered long enough to exact from Kitty and Kieran, then from Aaron and Lolly, confessions of true love, all in the presence of the pig, which, on some level of submerged consciousness, seemed to confer on the episode a legitimacy that could never be revoked.

Now, studying the mountains, the high rounded hills off to her right, searching for some means to avoid answering Aaron's earlier question, Lolly found herself at a loss. Apparently her quick-wittedness had abandoned her. She could say nothing but an undirected "What?"

"Never mind," Aaron answered. "You wouldn't tell me anyway."

"How do you know if you don't ask?"

"I did ask. And you gave me the only answer I'm going to get. Which was no answer."

A mist had begun to creep over the top of the nearby hill. Lolly, relieved to have a subject other than the one Aaron had introduced, took note of the obvious and said, "Oh, look. A mist is coming down, and we're going to disappear."

"How convenient."

"You're sulking. Why are you sulking?"

"Because you want to go—for reasons of your own—to look at where Declan Tovey was buried."

"Why would I want to do a thing like that?"

"Simple. Because he was your lover."

"He was Kitty's lover."

"And Kitty said you were."

"Kitty McCloud, your aunt though she may be, is not a reliable source of information, especially in matters pertaining to her early adventures. What need had I for Declan Tovey? I had my pigs. I had a calling and I gave it all I had—and more. The way I always do with anything important. You should know. You've been the beneficiary this past year gone."

After a moment's consideration, Aaron turned to look at his wife. "Is that true? I thought your novel was the most important."

"How can writing a novel be important?"

"It was to me. When I was doing it."

"Because you're a writer. I'm not a writer. Just because I wrote a novel doesn't make me a writer. Who can't write a novel if she's got half a head?"

"Fewer people than you think."

"Nonsense. I was too busy being your wife to do anything else, besides, of course, tending my pigs. But you, more than anyone, should know that. I wrote the novel to try to relax a little, to give myself some time off, to get ready for more of what we do better than anyone in history."

"Is that true?"

"I'll let you be the judge of that."

Aaron waited, then nodded. "All right then. If you say so."

"I did say so. Just now."

"I heard."

The descending mist had shrouded them completely, isolating them entirely from the world around. Aaron reached over and took his wife's hand. "I'll help you down." Lolly let her hand be held and, experienced from a life of climbing up rock walls and down as she was, allowed her husband to lead her safely into the meadow below.

"There'll be no grave," Aaron said. "I'll tell you that. Or the sea will tell you itself."

"We'll know when we get there. Come." Lolly led the way.

There was no grave. All the earth intended to be paste and cover to Declan Tovey's bones had been sent on with him, an unneeded recompense for his consignment to a watery end. Lolly and Aaron stared into the fog hovering a few feet past the edge of the cliff, swirling slowly in the updraft from the water below.

"I'm sorry," Aaron said. "You probably wanted to see the grave, and it isn't here any more. I dug it myself, deeper than it had been before, so Declan wouldn't get himself dug up again."

Lolly said nothing. Neither moved. The mist was cooling against their faces. The sea could be heard, its rampage somewhat stilled, but nothing was visible to either of them. The house could still be standing, the garden shed as well, but both would belong, as they so often had, to the rising mists, with no one to know whether they were there or not. They had always belonged to the mists. It was their age-old habit to dissolve into mystery, and this moment was a simple repetition, existence itself becoming doubtful and all proofs and certainties suspended.

Lolly broke the silence. "I saw him yesterday in Caherciveen when I was buying the bream we had for supper."

"Who?"

"Declan."

After he'd held off for a moment, Aaron said, "Lolly, you did not see Declan Tovey in Caherciveen."

"All right then. I didn't. And I didn't go to Caherciveen, and we didn't have bream. And we're not in Ireland. We're in Mozambique."

"You saw someone who looked like Declan Tovey."

"No one looks like Declan Tovey."

"People always look like other people. The gene pool of the world isn't as varied as most people think."

"Genes don't give you a scar over your left eye."

"Lolly, Declan Tovey's skeleton was found not ten feet from where we're standing."

"Maybe so. But he still made it to Caherciveen yesterday."

"Fully fleshed. Fully clothed."

"Yes. Fully fleshed. Fully clothed."

Aaron took his handkerchief from his back pocket and, without unfolding it, wiped it across his forehead. He looked to see if there was any mud, or better still, some hint of what he should say next. He put the handkerchief back into his pocket. "This is what happens when you write a book with ghosts in it."

"Declan was not in my book."

"No. But there were what you said were *real* ghosts. Not psychically induced apparitions or antic idiots playing games, but real live ghosts."

"Then yesterday Declan was a ghost."

"If it was Declan yesterday, it was not a ghost. There are no such things as ghosts. The fact is Declan is dead. His remains, such as they were, are out there somewhere in the sea."

"Be that as it may, I saw him yesterday. It had to be him."

"Lolly, there are no ghosts except in books."

"And why have you decided not to believe me no matter what I say?"

"I want to be helpful."

"You think I've gone off with my head, don't you?"

"I think you wrote a book about ghosts and the involvement was so intense that you're now living through parts of it yourself."

"If I thought that was true—that I'd live my novel—I

would have written a book about a woman married to a man who'd believe her when she said something was true and real."

"I told you. I'm trying to help."

"Then just believe me."

"Lolly, you and Kitty washed his bones yourselves!"

"I know that. I also know he's come back."

"He can't come back."

"Who said so?"

"Well, for one, Shakespeare said it. Hamlet said it. 'The undiscover'd country from whose bourn no traveler returns.' "

"Sure. 'No traveler returns.' Then what was Hamlet's father doing, turning up on the ramparts and later in his mother's bedroom, and him dead as a doornail? Answer me that."

"Now is not the time for Shakespearean exegesis."

"Of course not. Not after I ask you something you can't answer."

"All right then. Sometimes even Shakespeare was inconsistent. Henslowe was probably screaming for the script. They needed a new play—and fast. All writers are sometimes inconsistent."

"But I'm not writing this. I'm living it."

"I give up."

"Sure, you give up. You know I'm right and you're wrong. And I don't mean about Shakespeare. I mean about Declan."

"All right, all right. I'm wrong and you're—" He stopped.

Lolly waited for him to continue. He didn't. Instead he stared over Lolly's shoulder, into the distance, into the fog. His stare held.

"What?" Lolly asked.

Again Aaron pulled out his handkerchief, this time crumpling it in his fist. "Nothing."

"Oh?" Lolly looked over her shoulder. There, a dark form was making its way toward the edge of the cliff. Lolly sucked in a quick breath, held it, then let it go. In a hoarse voice she whispered, "Declan?" Then she called out the name. "Declan?" Aaron grabbed her by the arm. She called out more forcefully, "Declan?" She started to move away.

"Don't go," Aaron said. "Don't move."

"It's Declan. I know it is."

"You can't. The cliff is right there."

"I have to see him."

"You can't see him."

"But I just did. And so did you."

"It wasn't Declan. And I told you. The cliff—"

"I can prove it to you it's—"

"You can't. All we saw was someone in the fog. It could have been anyone. Anything."

"It was Declan."

"Lolly, he's dead."

"What difference does that make?"

Aaron didn't even try to answer. When Lolly spoke again, her voice was more subdued. "Can we just stand here? Just for a bit? Be with each other? And no one else, just the two of us? Here, where the house was. And now it's gone."

"And the grave."

"Yes. And the grave. That's gone, too."

Silently they stood. With his handkerchief Aaron brushed the gathering moisture from Lolly's brow. "Thanks," she said.

"Yeah." He shoved the handkerchief back into his pocket, then, after a respectful pause, turned and started back the way they'd come. Lolly followed. As they crossed the meadow Aaron said quietly, "You love him, don't you? The way you called his name."

"I love you."

"I know. Still, you love him."

"He's dead."

Aaron's response was ready. "What difference does that make?"

2

Standing on the rampart of Castle Kissane, Kitty
McCloud didn't know if she was more amused than
relieved or more relieved than amused. Perhaps both in
equal measure. More often than not she would repair to this
place of refuge—with its great sweep of County Kerry, its low
mountains and the turbulent sea ranged out before her—to
effect some mediation between herself and whichever intran-
sigent novel she might be writing at the moment. Her present
unburdened state, however, was in response to an e-mail from
her agent in Dublin, one Fiona O'Toole. Kitty had mentioned
to Ms. O'Toole her intention of taking on the only canonical
writer—Jane Austen—who so far had been spared her autho-
rial "correction." Charlotte Brontë, Thomas Hardy, George
Eliot, even Dickens, among others, had not been so fortunate.
Kitty, applying her considerable talents, would rectify the mad-
dening errors made by any number of her admired predecessors,
her work free of the ignominy the others so rightly deserved.

Gathering her forces about her, she had recently decided
not so much to "correct" Ms. Austen as to challenge her
outright. Kitty was determined to give her attention to
Pride and Prejudice (no less) for the simple reason that Jane

had too long been allowed to declare her novels—and their characters—fulfilled by providing marriages that were presumed to be happy. Kitty would now ask the unasked. What if Darcy, having married Elizabeth, were to abandon her for another woman? What would become of Ms. Bennett, a character Kitty herself often found insufferably perfect even with all the highly nuanced imperfections given her by her creator.

But now, via e-mail, this temptation to hubris on Kitty's part was exposed as the folly it would have become. The project was canceled, off, over, ended. And just in time. Had Kitty not so diligently ignored the efforts of her contemporaries, she would have been fully aware of the Jane Austen Industrial Complex. As Ms. O'Toole informed her, countless were the scribblings taking advantage of Jane's popularity. More than many were the authors who had exploited that good woman's achievements by trying to insinuate themselves into her company. Her ignorance exposed, Kitty was released from the infamy that would have blighted her renown had she honed her axe and given Jane and even Mrs. Darcy their forty whacks.

Still, she shouldn't waste time being amused and relieved. She was, after all, a writer, a calling that required for its sustenance despair, desperation, and even fears of inadequacy, this latter being an infrequent affliction visited upon Ms. Kitty McCloud. What she needed now, and quickly, was an inspiration comparable to the one that had inspired her most recent triumph: a correction of *The Mill on the Floss*.

In concert with muses of the highest distinction, Kitty had rescued Maggie Tulliver from the absurd fate devised by Ms. George Eliot. Kitty's gorge had risen to floodtide at her first reading of the novel, when she was an easily displeased teenager. As God was her witness, she would never allow

Maggie—the singular child who had run off to join the Gypsies, certain they would make her their queen—to wind up in
a dazed state in the company of an unworthy man, then return
to her brother, a prissy prick if ever there was one, just in time
to drown with him in the storm-roiled waters of the epony-
mous Floss.

No. She had vowed even then to make Maggie happy.
And make her happy she did—in her own inimitable way.
At a propitious moment, Maggie again meets the Gypsy boy
who, those long years ago, had led her around the camp on
his horse. He rescues her now from the rapidly rising Floss,
apparently still bestride the remembered animal. Their love
is sealed. As a boy, he had been, unbeknownst to Maggie,
the Prince of the Gypsies. Now come to full manhood, he is
King. Maggie Tulliver, Floss or no Floss, prick of a brother or
no prick of a brother, becomes, as God and Kitty McCloud
had ordained from the beginning of time, the Queen of the
Gypsies. (In actuality, Kitty believed deep down that, with
her writing, she was doing God's work—an unshakable belief
common to her kind.)

Just as she was about to move away and descend the winding stair leading to where her computer impatiently awaited,
Kitty found herself fixated on the slow progress of a lone man
who had turned onto her castle road. He was dressed mostly
in black, both pants and coat, with what seemed like a white
shirt open at the neck, the poor fellow looking for all the world
like a defeated warrior come back from a lost and distant war.
He wore no cap or hat. She took note of the thick black hair
falling across his forehead and the dark brows that failed to
distract from even darker eyes, eyes that in better times would

look out on the world with a challenging dare. Clutched at his side was a leather sack, heavy with what might possibly (but impossibly)be the implements necessary for a thatcher's trade.

This could only be (except it could not possibly be) Declan Tovey. Or (least likely of all) the ghost of Declan Tovey. Rebellious wrath arose in Kitty's breast. Her moment of relief was over. Hadn't she ghosts enough? Was her castle condemned to be a way station for every wandering shade who, for whatever reason, had failed to complete the journey from this world to the next? Considering the number of spooks said to be prowling the Kerry countryside, her castle, at this rate, would become a veritable repository for any and every phantom confused by an unjust demise.

As if to justify her complaint, she saw, off to the east, the slow progress through her apple orchard of the familiar ghosts of Taddy and Brid, the resident shades of Castle Kissane, both of them young and fair beyond measure. Taddy and Brid she accepted. They had been hanged in the great hall of her castle more than two centuries before. They had a right to possession. But what claim could be made by Declan Tovey?

Seeming to be fully fleshed, he was making his way down her road. But hadn't she herself—and Kieran and her best friend all her life, Lolly, and her nephew Aaron—already had considerable involvement with this man's skeleton? Neither hide nor hair had graced his bones. He had been identified not only by his clothes but also by the sack of thatcher's tools laid respectfully at his side in the unearthed grave dug in her garden. He was dead as dead can be. Had she and Lolly not prepared the skeleton for decent burial? Had they not washed with their own hands, using Kitty's most expensive and sweet-scented soap, each bone—the scapula, the patella, the thoracic vertebrae, the clavicle—one by one, then put them inside the fresh, clean clothing commandeered from her nephew? Had she not participated fully in the celebratory wake, with the man stretched out in a cushioned coffin fashioned from boards wrested from her own bookshelves? Had she not witnessed the slow slide of her ancestral home, garden and all, into the waves of the Western Sea, with the coffined bones securely inside?

Now he was come again, intent on yet another haunting of Castle Kissane. Of course, he *had* been murdered. This she acknowledged. But to return? Nothing could justify this intrusion. He had not been done in by her, not by her hand. Nor by the hand of—

Here her protestations stopped. At the wake, her now husband had boasted that he himself had killed the man, having struck him across the skull with the leggett, the most impressive tool of the thatcher's trade. Kieran had heard that she—*she, Kitty McCloud!*—had been called a cow-face by Declan Tovey. The murder was all too understandable. Kieran had obviously felled the blasphemous thatcher. If she had doubted Kieran's confession at the time, the proof of its validity was now coming closer to her castle courtyard. Declan had come to haunt his killer.

But another thought troubled her mind. If her husband had indeed murdered Declan, why was she, Kitty, seeing the man's ghost? Of course, she, too, had confessed to the killing, but it was only to protect her friend Lolly, who, Kitty had been convinced, was the actual murderer. Lolly certainly had good cause. Had Declan not preferred herself, Kitty, to the lesser Lolly? And did not Lolly verify Kitty's belief with her very own confession? But then, all three—Kitty, Kieran, and Lolly, each in turn—had laid claim to the well-deserved deed. Which was the legitimate claimant would probably never be known. But could a false confession alone allow even the innocent Kitty to be given the dubious privilege now being bestowed?

Kitty tried to foreclose all further speculations. She would surrender to the event, requiring no understanding, demanding no explanations. But before she could content herself with this reluctant resignation, an added complexity presented itself. Coming through the pasture grass beyond the courtyard sheds was her husband. Even in her distracted state, she had time to be annoyed that he was wearing, along with his everyday corduroy pants and a worn work shirt, the coat meant to be his Sunday best. Also, she had thought he was in the castle scullery—known in lesser accommodations as the kitchen—preparing, as was his habit, the evening meal. To her momentary puzzlement, she saw that there, in a heavily gloved hand, was a bunch of greens. Immediately she realized they must be nettles—or why the gloved hand? These she herself would simmer to a spicy broth, once the current situation had been resolved.

A greater unease came over her. Quite possibly Kieran, too, would see what she was seeing. Would he, before her very eyes, be confronted by the ghost of the man he may have murdered? As she watched, Kieran dropped the nettles. He had seen what she had feared he would see. Quickly, he leaned down and picked up the nettles. Then, with a sure step, he changed course and walked toward the advancing apparition.

Declan, in life, had been a man few would care to confront. Challenge of any kind would unfailingly animate his famous temperament: He could be, at one and the same time, both the most fearsome and the most irresistible. Women were known to capitulate after minimal urgings. Strong and brave men would usually manage to relax into camaraderie, some friendships sealed with an exchange of resounding thumps on the back or an occasional slap on the buttocks. No one was protected from a charm firmly grounded in a rascality so assured it never had to resort to arrogance. And besides, who would want to extinguish the least gleam that might diminish so compelling a radiance? Often enough Declan was identified with Lucifer himself, the Angel of Light, astride the threshold of heaven's gate, eagerly awaiting combat with a mere archangel. How could nothing more threatening than a fiery sword compete with the high pride that only an exalted and exultant sense of self could inspire? (As it happened, it had taken no more than Declan's own leggett to dispatch him when the time came to snuff out his own quite quenchable flame.)

In no way was it possible for Kitty not to be standing at her husband's side when he and the apparition would meet. She jumped, stumbled, and clattered her way down the winding stair. The great hall was crossed in what seemed a single bound and the door flung open with a ruthlessness that almost unhinged it. Having made an end-run maneuver that kept her clear of the visitor, she came to Kieran's side, where, with a breathless determination, she turned to challenge this latest haunting of her beloved castle.

But something was wrong. The ghost was talking—talking to her husband. He was speaking not of tenebrous things or sepulchral happenings, but of a subject so commonplace that he could be any Kerryman who had returned after a season's absence, expecting to be welcomed home.

"I wasn't looking for it to be that way," he was saying. "I went to the cliffs, and I was sure the house would be there along with the stretch of pasture, but there's not so much as a single stone to say where it had all once been."

"The sea took it," Kieran said, his tone as conversational as if he were dispensing information about any everyday happening.

"That I could tell. But it's a bit of a surprise to someone not that long away." During this last, he took note of Kitty standing there, her hand holding fast to Kieran's arm. "But you've got the castle," the apparition continued, "so I needn't feel too much regret, should I?"

"No." Kitty found it impossible not to whisper. "No need for regrets."

"But you miss it, the house."

"I . . . I . . . yes, I miss it. I think I miss it."

"A lot was lost."

"Yes. A lot. Lost."

"Taken into the sea."

"All taken." Kitty tried to achieve her husband's simple conversational tone, but she couldn't quite do it. "Yes. All. The sea. It . . . it was the sea that took it."

She did not say that the sea had taken him—or, rather, his bones—along with everything else, that she had seen the house become his private mausoleum as he and it sank, without struggle, into the eager waves.

"And the garden, too, went along."

"The garden. Yes. The garden."

"And all that was in it. Cabbages. Everything."

"Yes. Everything. Everything that was in it."

Kieran seemed quite willing to let Kitty do the talking, but she had no idea what she should be saying. She knew she was staring, unable to blink, transfixed. Her lips, too, had lost their easy, effortless mobility, their habit of forming words. Had he come to inquire as to the whereabouts of his remains, to be given some clue that might lead him to the place of his final disposal? Would he hold Kitty accountable for the disappearance of his mortal leavings? All Kitty could hope for at the moment was that, as Taddy and Brid were wont to do, he would vanish. Surely he had accomplished what he had come to accomplish: to announce his presence, charged with the promise that he would reappear from time to time and, in a revision of the usual ghost protocol, engage her and Kieran in conversation.

But he did not vanish. He simply shifted the sack he was carrying from his left hand to his right, causing the tools inside to clank against one another, a sound not unlike the rattle of collected bones. Was he about to throw at their feet this retrieval from the ocean floor? Would this meeting become a confrontation between the quick and the dead, between Declan Tovey's indestructible spirit and her and Kieran's challenged credulity? If Declan had come to accuse, let him. She was tempted to cry out, "Do it and be done!"

But before she could act on this latest impulse, she saw that something else was not right. Declan dead looked not at all like Declan living. This was truly his ghost. Gone was the amused invitation that dared the onlooker to search out the secrets implicit in his knowing smile. Apparent no more were the unsettling stares that had promised the presence of mysteries in the depths of his dark, dark eyes. Even the arched brows, full and black, seemed to have lost the sense of amazement that had unfailingly suggested that the object of his gaze possessed enticements that he could not be expected to resist. And the entire face, ever alive and eager, hungering to dispense pleasures as yet undreamed of, had fallen into disrepair—not aged, but lacking the upkeep that his indomitable spirit had always provided, the expectation of a profitable encounter, the offer of thrills heretofore inexperienced by the recipient of his attention.

The eyes were the most troubling of all. Still of unfathomable depths, they seemed to have taken into themselves a great sorrow, not drowning it, but giving it a refuge where it could dwell, guarding an implacable grief. The eyes' one source of life was a bewilderment, a searching, a quest that held fast a forlorn hope that might yet be fulfilled—should the gods bestow a blessing that could be well beyond even the powers of their divinity. His voice seemed tentative where it had been so self-assured before. A note of pity sounded somewhere in its depths, a complement to the sorrow in his eyes. And before Kitty could fend it off, a corresponding pity welled up within herself, already reaching out with a longing of its own that, if she weren't insistent, could summon again an old arousal.

"And none of the house," Declan said. "I mean not the house, that couldn't possibly happen, stones being what it was made of, but, well, anything that fell into the sea—nothing surfaced? Nothing came ashore? Or did you never bother to look?"

"Nothing," Kieran said.

"And Kitty, you . . . ?" Declan was looking at her with such needful pleading that she had to look down at her shoes, actually a pair of sneakers, footwear she had long disdained. So mundane, so insufficient to the moment were they that, ashamed, she looked up again and into the man's mournful countenance. "No," she whispered. "I've looked. And still do from time to time, but no, nothing."

She wanted to add, "Not even your bones, if that's what you're wondering." But she lacked the courage to introduce the one subject that hovered over everything being said: that he was dead. He was a specter. And then came an obvious afterthought: Perhaps he didn't know this simple fact. If so, how could she bring herself to tell him? How could she add, to the sufferings already too apparent, the stunned amazement, the unavoidable acceptance of his own death and eternal expulsion from the land of his birth? Perhaps it was himself he was mourning. The sorrows of Taddy and of Brid were as nothing to what death and insufficient resurrection had inflicted upon this man who had once stood indomitable astride all the bent world.

Again a surge of pity threatened to topple Kitty into a familiar abyss. She had not long since surrendered to the dangerous sympathies awakened by the mournful ghost of Taddy. And now she was being tempted by another urging toward an idiocy similar to the one she had so recently renounced: a helpless attraction to Taddy, to the ghost of Taddy. She loved her husband. He was magnificence made flesh. There could not possibly be a need for any other. Foolish she might be, but mad? The hapless victim of every needful spirit that might come to haunt her castle? Again she protested. This could not be allowed. It was enough that she was subject to these ghostly visitations. It was enough that she had managed to cling to her sanity and, at the same time, accept their reality and accommodate their presence. But to have demands made again not only upon her brain but also upon her heart was more than she was willing to accept.

If Declan Tovey, by the exercise of some shenanigans of unknowable origin, had been allowed to tread again upon Ireland's holy ground, let him limit his hauntings to the place of his burial, the cliff side and the beach where her house had

stood, where his grave had been. Or, were that not acceptable, let him return to the burial plot prepared for him, now
become sediment at the bottom of the sea. Even Kerry hospitality had its limits—limits, as everyone knew, that already
reached beyond the boundaries of infinity.

But Declan, having been consigned to realms not within
the known world, could no longer make legitimate claim to its
welcome. Kitty already had two ghosts—three if she counted
the slain pig, the very pig that with its undisciplined snout
had dug up Declan's buried remains. Her affliction caused by
the handsome Taddy should have granted her immunity from
a repeat contagion. She became impatient. She'd had enough;
she'd accept no more. "Go if you want," she said. "Go to where
the house was. And where the garden grew. Go down to the
water's edge at the foot of the cliffs and see for yourself what
might be there. The sea has ways of its own. What it might
yield today or tomorrow no one knows. But that's the one way
you might find out."

Kieran, either more brazen or more foolish than his wife,
asked outright, "Is there something in particular you're looking for? Have you lost something that you've a need for now?"

"Oh, no. No. Nothing. I only came to say I'm sorry it all
was lost. I've been away. It was a fine place you had, and all the
McClouds before. And now it's gone—and into the sea. Well,
it's an honored Kerry way to go, isn't it?" He switched his sack
from the right hand back to the left, signaling the end of what
he had to say. Except he had more: "But . . . I mean . . . if ever
you do find . . . No. No. Let it be."

With his persisting look of soulful mourning, he had the
good grace to lower his eyes so Kitty could not see what she
knew would be a deeper, darker depth than she had seen

before. Were she allowed speech, she would have begged him to disappear or to go—and quickly, too.

"Can you come in and have a bit of something to eat?" Kieran was saying. "If nettle soup is to your liking, no one makes it better than my wife."

Within Kitty rose the impulse to do away with her husband—until she was rescued by a sudden realization: Ghosts don't eat. Kieran, in his superior wisdom, was putting Declan to the test. If he were to accept, if he were to actually sit down and eat . . .

Kitty was spared the completion of her thought. A wan smile had come to Declan's face. "No. Thank you, no. I've got to be going back the way I came. Maude McCloskey up the road, she might want me to replace her roof slate with thatch. To preserve the old ways. Thatch was the original and the slate considered an improvement by her husband long moved away. She's thinking she might go back to thatch, so he'll see it if he should ever come home." He laughed less than half a laugh. "And God save us all."

"God and Mary, too," Kieran mumbled as the man turned and slowly started making his way back along the road, away from the castle, taking onto his once proud shoulders the full burden of his sorrows and his grief.

A ghost cannot thatch a roof. Untold times Kitty and Kieran had seen Brid at her loom in the tower room, and only once did any cloth appear; then it disappeared. At all other times the moving loom, with Brid's bare and muddy foot on the treadle, her hand threading gracefully in and out with the held shuttle, produced nothing. Kitty envisioned a roof thatched, then unthatched, the spectral reeds vanishing just as Declan himself could vanish.

This pleased Kitty somewhat. Maude McCloskey was the local Hag, the village Seer. That she would be permitted a visit by this newly arrived shade awakened a touch of resentment in Kitty, as if, in contradiction to her earlier thoughts, her proprietary right to see ghosts should not be infringed upon. If Maude's roof were to be thatched, then unthatched, the Hag would deserve this inevitable outcome for her intrusion into Kitty's territory.

Declan was halfway along the castle road that led to the turn that would take him up to Maude McCloskey's cottage. Kitty felt a slight urge to question his ghostly status. Maude, if anyone, would know she was engaging a phantom to cover her roof. Could there be another resolution to all these confusions, an unexplored explanation waiting to be considered?

But then she saw Declan stop. On a low stone wall sat Brid and Taddy, as if waiting to watch Declan pass by. With them was the phantom pig; it, too, seemed to be interested. Declan was observing them, even bowing slightly. Taddy and Brid made no noticeable acknowledgment, but that was their usual custom. She and Kieran had often passed or come upon them, and they'd give no special sign of recognition. But the spectral pig raised its snout in obvious salute. Declan lowered his bow further, then continued on his way. He and the ghosts were in communion. He was one of them.

"He's back! He's back!" Kitty's wrath had returned. "Another ghost! And Declan Tovey at that! Quick. Give me the nettles. I'll eat them here. I'll eat them now. Quick. Give them to me!"

Kieran, ever alert to his wife's sometimes impulsive demands, said simply, "Let me wash them first."

"No! I'll eat them as they are. And their sting be damned!"

3

eclan Tovey stood a few feet from the side of the narrow road that ran along the great rock cliff fronting the Western Sea. The breeze blew softly, lifting only slightly the black forelock that had fallen toward the scar above his left eye. His dark coat and pants, woolen and well made but more than slightly worn, were still damp from the ditch in which he'd slept the night before instead of returning to the Widow Quinn's, where he had his lodging. He had wanted to be at the sea before the sunrise.

A three-day stubble shadowed his cheeks and chin with bristles not quite as dark as the hair on his head or the curled tuft springing from the open neck of his shirt. There was a pebble in his right boot, but he would tend to that later. Casting his gaze out over the water, he was lost in a meditation of the horizon, the sullen clouds in the growing light meeting the indifferent waters, their pale purple and gloomy gray obliterating the line intended to separate the things of the earth from the things of the sky. Only the birds, cormorants and gulls, shrieking as they swooped and then rose again, seemed aware of the difference, taking full advantage of their ingrained knowledge to plunder the sea and escape to the clouds. A lone curragh rode the uncresting waves with an ease not usual on this coast.

Also unhurried was a boat, possibly a decommissioned freighter, headed for Skellig Michael, the island farther south, miles from shore. The boat was most likely laden with tourists come to gawk at the abandoned hermitage hewn from the island's crags and pinnacles, once home to the penitents of centuries long past, huddled as close as this world allows to the sheltering wings of Michael, the avenging angel himself.

Declan paid a momentary tribute to the island—how could he not as a son of Kerry, bred in the blood to revere the sacred precincts from which all Ireland had drawn strength and courage in the dark days only recently lifted. He, of course, was of two minds about the self-martyred hermits. To him, at times, it had seemed that with their denial of worldly pleasures, with their commitment to eat only what the barren ground would grow and what the sea and the sky might yield, they had brought into Ireland not the expected blessings, but a curse that had condemned people less eager for denial to experience—willingly or not—the same deprivations they themselves had so greedily embraced.

So pleased, apparently, was the Heavenly Father with the hermits' atonements that He decreed that the entire people from whom they'd sprung should be given an unending opportunity to replicate their extravagant austerity. When Skellig Michael had exploded into the air from the rock bottom of the sea, it had been too hasty in its eagerness for the sky to collect fertile sediments from the ocean floor, and too exultant by its expulsion from the netherworld to allow the watery sea time to erode its craggy stones to a scape more homely if not more hospitable.

That Skellig Michael was a holy place none could argue, but to Declan, living in the land that had made possible its sanctity, born a recipient of its example and a child of the enforced replications of its hardships, all Ireland was, by indisputable logic, equally holy—but with a holiness it had not invited and a blessing that could easily pass as a curse.

These unavoidable thoughts, moving at a measured pace through his distressed mind, prompted him to shorten his gaze and observe the great gaping space before him, where there had once been a house and where a garden had grown. It had belonged to an impossible woman, one Kitty McCloud, a writer of some repute. Her fame derived from an uncanny gift for both exciting and assuaging the suppressed libidos of unsuspecting females (and not a few males as well), convincing them in English, Irish, and languages that spanned the globe that they were simply indulging in a well-told tale, the adult equivalent of a bedtime story, when in truth they were submitting themselves to an onslaught against their most protected secrets. Declan had often wondered if Kitty herself was fully aware of her unique achievements. In his pride, he preferred to think he was the only one.

Mediated by her books, these truths descended into regions where the subconscious, in all innocence, engaged in deeds the day would quake to look on. The readers' conscious equipment assured them that these were fantasies, whereas in reality they were excursions into the seven secret places where the reader could range rampant and unconcerned among forbidden truths, thinking them no more than the crafty manipulations of an unscrupulous hack.

Declan had read Kitty McCloud's work, first out of mild curiosity—she was, after all, a conquest of his earliest urges—

then with actual interest, then in awe. He considered himself one of the few people who had deciphered the code and found his way into the inner temple where this votary of the truth labored away, secure in the knowledge that no one knew who she really was, where she had come from, and where she was leading them. Declan knew, but he would never tell—either about the code or about his youthful conquest.

And now her house and the garden had been taken into the sea, leaving behind an emptiness into which had rushed the giddy waves, reveling in this newly gouged cove. Gone, too, was the grave he'd dug in her garden, the grave into which he had placed with a tenderness uncommon to him the boy—sixteen? seventeen?—who'd been his apprentice, a cheerful and eager young man who had begged to be taught the thatcher's trade. The boy's name was Michael, and he'd come from an island in the north, which island Declan would never know. When he'd name one, the boy would always answer, "No. Not that one. Another one. To the north." When asked the name yet again, he would only say, "It has so many names, each different, depending on whom you ask."

"Fine. And I'm asking now."

"All right, then. To my family, to us, it's been always known as Kinvara. But don't say it to others or they'll claim there's no such place. But to us it's Kinvara. There. To the north." And he would point out to sea.

After Declan had buried the boy for safekeeping in the newly dug garden of Kitty McCloud, he had set out to the north, to find Kinvara and the boy's family, to bring him home so he wouldn't lie among strangers. More than a year of wandering had taken him to far places, to islands no map had ever shown, to villages unvisited by travelers, to towns where no one recognized from Declan's words a young man who had wanted to be a thatcher: he of the dark brown hair and deep blue eyes, the straight broad shoulders and the skinny arms but powerful hands; he of the marked cheek, the right one, where a thrown stone had missed the eye toward which it had been aimed by an older brother. He of the confident nose and the innocent lips, the negligible chest and the long thin legs, the happy insistence that he become a master of his chosen trade. He of the high laughter and low sighs, the easy smiles, the hidden sorrows and the big feet. He of the unknowable mystery of himself, all gathered together in the name of Michael—the Hebrew word the boy had told him meant "Who is like God."

His death was unexpected but not sudden. They had been thatching a cottage roof off a road that would end before it reached the top of a great hill, giving way to rocky pastures where the sheep would graze. The thatch was of combed wheat, guaranteeing long service and certain shelter. Declan had decided from the first that at least one layer of the old thatch should be removed, the gulley indentations filled with new reeds, creating a firm foundation for the next course.

It was while Michael was filling in the gullies near the roof beam of the high-pitched roof that, for whatever reason, he decided to stand upright, perhaps to relieve a crick or a cramp, maybe just to be free of the blunted scent rising from the reeds. He slipped, he slid, he fell, and Declan was helpless to do anything but cry out, "Don't!"

Michael's head hit the flat stone sunk in front of the cottage door. But no sooner had the boy straightened himself out full length than he sat up, raised both his arms, looked at Declan, and smiled and shrugged, congratulating himself for not having been subject to the punishment he deserved for contradicting his master's instruction about not taking unnecessary risks.

He got up, put his foot on the bottom rung of the ladder, and made the ascent, unfazed by the fall and the flat stone. Together he and Declan worked until sundown. During the walk back to the truck Michael stopped, went to the side of the road, leaned against a fence bordering a sheepfold, then carefully began lowering himself onto the ground, his eyes showing surprise more than hurt. He lay back his head but had not yet straightened his legs out in front of him when the legs simply fell sideways and his body tipped slowly toward the ground. He had died.

Declan sat down next to him and drew his body into a sitting position. To keep it from tipping again, he put his arm across the boy's shoulders and drew him closer. Declan would wait a moment, then take the body to the hospital in the next village and report what had happened. The authorities could then locate the boy's family and arrange for a proper burial.

The moments passed and still they sat there. Then Declan recalled all those times when he had been too tired to roam (if such a thing were imaginable)and the boy would recite the old tales and legends sent down by mouth or set down by a seanchaí, stories retrieved from ancestral memory. Some Declan remembered, like Finn MacCumhaill tales, and some he'd never heard, like "The Old Woman in the Chest" and "Crooked Tadhg's Way to the Island." But now the boy was dead, there, against his shoulder.

Slowly the dark came down. A half moon rose over the hill. Declan went to the truck and opened the door on the passenger side. Then he went back, crouched down, and raised the body in his arms. The legs and arms dangled freely, but the head was held in the crook of Declan's arm. He propped the boy on the seat and lowered the head onto the his chest.

Declan went around to the driver's side, got in, and started the truck's motor. He saw the lowered head. It looked as if the boy felt he had done something shameful and had forbidden himself to hold his head high. Declan put his hand under the chin and raised the head. He leaned it against the back of the seat, but again it fell forward. Declan put the truck in gear but couldn't place his foot on the accelerator. The head should not be lowered in shame.

He reached his arm over, drew the body closer to himself, and let the head rest on his shoulder. The truck drove off.

As they went slowly along the dark lanes, Declan realized why he had waited so long to take up the body. He had come to know that he would never deliver the boy into the hands of others, who might bury him in common ground if his family couldn't be found. He, Declan himself, would find them in the far north. This thought advanced from a decision to a determination to a vow. For now he would simply bury the body in a place where it could safely wait for his return.

Her house had been dark when Declan reached the garden of Kitty McCloud. He had seen the newly turned soil plowed two nights before by Kieran Sweeney, sworn enemy of Miss McCloud and all her kin, who loved her above all women in the world but was forbidden by an age-old feud to declare his ardor. Still, every year since Sweeney was fifteen he would secretly, with his small plow, prepare her soil for whatever she might choose to grow, usually cabbages.

The plowing was not especially deep, so Declan, with a spade—an implement for cutting peat from a bog bottom—he found leaning against her tool shed dug down to a decent depth. The grave would be only temporary, until he could take the young man home to the north. After a moment's pause, he sat down next to the hole he'd dug and pulled off his right boot. He thrust his hand inside, felt around, then upended the boot and gave it an impatient shake. Out onto the ground fell a coin, gold and imprinted with the profile of the monarch who had reigned more than two centuries before, George, third of that name. He picked it up and held it between his thumb and forefinger. As he turned it over, then over again, he wondered why he'd felt a strange compulsion to place it in the grave, but after looking at it a while more, he shrugged, put the boot on, and slipped the coin back inside. To have buried it with the boy would have bestowed on him the highest honor within his power to give. For generation upon generation it had been passed along, from the time of the imprinted monarch to this present day, a token of a great deed done by Declan's ancestors and sacred to their memory. It was his duty to pass it on to the next generation, and it had been an aberrant thought to even consider burying it alongside the fallen apprentice. The boy was not his son. He was his apprentice. Declan did, however, take off the baseball cap he always wore and placed it on the boy's wounded head. And, even though the youth had not yet completed his apprenticeship, Declan, bowing to an instinct he felt no need to understand, placed his sack of thatcher's tools inside the grave.

As he was lowering him into the opened earth, he could feel again the cold ground he'd been digging. He lifted the body back up and leaned it against the mound of earth, then took off the coat he was wearing—the one with the brass buttons—and, slowly, carefully, and not without difficulty put it on the boy.

It was when he was buttoning the coat that, informed by a prompting from nowhere, he realized he could not do what he was doing. He could not place the body in the ground. He could not accept that he must leave him there, alone and in the cold. He could not believe that the boy was truly gone, that he, Declan, had lost him. Forever. And that he would never see him again working away with the reeds on the rooftops, or hear again the happy voice telling tales from the distant past. Then, without warning, came a still more unacceptable truth. The boy in the grave would be alone. And with that came another thought: The boy had always been alone, a loneliness he had accepted with good cheer and an indifferent resignation. Declan had seen it in the isolation of the work, in the chattering and the tale telling, but he had never been aware of it until now. Recollecting it now, he reached a depth within himself he hadn't even known existed. His heart broke, allowing the entry of a grief so profound it would find there a place where it would dwell forever.

Slowly Declan lowered the boy back into the grave. Quietly he covered the body, making sure that the earth looked undisturbed by anything other than Kieran Sweeney's plow. He made his way back to the truck, stumbling twice. Then he set out for the north.

Declan had neglected to say a prayer, but remembered on the second day of his journey. He paused near a well and, before he drank, stood silently, inviting God to select from the confused vocabulary that crowded his mind and his heart the words He considered appropriate to the event. Declan drank but half a cup. Then he gave the rest to the ground at his feet and continued on to search out Kinvara.

A mist had come up from the water, reminding Declan as he stood atop the cliff that the sea had ways to protect its secrets. While sometimes gentle, as now, it was potentially fierce and terrible. No longer could he see the curragh, no longer make sure that the boat had arrived safely at Skellig Michael. The gulls could be heard but not seen, their cries out of the clouds mocking any and all who might try to compete for dominance of the mist. There was no sea, no sky, and even the land was beginning to dissolve.

From a distance, then closer by, came the sound of a car, or more likely a truck. Declan would wait until it had passed to make his descent down the stone steps to the beach below. The ancient passageway from the McCloud house to the sea had been an escape route for hunted priests in the days of suppression. Now, the stairs alone had survived the rampage that had delivered the house and the boy's grave to the undeserving waves. Now he could tell it was definitely a truck, its arrogant growl too explicit to be mistaken for anything other than that. To his distress, it did not continue on by. It had stopped far enough away to be invisible, but near enough for him to be seen should the mist shift or be summoned back into the waters below. Now he could hear voices that managed to be intense but hushed. He might even have heard his name, but that could be an illusion prompted by the damage done to his concentration by the ear-numbing sound of the truck.

He walked along the edge of the cliff, cautiously, more slowly than he'd prefer, but at a pace acceptable under the circumstances. He did not want to go as the house had gone, as the garden had gone, as the grave had gone—pulled from the heights down into the closing waters. A little way back from the cliffside he found the first of the steps hidden under some overgrown weeds. He began the descent, still cautious, still slow. The voices had faded or, possibly, ceased altogether. He doubted that anyone had seen him.

The rising shroud had enveloped him, taken him into itself, with the whispered promise that it would protect him in this moment of need when he sought nothing but solitude, a separation from the world and all the people in it. He would make his search unseen, unchallenged.

He reached the bottom of the stairs and stepped onto the strewn beach, stumbling on a stone, his progress from then on limited to lurches and sudden fits of thrown balance. It was not that he ignored what was at his feet. The mist wasn't *that* dense, but his eyes had been instructed to disregard anything set in his path and keep themselves alert for any least object the sea might have decided was no longer of interest to itself. He was foolish enough—*crazed* might be the better word—to hope he could find a less primitive entity than salted kelp. He was foolish enough to expect that there at his feet might be a shred of clothing, the cap maybe, or the saddest prize of all, the wounded skull where the fish might have made their home. Anything. Anything at all that he might hold long enough for him to know that there, in his hand, was some remnant of the lost boy. He wanted to hold whatever it might be long enough to feel he had said the final farewell he had saved for the moment he would bury the youth in the soil of Kinvara.

Should he find anything, words might come to him. He would say them, wait for the tide, then return to the grave what had been given by the sea. Declan asked no more. He wanted to be a participant. He wanted to be included in the obsequies. Michael should not have been sent to this lasting rest either in Kinvara or in the sea without some sign, some gesture, some final permission to take leave of this world, to know of Declan's surrender of the boy to the peace that only the grave can give.

Driftwood there was in abundance, some pieces smoothed, polished clean, others, more recent, rough and splintered, torn loose from a sunken boat and sent back to a world that no longer had any use for it. Kelp and weed, frothing as if they were a strung series of mouths gone mad, marked the farthest reach of the receded tide. There were plastic bottles, none capable of offering the final fulfillment of beach glass, its magical colors rivaling the panes set into church windows at a time when it had been thought that faith and glory were one and inseparable. He did find a shoe, but it wasn't Michael's. He didn't even bother to pick it up, much less look for its mate.

He stopped and turned to face the sea. The swelling waves had given him nothing he had sought. He would not complain. The sea was the sea. To rage against it defined absurdity.

The tide had turned again. The beach was narrowing. The mist was being drawn up into the low clouds above. Declan turned to his right and gave one last look at the stretch of beach ahead. Whatever it might hold would have to wait for another time. For an instant the thought came to him that he would continue his search, that the incoming tide would continue its advance at whatever speed it preferred. He would go on. The tide would rise. It would reach the foot of the cliff, and it would continue to rise. Declan's feet, his ankles, calves and thighs, his chest, his shoulders, neck and head would accept the water's arrival, and still he would continue on. He would be drawn into Michael's grave, where he would find the boy waiting, shifting slightly as the swells moved overhead. He would be as he had been when Declan had placed him among Kitty McCloud's cabbages.

The water had come closer. The thought, the intent to seek further, passed on. Declan would go no nearer to where the boy would be. He would simply endure—and give thanks that his grief would never end. There would be other forays, other gleanings, perhaps a finding.

On the beach, about ten feet from the bottom of the stairs, tipped up against a stone, was a book, opened. He stooped and picked it up. Most of the pages were stuck together, sodden, suggesting a long immersion. His nostrils took in the full salt scent the book released as, with limited success, he tried to flip his way through. It was as though the words had been set down not in print or even in ink, but were the product of tears fallen one by one onto a piece of paper and then gathered together to become a book. That the book should be drenched seemed only right. Declan read the words on the title page: *The House of Mirth*. "By Edith Wharton."

It was from the shelves of Kitty McCloud. That much he knew, a book that might require one of her famous "corrections." Would he restore it to Miss McCloud? That it had come from Michael's grave was a claim he could rightly make for himself. But of what interest was it? Could the sea possibly exchange it for something more intimate? The baseball cap, for instance.

He would return the book to Kitty. It was hers, not his, nor was it Michael's. Let the cap come. That he would accept. Nothing less.

4

The cross-eyed pig screamed and squealed as if it were being tormented by a thousand pig demons—even though it was merely being encouraged to walk the ramp onto Lolly and Aaron's truck for transport to Castle Kissane. Head raised, ears pulled straight back, it entreated whichever deities might be attentive to the lamentations of a pig to take pity on its plight, honor its dignity, and smite its tormentors. In partial answer to its prayer, it was awarded new modulations: a more varied pitch and an increase in decibel levels that reached the limits of human hearing.

Aaron gave its hams another slap. The pig, believing itself a horse, reared on its hind legs and would, if it could, have trampled Aaron with its cloven hoofs. "Tell it it's going back to the castle, not to the slaughterhouse," he told his wife.

"I did tell it. It won't listen."

"I can't hear. It's making too much noise."

Lolly, fortunately, had a history of enjoying confusion and calamity, an idiosyncrasy that was a help with the situation now. Adding her happy laughter to the pig's pleadings, she climbed the ramp onto the bed of the truck. After she'd gone as far as the back of the cab, she turned and called out to her husband, "Come on up."

"What?"

Lolly mouthed rather than spoke the words.

Aaron understood. "Why?" he yelled.

Lolly made the appropriate gestures, inviting him to join her. He climbed the ramp. As soon as he was aboard, Lolly kicked away the ramp and put in place the tailgate that fenced the bed of the truck. The pig became silent.

"Face the other way," Lolly said. "And come back here." She returned to the far end.

Aaron followed. "What are we doing?"

"We're letting the pig know we're going without her and leaving her behind."

"We are?"

"We're pretending. Surely you know how to pretend."

"I guess so."

"Then pretend."

Aaron, with a nonchalance so fake even a pig couldn't accept it, looked to his left, then to his right, then up at the sky.

"You're not pretending. You're acting. Pretend for real. Pigs aren't stupid, you know."

Aaron decided to do nothing, an action at which he was more than particularly adept. The pig, moving slowly onto the fallen ramp, came to the end of the truck and snorted softly. Without moving her lips, Lolly said to Aaron, "Don't do anything. Let her beg just a bit more to make sure she got the message."

Aaron stood at his wife's side, trying with all his might to clear his mind of all the thoughts racing through it, the least of which would force from him some gesture, some shifting of his feet, some stretching of his neck. It was not easy for him to pretend upon demand.

After the pig had repeated its soft snortings three times, Lolly, in mercy, removed the tailgate, jumped down, replaced the ramp, and watched as the pig trotted aboard. It went directly to Aaron and rubbed its ringed snout against his pants leg. "You'll have to stay there with her. I don't want her to think she's been tricked," said Lolly. She shoved the ramp up onto the truck bed, told Aaron to replace the tailgate, then went around and climbed into the cab. Smiling widely, she waved through the rearview window, thumped twice against the back of the cab, and drove off to Castle Kissane.

Until now, neither Lolly nor Aaron had been able to figure out what to do with this particular pig. It seemed to be subject to fits, but the summoned veterinarian could find nothing wrong. Various tests validated his prognosis. For the inexplicable episodes of screeching and screaming, no explanation presented itself. And when it repeatedly butted its formidable head against the fences of the penned area, desperate to be set loose, there were fears that it would damage itself, to say nothing of the pen. Also, it would shriek, snout raised skyward, to ward off any other pig that might come too close, creating around itself an impenetrable barrier that none of the other pigs would dare to violate. Intermittent periods of repose seemed more the result of exhaustion than the arrival of some newfound serenity.

This behavior could not continue. It agitated the entire herd. Loss of appetite was the most disturbing symptom. Here, too, the veterinarian could offer nothing but a shake of his head. But if a pig doesn't eat, it doesn't fatten. And if it doesn't fatten, then its sole purpose for being a pig is nullified. A trim and slender pig is not what nature had in mind when the species evolved to its present preferred state: gross and repellent. Slender and cuddly was not an acceptable alternative.

To isolate the pig achieved nothing. The farm's acreage, limited as it was, failed to provide a place that would enable the animal to be out of earshot not only of the herd but of Lolly and Aaron themselves,—not to mention their neighbors. Slaughter was the only solution. This pig, after all, had once been chosen from among the entire herd for such a fate. Its eviscerated, spitted, and roasted carcass had been the intended centerpiece of a communal celebration, a general rejoicing justified by Aaron's aunt Kitty and her husband's having taken possession of Castle Kissane, a bit of real estate distinguished more by its want of lordly proportion than any claim to an imposing dynamic. A castle, however, is still a castle, with a dank dungeon as well as a great hall crowned with an iron chandelier that could accommodate a hundred candles.

The chosen pig, identified by its crossed eyes—the very pig now being carted back to Castle Kissane—had been granted a reprieve by a mistaken last-minute substitution. Another pig had been sent to the spit in its place. Since the sacrificed animal had a somewhat special history, including its unearthing of a skeleton and the eventual pairing of Kitty as well as Kieran, Lolly and Aaron, the loss prompted a revulsion against the spared beast. (That Kitty had made the mistaken substitution was also a factor.) The living animal was forthwith returned to Lolly and Aaron.

But the pig now being returned was no longer the same pig they had chosen for the feast. At the time, it had been as fat as the overstuffed sausage its lesser parts would one day become. Its temperament had been exuberant but agreeable, with no suggestion of rebellion. Now it had become a malcontent, forever outraged by some unknowable deprivation (unless, of course, its discontent derived from having been denied the honor of being spitted and roasted to a crisp succulence and devoured pitilessly by the ravening guests).

That this could be a legitimate complaint, no one would deny, but so excessive was the pig's distress that all sympathy was withheld. The animal must now either calm down or be hauled off to the slaughterhouse, fattened or not fattened. Or, worse, sold to what was known as "intensive," a fate Lolly would never allow for any Irish pig. Her animals were the beneficiary of her insistence that she would be a swineherd if she so chose, even if she were the last independent pig person in all of Ireland. She was determined not to relinquish her calling. In her family, swine-herding reached back to the days of Queen Maeve herself. Never would any pig of hers be confined to an overcrowded area, there to be mechanically fed, with no human hand to give it a slap, no befouled boot to give it a kick. Better the butcher than "intensive."

But before Lolly could say the words aloud—which would make them irrevocable, since she was never known to change her mind—her American husband had made a proposal of his own. They would return the animal to Kitty and Kieran. They were the ones responsible for its current plight. It was at Castle Kissane that the tragic exchange had taken place. It seemed only fair that they should be made to deal with the consequences of their error. Let them suffer the loss of sleep, let them hear the constant cries, let them try what consolations they might. If they didn't want to fatten it, well, that would be their decision, not Lolly's or Aaron's. There would be nothing to trouble their conscience.

•

When the truck reached the castle, Aaron saw Kitty weeding the vegetable patch near the courtyard. As the truck came to a halt, his aunt dusted her hands against her faded jeans and, seeing Aaron in the back of the truck with the pig, called out, "Which one has come to stay? The man or the pig?"

Lolly got out of the cab. "Take your choice."

"The one's too skinny. I'll take the fatter one, even if it's a bit skinnier than I remembered it."

Aaron, an American by birth and not yet accustomed to Irish ways, all but sighed at this display of what he had come to accept as Kerry wit. He removed the tailgate and shoved the ramp into place. He then made the mistake of giving the pig an obligatory slap. The full force of its earlier lament was given new voice. The stubborn refusal to cooperate returned with added resolve. It rooted itself to the bed of the truck, daring one and all to infringe upon its right to be intractable.

Aaron walked down the ramp, went to his aunt, and mouthed his hello. She in turn mouthed hers, then called out to Lolly loud enough to best the noise of the pig's complaints, "Is this what you're leaving us? I'll take the skinny one after all."

Aaron walked over to pretend—his recently acquired expertise—an interest in the garden, thereby distancing himself from the pig. Because he was in Ireland and not America, he allowed himself to engage in some specious reasoning: A pig was woman's work. Not only was it a tradition that the women of the house looked after the animals, but it was a known fact that women had an instinctive sense when it came to understanding nurture. Lolly had known how to get the pig onto the truck. Aaron, therefore, felt it was perfectly permissible that she dip down into her instincts and retrieve the one unfailing gesture that would bring a docile and amiable sow from the bed of their truck onto the castle grounds. It was no concern of his.

Lolly, unable to abbreviate the witty exchange, yelled back to Kitty, "They're both skinny. The pig came back to us fat, but it hasn't eaten since. With all the ructions it's been raising, we'd take it to the butcher in a minute, but we can't until it's put on a bit more bacon. If you and Kieran would just make it more eligible, we'd be obliged."

At a fair remove from the courtyard chaos, Aaron walked around the periphery of the garden, the fresh greens promising vegetables he couldn't identify. It was into cabbages that the dead Declan had been deposited. Aaron couldn't help wondering what might lie beneath the soil he was stepping on now. The castle had a dungeon. Was it into this ground that its occupants had been released? The fact that he and Lolly had put a ring through the delivered pig's snout would at least prevent it from unearthing yet another heap of bones, thereby repeating the havoc Declan Tovey had brought with him from the grave more than a year ago.

As he stood at the far end of the garden near a mound of uprooted weeds, Aaron looked back at his wife, his aunt, and the pig. To his surprise, things seemed somewhat under control. The pig was off the truck and sticking its snout through the rail of the handsomely crafted pen Kieran had built for it during its previous stay. If Aaron interpreted the action rightly, the pig was asking to be put back where it had lived for that brief time before it was the be the star attraction at the castle feast. That it wanted to be penned up was further proof of its derangement. Should they consider having the sow tested for Mad Pig Disease? The animal was now in the custody of Kitty and Kieran. She was their problem.

Now that the pig was quiescent, Aaron made his way back to his waiting wife. He stopped when he saw entering the courtyard a small, rattletrap truck, nearly on the verge of falling apart completely. It was obviously having a fit—one that might prove fatal if the motor wasn't cut off within seconds. The motor was cut. A man got out. Aaron saw his wife take two steps back at the sight of him. His aunt took one step forward. The man hadn't moved away from the truck, suggesting this was not meant to be a prolonged encounter. He had even kept his hand on the door, possibly to expedite a quick getaway should that prove advisable. With the other hand he was holding a book.

The man's pants, coat, and cap replicated almost exactly the clothing worn by the aforementioned unearthed skeleton—before it had been given improved attire more worthy of the laying out, including Aaron's last good shirt. Could this be the man Lolly had seen in Caherciveen and mistaken for Declan Tovey? Aaron snorted with pleased relief. The mystery was solved. It was the similar clothing that had caused the mistaken identity.

Lolly turned and went quickly to the cab of their own truck, opened the door, reached in, and pulled out what he knew to be a fresh ham wrapped in yesterday's *Irish Times*, brought to thank (that is, to bribe) Kitty and Kieran for relieving them of the impossible pig.

"Here's the ham I promised," she called out, a needless explanation. The man's arrival had obviously unsettled her—which was understandable. Even Aaron, who had never seen

Declan Tovey, could agree to a resemblance to what had been described. Wielding the ham in her hand like a primitive club, Lolly continued to explain herself. "I'll put it in your kitch—I mean your scullery." She ran to the door leading into the great hall, entered, and neglected to close the door behind her.

At first, Aaron thought his first responsibility was to check on his wife. He would explain, patiently, what was happening. He was certain that Lolly would be grateful for the correction of her misidentification. Curiosity, however, got the better of him. Before going to his wife, he would accumulate more information, enough to settle the issue once and for all. This must be a Tovey relation newly come into these parts. Or, more likely, someone from the same gene pool as the departed—a possibility he'd already suggested. Lolly would be uncharacteristically shamed to have thought they were being visited by the risen dead, a spirit too impatient to wait for the final trump.

With a step firm and purposeful, Aaron approached. The man had handed Kitty the book. She was staring down at it, then up at the man, then again at the book. She lowered it to her side. She obviously knew the man, and the man knew her—well enough for him to have brought her a book. This implied an intimacy impossible between strangers.

The man was speaking Irish, as was the custom in western Kerry. Kitty was answering in Irish. Aware that Kerry courtesy required that conversations in the company of those denied acquaintance with the native tongue should be conducted in English, Aaron continued toward the man and his aunt.

Their talk continued, in Irish. Aaron, not adept at languages—especially one as seemingly difficult as Irish, with its impossible difference between what was put on the printed page and what was pronounced in actual speech, its insistent dismissal of the phonics on which he'd been schooled—could make out little of what was being said, despite his wife's repeated attempts, during the year since their shared entry into bliss, to teach him the language to which he was a rightful heir, being the son, as he was, of both a Kerry father and a Kerry mother. As far as he could determine from what he thought he could understand, the book had been washed ashore, no doubt from the engulfed McCloud home, but beyond that he could discern nothing. Apparently the man presumed Aaron to have been Kerry-born and Kerry-bred. Aaron expected his aunt to make the required correction, but she was obviously too unsettled by the man's presence to take her nephew's needs into account. Indeed, at the moment, she was not speaking with the casual ease consistent with her nature. Far from it. Stammering and giddy laughs punctuated her words. It seemed this Declan Tovey look-alike had had a certain effect on Kitty, and he should make allowances.

Having waited long enough for common courtesy to assert itself, Aaron held out his hand and said, in English, "I'm Aaron, Kitty's nephew. Lolly's husband." The man gave his head only the slightest turn, his Irish sentence uninterrupted. Not one to waste a gesture, Aaron raised his hand and scratched his forehead.

What he had failed to achieve—getting the attention of his aunt and the man—was accomplished by the pig. It had stayed at the pen and, between snorts, seemed transfixed by the empty space inside. For a moment, Aaron thought he could understand what the man said next, but his translation immediately informed him that he was mistaken in his assumption. He had thought he'd heard the man say, in Irish,

"It wants to get in. To be with the other pig." Since there was no other pig, it was readily apparent that Aaron's linguistic ineptitude was persisting despite his best efforts. The pig was staring at nothing. Which meant that, in his incompetence, Aaron was obviously in continuing error and should end his effort at even minimal understanding.

To further persuade him that any attempt at comprehension was an exercise in futility, he thought the man said the English equivalent of "They can't be together. Is that the truth of it?" Which made less sense than anything that had gone before.

His aunt made a few mumbled sounds, then spoke up, too loud at first, then with a more moderated voice, but in words that only increased his exasperation. "No. I . . . I mean I don't know. I don't know if they can be together or not."

Whatever she might have actually said, it brought a smile to the man's face. His teeth were perfect, the smile, even to Aaron, dazzling. After a few more words Aaron didn't even try to understand, the man started toward the pen.

With a nervous glance at Aaron, his aunt blurted out a torrent of words that seemed to plead with the man to ignore the pig, the pen, and return to their previous conversation.

But the man was unheeding. He lifted the latch and opened the gate. The pig, as if relieved of a great anxiety, moved with an almost dainty step into the enclosure. The man shut and latched the gate. Quiet now, the pig looked skyward, trying, it seemed, to discover within or beyond the clouds overhead the source of its apparent newly bestowed serenity. As if still surprised by this change in its temperament, the pig's crossed eyes searched the pen, hoping to find some hint of what had brought about the transformation. But seeming to find nothing that might explain its wonderment, obviously unable to see the ghost of the pig it had so contentedly known in the days before the fated feasting, it simply stood there, allowing a benediction to descend, no longer requiring that it know from whence it came. All Aaron could do, deprived as he also was of noting the slain pig's presence, was to snort his perplexity, then make one last attempt at inclusion in the continuing conversation. So he said, in English, "See? I knew here at the castle is where the pig wanted to be. It likes being by itself. We should never have taken it back. It should have stayed here. Look at how happy it is, being here all by itself. Right?"

The man looked at Aaron as if offended that an imbecile was trying to insinuate himself into a conversation for which he was so obviously unqualified. To lessen the befuddlement brought on by Aaron's words, he said, "Alone?"

Kitty, aghast as if the word *alone* required an immediate change of subject, turned to her nephew and said, "I've been rude. Forgive me. Rude. And thoughtless. We're happy to have the pig here with us. Anything to oblige. Good. Good for it. I mean, good for us, too. That it likes it here."

With this, it occurred to Aaron that his own presence was as disconcerting as that of the Tovey look-alike. Had it been Declan Tovey himself, such a response from his aunt might be understandable. Aaron was, after all, married to an object of the departed Mr. Tovey's affections. But this was not Declan Tovey—which made his aunt's behavior that much more inexplicable.

As if sent by the merciful gods to release his wife from whatever had taken hold of her, Kieran was seen coming toward them, lugging the wheeled apparatus for spraying the apple orchard. After a less-than-welcoming intake of breath at the sight of the visitant, he took a quick look at the pig and gave it a resigned shake of his head. Then he, too, saw fit to speak in Irish, as if the pig were a subject unfit for Aaron's consideration. He said something about the pigs certainly getting along together. Then Aaron had a thought that should have come sooner, even taking into consideration his limited and scrambled sense of the language: Kieran, like Kitty, had so deeply missed the sacrificed animal that had once occupied (to its disadvantage) the latched enclosure with the pig now in undeniable residence that they kept making references to it as if it were still a corporeal presence. Pleased with himself for the insight, he became less dissatisfied with his linguistic disability and more accepting of his exclusion from the conversation, which, no doubt, would continue to assault his questionable sense of adequacy. Kieran, having reduced his show of displeasure with the man to a neutral, almost indifferent stare, put his arm around his wife's waist and drew her close, as if she were in need of protection. Kitty, in turn, glanced up at him with a sad but grateful smile, expressed more with her eyes than with her lips.

The man made no move at all, impervious to the discomfort he was causing. Kieran removed a glove and wiped the back of his hand across his mouth either to signal a readiness for combat or, more likely, to give himself more time to think of what he might say.

He shouldn't have bothered. The man was speaking again. In Irish. Kieran listened. Aaron heard mention of a Maude McCloskey, a woman who lived a ways up the road and was said to be somewhat peculiar. When the man stopped speaking, Kieran responded, still in Irish—which Aaron may or may not have deciphered. Thatching may have been the subject. The man nodded what proved to be a farewell, turned, and went back to his contraption, his head bowed, seemingly lost in thoughts far from what he had been discussing with Aaron's unsettled aunt and her unwelcoming husband. What a sad comparison the man made to the departed thatcher Aaron had been told so much about, with his huge pride, his unconquerable daring. Aaron came close to pitying the man, but was prevented from completing the impulse by his lingering resentment at the man's indifference to Kerry customs and his dismissal of common courtesy.

The man paused a moment in his advance, looked over at the pig, then continued on. Without a backward glance or gesture, he got into the truck, started the motor, made the necessary turn, and headed up the castle road.

Aaron's expectation that some explanation—in English— of what he had endured would now be forthcoming was sorely disappointed, because his wife chose exactly that moment to emerge from the castle and summon him to their truck. After hurried farewells and a terse repetition of gratitude for Kitty and Kieran's having accepted the pig and her hopes for its assured obesity, she then drove them away from the castle, away from the pig, and away from the day's confusions.

Aaron used the ride home to try to sort out the unnerving happenings—and the no less unnerving conduct of everyone concerned, especially his aunt. Lolly was of no help. References to a second pig were of no interest. Until, of course, Aaron mentioned his aunt's agitated conduct, as if she were suffering some temporary derangement in response not only to the man's presence but to his repeated insistence that a second pig was in the pen. Lolly scoffed. "Of course she's deranged. Crazy. Crazy about Declan Tovey. I had to get myself away from the two of them with that ham we brought. I didn't want to see what was surely going to happen. I know she's your aunt, but you have to face facts. Kieran Sweeney settled for decidedly experienced goods."

Aaron almost reminded his wife that this was hardly Declan Tovey. A facsimile perhaps, but they both knew where the actual thatcher was at that very moment. Rather than take up yet again the subject of look-alike versus ghost, he decided—prompted by his wife's reference to his aunt and her younger life—to revert to his wife's comment about his aunt's youthful "experience." "Strange. *Experienced* may not have been her exact word, but it comes close. My aunt said pretty much the same about you and Mr. Tovey just before we were married."

"Of course she did. My best friend. Accusing me of what she'd done herself. Trying to make sure Sweeney—poor deluded man that he is—would never believe the truth about all her goings-on. Really." She relieved herself of a sigh.

"Strange. When I mentioned what you'd said about her and Declan right after we found the skeleton, she said almost the exact same thing. Except it was about you accusing her."

"She's the one telling the terrible lies. I'm the one dealing in fact, not fiction."

"Again, her exact same words." He made no attempt to suppress a smile.

"You needn't be so pleased. I *am* your wife. And if you want it to stay that way—"

"My aunt making up stories or not making up stories is, at the moment, beside the point. What's more important is what she was saying to Kieran while that man was still there."

"What was she saying, liar that she tends to be?"

"It was in Irish . . ."

"You don't speak Irish. You try. But it's better you don't."

"I won't argue with that. All that nonsense about the pig—well, let it go. But what I also may or may not have picked up is that the man was offering to thatch the roofs of the courtyard sheds. For nothing. Something about Maude McCloskey's husband maybe coming back, so she's changed her mind about her own roof. But the next thing I think I understood—if I got any of it right—was Kitty telling Kieran after the guy left, 'He sees our pig the same as we do.' Whatever that might mean."

"No more about the pig if you don't mind. Are you ready for the real truth?"

"Probably not. But go ahead."

"That was Declan Tovey. In the flesh I might add."

"Oh? And now who's deranged?"

"I knew it was Declan the minute he stepped out of his truck."

"You mean your Declan was the only thatcher who could drive a truck?"

"Try not to be quite so smart."

"I'm trying to stay sane. Next you'll be back to telling me it was his ghost."

"It wasn't his ghost. Ghosts don't smell. At least not like Declan Tovey. I'd know that smell anywhere. It's like . . . it's like . . ." She stopped, unable to go further.

His expression gone deliberately blank, Aaron turned and looked at his wife. "Like what?"

"Like Declan Tovey," she said quietly.

Tempted to ask how she had become so familiar with the

scent of the man's flesh, he resisted. He'd resort to the obvious, to the question that now had to be asked. "Then who was that who took my best shirt with him to the bottom of the sea?"

"I haven't the slightest. Probably someone Declan murdered and put in with the cabbages. Who knows?"

"Aren't you even interested in finding out?"

"I gave up a long time ago trying to know or even to speculate on the doings of Mr. Tovey. But he must have done something that makes him go looking to see where his handiwork went, haunting around the old place on the cliffs that made us think he was a ghost."

"Not 'us.' You."

"Same thing."

"If you say so."

"I just did."

"Fine. But why would he murder someone?"

"How can you not know that? He was jealous."

"Of who?"

"Of whom. I was a writer once, don't forget."

"All right. Of whom?"

"Ask him."

"So he's capable of killing someone because he's jealous?"

"Well, I would hope so."

After an extended pause, Aaron said, "You don't think he . . . well . . . he's jealous of . . . well . . . of me, do you?"

"Ask him."

"Am I allowed to suspect he might have a reason to be jealous?"

"You're allowed to do anything you want. You're an adult."

"Including thinking he might murder me?"

"Ask him."

"The idea doesn't . . . well . . . disturb you?"

A small smile came to Lolly's face. "All right, then, I'll ask him myself. And if he says yes, I'll do anything I possibly can to persuade him not to. Does that satisfy you?" After a quick giggle, she leaned toward her husband and pecked his cheek.

Aaron turned to look at his wife. Her smile had broadened and the glint in her eyes intensified as it was refracted from the windshield, making her enviable auburn hair seem even more lustrous. Never had he seen her as beautiful as she was at this present moment. But he was no longer quite so sure he was that pleased that his wife had regained all her mirth.

Added to his unease that a fully fleshed Declan Tovey had now come among them was the unavoidable revelation that his wife was not, as she had claimed at the skeleton's wake, the one and only murderer of the then presumed thatcher stretched out in the coffin before her. Instead of being relieved to discover that the most beautiful woman in the world, now seated next to him, was innocent, he was given the realization that this latest truth was merely prologue to yet another: He had not married a possible killer. "Can you love someone might be a murderer?" she had asked him after the remains of the obviously murdered man had been drawn down to the sea and Kitty's house along with them. It had been Kieran who, taking in his hand the hand of his lifelong foe, one Kitty McCloud, said, "I can" (in consideration of the confession his aunt had offered at the wake), after which Lolly, ever Kitty's competitor, had been compelled to claim the crime as her own. His aunt had answered Kieran, in tones that defied contradiction, "I can," knowing that Kieran, not to be outdone, had also confessed.

Aaron, subsumed in this orgy of admissions, had, without pause, taken Kitty's hand in his and had ardently proclaimed, "I can!"—surely the most courageous utterance he'd ever made. He could, and did, love a woman who might be a murderer.

But now, the bravery that had been so nourishing to his self-satisfaction, to say nothing of its considerable contribution to the oddity of his marriage, had been nullified. Should he feel diminished? Should he admit that his marriage was not the brave and generous deed he had so smugly thought it to be? Before he could even articulate the questions to himself, they were set at a remove for consideration at some distant date. The day had already been challenging enough. Surely a postponement was allowed.

They made the turn toward home, toward the pigs that greeted them with a chorus of shrieks and squeals, a cacophony in which Aaron thought he could detect some strains of derisive Irish laughter.

5

Maude McCloskey was the local Hag—or, to put it
more respectfully, the village Seer, a woman reputed
to have Cassandra-like gifts enabling her to perceive
truths and knowledge hidden from the common eye. She was
not exactly Kitty's favorite. Most likely it was envy. Kitty, as
a writer, considered herself a truth-teller capable of creating
a past, a present, and a future, and she resented that Maude
could so effortlessly achieve somewhat comparable results
without having recourse to the endless days and nights of hard
labor required of Kitty herself.

Still, a summons from a woman of Maude's peculiarity
could not be ignored. Teatime was the specified hour. What
the woman wanted from Kitty would be revealed soon enough,
but it was a fairly good guess that it concerned the latest intrusion into Kitty's already challenged life. Declan had had traffic
with the woman—first to thatch her roof, then not to thatch
her roof—and it was not impossible that his and Maude's
negotiations had ended with some of Maude's curiosities left
unsatisfied.

Even though, as far as Kitty could figure out, the woman
knew nothing of Declan's previously presumed demise and his

perturbing return, she might have some awareness of his ability to see the castle ghosts. It was Maude, after all, who, without being able to see Brid and Taddy at Kitty's wedding feast,
had identified them by name from the descriptions given.
Maude knew of their existence and of Kitty's privileged relationship to them.

Did she hope to exact from Kitty some addition to what
she already suspected—that she could see Taddy and Brid?
Was Kitty now to inform the all-seeing Seer? This had its
appeal, a turnabout that tempted Kitty to commit the unfor-
givable sin of smugness. To overcome the temptation, she
decided she would be wary and uncooperative while sipping
her tea. If Maude's divinations weren't sufficient to her needs,
scant help would she get from Kitty McCloud. And besides,
Kitty had more than several questions of her own. According
to her plan, her highly developed talent for manipulation, for
dissembling, for getting what she wanted without having to
demean herself by asking for it, would be activated to the full.

With anyone but Maude, she could bring into play the
full force of her formidable resources. So the coming interview could require a bit more expenditure of her talents than
usual, and she felt some anxiety about their effectiveness with
the oracular Maude. What helped her calm even this minimal unease, however, was a sense of challenge. Quite possibly
she was the equal of Maude McCloskey when it came to psy-
chic ability. Maude's aptitudes were limited to the reportorial;
Kitty's were engendered by creativity. Kitty could draw upon
anything within her imagining—a resource vast and varied.
Maude was stuck with reality, be it past, present, or yet to
come—a decidedly limited capability compared to the skills of
the cunning operator Kitty McCloud knew herself to be.

Maude, Kitty hoped, would pass on some knowledge concerning the return of Mr. Tovey. That he had not come in spectral form was now accepted. But who, then, had been put into her cabbage patch? Then, too, why was Declan allowed—with an ease that suggested long acquaintance—to see Taddy and Brid? And the ghostly pig as well? Her first reason for engaging him as thatcher was that, in time, she could be fairly direct in addressing these issues.

Her second reason, it should be noted, was her determination to reclaim the great hall, relieving it of cow flop and the piles of reeking straw, to restore its ancient austerity. It was an offense to Kitty that the hundred-candled chandelier from which Taddy and Brid had been hanged should crown a space given over to cows, peaceable creatures though they might be. She and Kieran had waited far too long to bring back the cold dignity that would be a more fitting memorial to the martyred pair. The flagstones, enduring repositories of the gunpowder still capable of sending the castle heavenward, must be unsullied, a tribute—inadequate as it would always be—to the fair Taddy and the incomparable Brid, a reminder of Hanging Lord Shaftoe's perfidy that nothing could expiate except a damnation that would outlast eternity itself.

So calmed had Kitty become with the appointment soon to take place that, as she climbed the first of the three hills that led to Maude's cottage, she found herself reverting to a long-time habit: She would work while she walked. Declan's delivery of *The House of Mirth* had unsettled her. It was the one and only retrieval from her departed house. That in itself should have been enough to trouble her mind. Why had it been sent back—and nothing else? But, she reminded herself, she *was* a writer. And the novel by Mrs. Wharton, aka Pussy Jones, had, by its presence on her shelf, been considered a candidate for correction. Now it had made a somewhat insistent re-entry, demanding honest consideration. Kitty could claim that she didn't believe in signs or omens, but she also hadn't believed in ghosts—and look at her now. While striding down the far side of the hill, her mind wandered back to Declan's delivery of the book. From there it was one step further to recall his mention of having seen Maude. And from there it was a half step to a thought that hadn't occurred to her before. Had Maude invited him? Or had he sought her out? Had they met by accident? Was talk of a possible thatching a pretext for their meetings? Maude and Declan had no shared history that Kitty knew of. Could it be possible . . .

As soon as this absurdity introduced itself, it was intensified. Kitty couldn't help it. What had suggested itself was not possible. Declan couldn't! For all his iniquities he did have *standards*. Kitty herself was surely the living proof of that. Never would he descend so low as to . . . No. He wouldn't. Not Maude McCloskey. He couldn't. Not Declan, who had been made familiar with such splendors that he could never, *never* defile the supreme glory provided by Kitty herself by trying to replicate it, much less best it, with such inferior offerings.

Kitty pressed forward, going up the road and down with even greater determination. As she climbed the second hill, Peter, Maude's eight-year-old son, came alongside on his bicycle, his backpack filled with school books strapped in place on the handlebars, his dog, Joey, trotting at his side. He stopped. The dog stopped, too.

Peter's toes touched the roadway to balance the bike as he began to walk next to Kitty. "Is it all right I'm with you? You look so far away with your thinking." His clothes were disheveled, his sweater twisted to the side, his shirt tugged out of his pants, the pants muddied at the knees, and his untied shoes covered with bits of turf. His right cheek was stained with grass, and there were scratches among the beads of sweat. His hair, however, was the same as always, a comb being an accessory unknown to his toilette.

It was Kitty's assumption that the faithful dog had arrived too late to participate in the schoolyard melee where its famous courage on its master's behalf might have been of some use. "Because I'm skinny, he's trained to bite anyone who touches me at school," Peter had explained when, the year before, the dog had bitten her when she did no more than affectionately touch Peter's cheek. Where had the dog been when its services could have been put to good purpose?

In answer to his question about her faraway look, Kitty said, "I was fussing in my head over the book I'm considering for my next project."

"Oh, a book. Of course. My mother says you're one of the great ones. Is that true?"

Kitty paused not at all. "Well, who am I to contradict your mother."

"She says you see things no one else can see. Is that true, too?"

"Well, that's why writers write. (That both Peter and his mother were known to possess extravagant capabilities of this nature she would not mention.)

"Oh, is that why you write?" He rubbed his distressed cheek. "I thought it was to make money and buy a castle."

"One can hardly dismiss the unintended fruits of one's labor, can one?"

"No, I suppose not. And it would be a sad thing not to have you and Mr. Sweeney there, such a fine place and no one to live in it. It wouldn't be right. Is it coming to tea you are?"

"Well, your mother was kind enough to invite me."

"Then it must be she has things to tell."

Kitty's interest expanded. "Did she say that?"

"She doesn't have to. It's usually why she asks people to come. And I'm glad you'll be there. With you in the house she won't beat me for playing football after school when I should be home doing chores."

By now they were walking side by side, Peter instinctively placing the bicycle between Kitty and the dog. "Beats you?" Kitty asked. "With Joey there, too? And he does nothing the like of which he did to me that time?"

"Oh, he helps her. He nips at my ankles while my mother sees to the sides of my head."

"Could it be your clothes all messed and your face given a good drubbing that brings it all about?"

"My clothes? What about my clothes? Can you tell I've been playing? And my face? What's wrong with my face?"

"Peter, you've been playing football. It's either that or someone dragged you along through the mud."

"No one has dragged me. I'm the best on the team and they all know it."

"You?" Kitty immediately repented the amazement in her voice. Quickly she added, "I didn't even know you played."

"You didn't? Everyone knows I play. Everyone knows how brilliant I am. And you didn't know that at all?"

"I do now."

"You're surprised because I'm short and I'm skinny. But that's why I'm so brilliant. When you're short and skinny, the first thing you learn is to run. Fast. So many times there are when you have to get away. And I learned—because I had to. Now I can outrun anyone. And the ball, so many times things were taken away from me. But now, running, and my foot guiding and kicking the ball, I dare anyone to try to get it away from me. They never do. Well, hardly ever."

"I must come watch."

"Oh, no. Today was the last time for a while. I worry it wears my mother down to beat me. She starts losing her breath, and she's only through with one side of my head and the other side still to be done. I can't do that to her. Not for a while at least. And before I forget, my mother says you're an old friend of Declan Tovey's and maybe you could talk to him and tell him he should take me on and teach me the ways of a thatcher. My mother said she asked him and he only spoke two words: 'No. Never.' And he'd give no reason why. My mother says it's a dying art and I should learn it before no one knows it at all. But he, Mr. Tovey, he wouldn't take his words away. Except maybe if you talked to him—because he's your close friend, my mother says, and people do things for close friends. Can you do that?"

Well, thought Kitty, now I know the reason for the invitation. Then, unable to restrain herself, she had to ask, "But isn't your mother a close friend of Mr. Tovey's, too?"

Before he could answer, there was Maude herself at her open door and Kitty and Peter not ten feet away, Maude in her black skirt and white blouse that, to Kitty's thinking, almost replicated the school uniform that represented the first flowering of Maude's approaching glory. It is not uncommon, Kitty thought, for people to cling to the costuming they believe contributed to the allure of their youthful days, but it had always bewildered Kitty that Maude had felt the need. True, she, like Kitty herself, had been a bit late coming into her destined splendor, but most surely it had arrived by now. And Maude could well afford to clothe herself in raiment better than that imposed upon a gawky girl in school.

The woman, her lips given over to a happy and expectant grin, said, cheerful as was her way, "I knew it was you."

Of course she knew. Maude had invited her. Still, the words bothered Kitty. Did the Hag's clairvoyance track her every move, or did Kitty have to come within a given radius to have her movements observed? With a cheerfulness confidently competitive with Maude's, Kitty said, "The promise of a boiling kettle? How could I not be here?"

"Yes, it does enjoy a good whistle now and then. As who doesn't." She stepped aside to let the chatelaine of Castle Kissane cross her threshold. Which Kitty did, hearing the words the woman spoke to her son: "And you, young man, might want to change from your good school clothes before I have a chance to see them all messed and ruined the way they are."

Peter rushed past Kitty and through a door to the right, his shirttail flapping in the breeze his swift passage had created.

"The girls, Margaret and Ellen, are at play practice, the school pageant," Maude said. "Singing, dancing, as only they can, the loves. They'll weep to know they've missed you. Sit yourself down and I'll be back in a jiffy. You'll probably hear the kettle as well as I."

"And a lovely sound, too."

"The best there is."

Nearly knocking over a small table to the left of the

kitchen door, Maude managed to make it out of the room. For all her Seer-like attributes, she had been denied the simple gift of seeing what lay directly in front of her.

The television was on but the sound taken down. Kitty couldn't believe what was being shown. A rerun of a popular miniseries of *Pride and Prejudice* with an actress whose name was, if Kitty remembered correctly, Jennifer Ehle as Elizabeth, and Colin Firth, handsome beyond bearing, playing Darcy. Both, with unutterable charm, were testing their true feelings one for the other, just to make sure that several added episodes would be necessary, a succession of scenes, until Ms. Austen decided she'd been delighted enough and would, with infinite subtlety and unmatched skill (unmatched, of course, now that Kitty McCloud had abandoned any efforts at improvement) ease them into a presumably secure fulfillment.

Kitty forced herself to watch. They were still at it, Darcy so pridefully polite and Elizabeth so protective of her prejudice against the man, that it was all Kitty could do to keep herself from rising up, going to the television, and giving them both a slap.

No kettle had ever sounded, but, before long, Maude came in with the tray. "The tea has gone off somewhere, but this should do." She set the tray down on the table at the side of her chair, then went to the television and turned it off. "We don't want them watching, do we?"

Kitty could see on the tray the teapot and two cups and saucers. In each cup was an olive. Maude sat down and poured a clear liquid into each cup, the sound of ice cubes rattling inside the pot. "Since you've had your years in America, I thought this might be appreciated. I did, of course, change the recipe a bit, but shouldn't one always?"

"Oh, yes. Surely." Maude was up to something. But then so was Kitty.

Maude held out the tray toward Kitty. "You first."

"I'll take this one. It has more in it."

"Spoken like a true American." Her voice was under-scored with a waiting laugh. After she had put the remaining cup on the table next to her, she set the tray down on the floor in front of her chair. The two women, teacup in hand, saluted each other. Kitty took a delicate sip. She saw nowhere to set down her cup and saucer, so held them until Maude, after a less delicate sip, set hers down on the tray at her feet. Kitty took this as permission to place her own cup on the carpet.

"Oh, no, dear, not on the carpet. It wants to be cleaned and I haven't done it." With the toe of her shoe she nudged the tray toward Kitty, placing it within reach. "Here," she said, "surely this can accommodate more than one."

Next to the teapot, Kitty saw a bowl of olives. Teatime was obviously going to be an extended session. Taking her cue from her hostess, before putting her cup down, she took a second sip, not as delicate as the first. Then she set the cup and saucer on the tray next to the bowl of olives. As she leaned down, she had a vision of herself and Maude toppling over onto the tray at teatime's end, when they both would have quaffed their fill. Kieran would have to come and cart her home.

This, she decided, must not be allowed to happen. And besides, before the visit had come to an end, she would have teased out of Maude some sensible explanation relative to the confusions she brought to the Hag's door. But would Kitty herself be wiser as to what Maude had in mind when she'd made the invitation? Peter's interest in thatching did not completely explain the woman's willingness to upend her gin bottle and indulge in this extravagant show of hospitality. What did Maude want from her? Had Peter told her about last year's revelations, Kitty and Kieran's shameful family history? Did Maude know that an ancestor of hers and an ancestor of his had pledged to blow up the castle and had then gone off to Tralee to alert relatives about their coming marriage? Had Maude, in a Haglike moment, been informed of the discovery of Declan's bones and their wind-induced burial at sea? Had Maude made herself present at the wake with no fewer than three confessions of murder and no judgment available as to the identity of the actual despatcher?

If Kitty were to be confronted with all of this, she would admit nothing—and ask for a double dose of olives in the next round of their contest. Let Maude believe what she believed, see what she may have seen. She'd get no verifications from Kitty no matter how many olives had been consumed.

After Maude had taken another considerable sip, she leaned back and provided the opening gambit of the game that was sure to follow: "It would seem Declan Tovey has come back to us."

Kitty made her next sip a Maude-sized gulp. This accomplished, she looked forward to eating the olive, but that would wait until after she had said, "He was a long time away. Have you any idea of where he might have gone off to?"

Maude, too, drained her cup. "I thought surely you would be the one to know, close as the two of you once were, unless it be Lolly McKeever—or is it Lolly McCloud now? Well, no matter. But one of you or the two of you must still be aware of where he might have gone and what he's up to now that he's back."

"Really?" Kitty picked up the olive, turned it over between thumb and forefinger, then dropped it back down into the cup. "It's been my impression that you yourself had by far the greater claim than anyone to the doings of Declan Tovey."

"I? Oh, no. I could never presume to be privy, as it were, to privileges bestowed upon many, but never, shall we say, never *accepted* by some. Among the deprived I number myself. On some subjects I know so little. But you—"

"For all the many times he was among us, surely he impressed you sufficiently for you to—"

"I was never very impressionable in that way. Unlike some. I had, as you know, distractions not of my own choosing. So it could be that I was inclined to engage myself in other 'pursuits.' Yes. Other. But you . . ."

Kitty popped the olive into her mouth and began to chew vigorously, clamping down on the pit. But rather than admit to her distress, she said, chewing more slowly, "So he made no impression when you saw him last? And you had not even the curiosity to ask where he'd been? Could it be that you already knew?"

Competitive to the last, Maude, too, popped her olive into her mouth, but sucked on it instead of chewing. Then, holding it in her right cheek, she said, "I had no reason to ask. Of the two of us, you must be the more knowledgeable. Don't forget, Kitty dear, as I mentioned on other occasions, you know a great deal. Sometimes I suspect you surpass even me in, well, in perceptions and events that would, at best, invite my envy. Don't forget, I myself have told you, you are a prophet. In this instance, I know whereof I speak. It's in your writings. You know truths unsuspected by the rest of us. You have God's greatest gift: an imagination. What is to prevent some power you already possess from extending its range, so that an unheard voice might say, 'Don't stop. Keep reaching, farther, farther.' I know many things and that is one of them." Now she began chewing. Rapidly. So rapidly that she soon pulled the pit from her mouth and put it on the tray. Kitty did likewise.

As she poured from the pot, Maude asked more quietly, "Have I gone too far?" She dropped an olive into each cup. There was a minor splash.

"No," said Kitty. "It's all right. It's just that I'm not used to anyone knowing what my writing is really about." She drank.

"Not just your writing. You. You, Kitty McCloud. The gift is yours. Don't be afraid. Accept it. I did. And my dear sweet Peter, he has accepted it, too, child that he is. Now it's you must do it." She drank.

"I . . . I'm sorry, but I don't really understand." Kitty drank some more.

"Have another olive. And here's a bit of something to wash it down." She started to tip the pot.

"Oh, I mustn't."

"When did that ever stop you?" Maude poured, and for herself as well. "There's nothing to understand," she said. "It's beyond understanding. That's the point. You speak of Declan Tovey. You think I know what I don't know. And I don't, I promise you. I know only what everyone else knows about most things. Now I'm talking about the tales, or the common gossip that keeps a long night from getting longer. What we were talking about before wasn't, of course, rumors. You and Lolly McKeever. And Declan Tovey. Those are facts. What I mean now are the old stories. Ancestors, Taddy, Brid, you remember all that, I'm sure. Oh, and by the way, do you still

see them? Taddy and Brid? At your wedding feast, remember
how they were there? You didn't even know their names. And
you the only one could see them. Are they still about?"

"We . . . we were talking about Declan. About ancestors."

"Oh, yes. That. But you must know about it already.
Declan and the hanging in the castle. *Your* castle I might add."

"Declan and the hanging?" Kitty wondered if now was the
time for another sip. She decided it was.

"Surely you've heard it all from the time you were born."

"Tell me now, so I'll know whether I know it or not."

"A tale is all it is, except the Toveys themselves always
told it as gospel truth. And who could blame them, claiming
to be descended from heroes and all that."

"No. I don't know any of this."

Maude chose to laugh. "Don't tell me the McClouds paid
no attention to what was said for centuries at every hearth in
the village."

"Possibly. But what is it about Declan being descended
from heroes?"

With an eager smile, Maude replenished the cups. "You'll
stop me when it becomes familiar. Promise?"

Kitty took a generous gulp. "Promise."

"The hanging. You know about that?"

"I do."

"Good. We'll start with that. And you'll speak up if you've
already heard—"

"Yes, yes. I promise."

"The hanging. The gunpowder. A Lord Shaftoe coming
back after a few generations gone, two centuries and more ago.
He hears of a plot to blow him up. All that you know. We
talked about it at the wedding. But here begins the Declan

part. His lordship demands to know who's plotting against him. The villagers, the cottagers around, some, he insists, must know. The miscreants must be informed on. But no one speaks up—probably because no one really knows. Hostages are taken. Brid. Taddy. Lovely it's said they were. Young and to be married one day. Either the plotters be delivered up or the young ones hanged."

"All this I know." Kitty's patience was being sore tried.

"Well, then, here comes Declan." Maude lifted the pot and poured again. Kitty did not protest. Maude went on. "Ancestors of Declan, an old man by now, and an old woman, they present themselves to his lordship. He expects them to confess, which in its own way disappoints him. He had looked forward to stringing up someone young and with a whole life to be lived. But then he's not disappointed after all. The old couple had come not to confess but to offer themselves in the hostages' stead. They plead. 'Let them live. Let ourselves be hanged and they go free.' But his lordship will have none of it."

She took a goodly gulp. "Why the stupid fools didn't simply confess, get themselves hanged, and be done with it, no one really knows. The Toveys have always claimed that the old man, the old woman, thinking themselves about to be dead, were afraid to tell a lie and be damned for it. Believe it or not, that's what the family has claimed."

Maude plunked another olive in each cup. Kitty began to make a gesture of protest, but changed her mind. Maude poured. After she'd set the teapot down, she went on. "To reward the old woman and the old man for their insolence in coming before his lordly self without naming the names he had demanded, he had them whipped and sent home. And to the villagers, seeing them in pain and with the blood showing through their clothing, and begging an explanation, the old couple tell their sorry story. Just as you've heard it now. If it's gospel or not, I'll leave it for you to decide." She raised her cup and held it out in salute to the tale she'd told.

With only the slightest hesitation, Kitty responded with her own raised cup. And how could she not? Maude, possibly knowing exactly what she was doing, had given her some information she'd neglected to hope for. Naturally, Kitty was a bit disappointed that more had not been required of her own gifts for manipulation, but she could hardly register a complaint. It was a triumph, and she must not deny herself the pleasures it had offered. Now she knew. Declan's ancestry, like hers, like Kieran's, had made possible his sightings of Taddy and of Brid. What Maude had said might have been only a village rumor, but it was not impossible that she had given the tale this lesser designation—as opposed to an outright vision proceeding from her Seerage—to diminish the authority and spare Kitty the accusation that she was inventing from first to last what she'd given.

Kitty had no trouble believing. It all made sense—if such a word could be applied to something so totally contrary to the common definition. She emptied her cup. Maude emptied hers. The moment demanded nothing less.

Now Kitty understood the reason for her summons. Judging other people by her own example, she had expected an unending exchange of manipulations: Maude determined to know what Kitty knew about Declan, Kitty equally determined to exact from the Hag any knowledge she might have. And here Maude was, deliberately telling Kitty a not improbable story relating to Declan and Brid and Taddy. Kitty and

Kieran's ability to see the couple proceeded from a truth less heroic. Their ancestors had (unwittingly) been responsible for the hanging. Declan's ancestors were much the opposite. And Maude had helped her to know it.

There might have been an element of spite in the telling, Maude reveling in the disparity of ancestral contributions to the fate of the young martyrs, but Kitty was too grateful to give that particular reading to Maude's motive. The woman had done a good and generous deed, and Kitty would concentrate on that to the exclusion of other more satisfying possibilities. Friends they would be from this moment on.

Maude was reaching for the olives again when Peter came into the room. She leaned closer to Kitty and whispered, "Let me get the child out of here and we'll have still another. I don't encourage myself to do it in front of family. You understand." She turned toward her son, now changed into jeans with the obligatory rip at the knees and a T-shirt smaller than those worn by boys in this day and age. It barely reached mid-thigh, much less to his knees. "Be a good boy now and run along. You've chores. And if I'm not mistaken, you're a bit late. Is that true?"

"Yes, Ma."

"Then do as you're told. And say goodbye to Mrs. Sweeney. No. To Ms. McCloud."

Having paid minimum attention to what his mother had been saying, Peter reached down and picked up one of the olive pits from the tray. Kitty suspected it was one of hers. With a mixture of curiosity and concentration, he began turning it over, staring at it.

Kitty knew immediately what he was doing. He'd done it before, once with a piece of dried mucus picked from his nose, another time with a button popped from Lord Shaftoe's shirt when the man had tried to jump to his death from the castle parapet and was rescued by Kieran. Peter would now offer some revelation. Kitty had no choice but hold her breath.

But before the boy could speak, Maude reached over and plucked the pit from his fingers. Gasping as if struck, Peter looked in bewilderment at his mother. "Now run along, son. And say goodbye to Ms. McCloud. Or must I say it yet again?"

Peter blinked and turned his head away as if trying to remind himself of where he was. He looked down into his empty hand and blinked again like one awakening, puzzled by a dream already escaped back into the world from whence it had come. "Oh. Yes." His bewilderment had not quite dispersed. "Well . . . goodbye, Miss McCloud." He paused, then added, "Did my mother ask you to talk to Mr. Tovey about me thatching? To learn the trade? I . . . I'd like that. You'll ask him, then?"

So mournfully lost did the boy seem that Kitty had to say, "I'll do what I can, surely."

He nodded. "Yes. And thank you." Without looking at his mother, who was still holding the olive pit, he started out the door, turned to take one more perplexed look at Kitty, then closed the door behind him.

"Finish up so we can have another." Maude was still whispering. "And do ask Declan. It would mean so much to the boy."

Kitty put her hand over her cup. "Oh, no. No more. I think I've had enough. And it . . . it's very kind of you. Very kind. But I'd better be going. Too many olives disagrees with me. I can't understand why."

"Me, too. I can't understand it at all, either." Maude picked up the pot and filled Kitty's cup to the brim. Kitty watched, not particularly displeased. "Now tell me," Maude said, "you are coming to see the girls in the pageant, aren't you?"

Kitty realized the official business had been tended to. The social moment had arrived, and she must give it equal attention. The time for revelations had passed. Maude, knowingly or not, had given Kitty the ancestral justification for Declan's ability to see the ghosts of Taddy and Brid, the apparent reason for the teatime invitation, and Kitty knew better than to press for more than had already been said.

"Margaret plays broccoli," Maude continued. "Very convincingly, I'm told. Poor Ellen is rutabaga and takes it personally. But once she starts to sing, she'll feel she's a nice plump tomato and will do quite well. You *will* come, I'm sure. You'd never forgive yourself if you didn't. And look, there's plenty more olives and it's Margaret doing supper. Colcannon, of course. Her specialty. So we don't have a worry in the world."

Kitty reached for her cup. She was beginning to agree.

6

The night was cool, almost cold, but not cold enough to suggest to Aaron that this was the Christmas season, during which time Americans of competing persuasions went to performances of Handel's *Messiah*. Lolly had explained that in Ireland the oratorio transcended seasons. *Messiah* was, after all, an Irish work. She didn't go so far as Kitty with her insistence on Shakespeare's irrefutable Irish lineage and claim that Handel was her countryman, but she did point out that the oratorio's world premiere was not held in any of the grand halls of Europe, nor was the honor given to London. It was at the Music Hall in Fishamble Street in Dublin, the one city in all this world that could assemble an audience worthy of its glory.

Lolly, not having been to college in America like her husband's aunt, was a bit less nationalistic than Kitty. Still, she had been somewhat susceptible to Kitty's proofs of Shakespeare's indisputable origins. Lolly had been directed by Kitty to the bard's historical tragedy *Richard II*. Kitty explained to her that, at the beginning of the play, Richard is a hedonistic tyrant. Then he goes to Ireland. When he returns, he's a great metaphysical poet. Was this not a clue intended by

Mr. Shakespeare to reassure those capable of sufficient scrutiny that he was indeed of Gaelic blood, a claim it would have
been mortally dangerous to make while the Virgin Queen was
squatting on the throne of England?

Lolly had accepted this as a possibility. Then Kitty, to
make her proofs incontrovertible, steered Lolly to *Hamlet*, act
I, scene v, line 136. And, lo and behold, the Danish prince, in
the cold castle of Elsinore, when assuring his friend Horatio
of the validity of the ghost of his father he'd just seen, cries
out as witness to the truth of his words, "By Saint Patrick!"
The only saint invoked in the entire play. Unbeknownst to
Lolly, Kitty had considered one further proof, this one also
involving the Prince of Denmark. In act III, scene iii, line 73,
when Hamlet, stirred to vengeance, is passing by his murderous Uncle Claudius at his prayers, he says to himself, "Now
might I do it pat." That final invocation of the saint, though
admittedly more subtle than the previous proofs, could, she
felt, surely serve her cause, but she had decided not only that
its degree of subtlety might cause it to be resisted as a proof,
but also that any right-minded person would already be sufficiently persuaded by what had already been offered. Kitty
had therefore said to Lolly, regarding act I, scene v, line 136,
"Patrick's the only saint invoked in the entire play!"—with an
emphasis suggesting that it would behoove (wonderful word,
behoove) Lolly to subscribe to Kitty's promulgation. Lolly subscribed. More or less.

The drive to Caherciveen for the performance was quite
pleasant, and the dinner in a seafood restaurant across from
Valencia Island even more so. Aaron was genuinely impressed
by the great fortresslike church where the oratorio would be

sung. Lolly pridefully explained that the church was a memorial not to Patrick or Brendan or even Michael—to say nothing of Mary in all her many guises—but to Daniel O'Connell. It was he who had persuaded the Parliament legislating from London, in their famous enthusiasm for tolerance in their relationship to their presumed inferiors, to bestow on the *real* Irish the Catholic Emancipation. Lolly's use of the word *real* was to distinguish the indigenous people from the Anglos of Irish pretension who, in their Ascendancy, had no need of legislated rights, those having already been implicit in their proud birthright as subjects of the Crown.

Great gray stones rose toward the darkening sky, the church itself a massive example of the Gothic that had decided to be imposing rather than majestic. Before they had reached the gate leading through the iron fence, Aaron had said, and not for the first time, "She's going to be in the chorus. I know she is."

Lolly, more amused than exasperated, said what was expected of her. "You know nothing of the kind."

"It's an American chorus on tour. Lucille ran off with a member of our church choir. They're both going to be here, I know it."

"This Lucille of yours—or formerly yours—and her gentleman friend . . ."

"He was no gentleman. Lucille was my wife."

"Be that as it may, if I remember correctly, they sang in an obscure church tucked away somewhere in New York. And now they're touring the world singing Handel?"

"It is not an obscure church. It's St. Joseph in Greenwich Village—founded and bankrolled by the Irish, I'll have you know, the best parish in the known world."

"Fine. But that hardly qualifies your wife and her . . . abductor? . . . to advance to a world-class chorus come all the way to County Kerry, just so she can taunt you and make you into an idiot blithering about crises that will never come about."

"You'll see her for yourself."

"I can hardly wait. Except that she's elsewhere at the present time. And, I might add, it doesn't take a Doctor Freud to suggest that all this about seeing her is a disguised wish that you *will* see her. Can't you be a little less obvious?"

"Oh? I'm obvious, am I? And what about someone who just a few weeks ago saw what I'll call 'an old acquaintance' thought to be about two years dead and convinces herself that some moving shadow off in the fog is no one but him and calls out his name for all to hear. 'Declan!' she cries. 'Declan!' Does that say anything about obvious?"

"I thought it was his ghost. And I did nothing to summon him. Nothing."

"Not consciously. But subconsciously . . ."

"I saw him. You saw him."

"I did not see him. Not then. Later, at the castle, but not then. I saw a dark figure walking off into the fog. That's all you saw. And then heard 'Declan! Declan!'—as if pleading for some deepest need to be fulfilled."

To close down the subject, Lolly, in her aggressively agreeable voice, said, "All right. All right. Let it go. Let it go."

They passed through the gate and followed the path leading through the well-kept lawn to the portals of the church. "And let me say this," Lolly said, breaking her own truce, "I never want to see him again."

"Nor I Lucille. So can we, as you so charmingly proposed, 'let it go'?"

"We'd better. And don't think of it anymore or we won't hear the music."

"I'll hear it. And it will be Lucille singing it."
"Stop!"
"All right. All right."
They went inside.

Lucille was one of the first to enter the sanctuary. There was applause. She was the fifth chorister in the second tier. Aaron didn't know whether to feel aghast or exonerated. He decided to be both. Lucille was wearing, as was the entire chorus, a red robe that Aaron immediately saw as most appropriate: She was a scarlet woman if ever there was one. Lucille was a slightly lighter blond than he remembered, but her fresh beauty still glowed, a beauty that was her irresistible allure, a beauty that had enthralled all too easily the baritone with whom she had run off. Aaron elbowed Lolly. Still staring at Lucille, who was busy licking her lips, unmindful of the weird workings of the world that had brought both her and most likely her former husband to this distant place, a coincidence usually reserved for—nay, demanded by—fiction of the Victorian era, Aaron spoke the sideways words: "Second tier. Fifth from the left."

Lolly looked first at her husband, then toward the sanctuary, now filling with the last members of the two-tiered chorus. "It's not Lucille," she muttered.

The soloists entered. Everybody clapped, including Aaron and Lolly. Before the applause had stopped, Aaron repeated the word: *Lucille*.

"It can't be."
"I know it can't. But it is."
"She's too young for you."
"She's a year older."
"It's *still* not Lucille."

"You've never seen her before. How can you know?"

"She's too pretty."

"Too pretty for me? Is that what you're saying?"

"I've already said it."

"So you're saying I could only get an ugly woman for a wife?"

Before an answer could be given, the conductor, mercifully, entered. After bowing to the audience, acknowledging the welcome, and picking up the baton, he lifted his arms and bid the chorus to rise. The music began. What Lolly and Aaron heard or did not hear was anyone's guess.

At the intermission, no consultation was needed for the decision to go out for some fresh air. The sky had misted over and the half moon was a pale blue off to the east. Lolly and Aaron went past all the other Handel enthusiasts and stood apart near the iron gate. To occupy themselves, they each made a show of regarding the impressive tombstones marking the burial plots of ecclesiastics long departed. They said nothing. Finally, Aaron spoke. "Should we leave?"

"Why leave? We've come all this way."

In a slightly saddened voice, Aaron said, "You think I'm making this up. But I'm not."

"I understand." Lolly raised her hands in a gesture of mock surrender. "I really do."

"What do you understand?"

"That you have some wish to see the woman once your wife named Lucille. And I understand. As I said, I really do."

While Aaron was formulating his reply, another voice was heard. "Aaron! Aaron McCloud! Is that you?"

A woman in a red robe was coming toward them, making

her way among the tombstones. A few feet away, she said in tones not far removed from a shriek, "If it isn't you, I'm hallucinating. Am I?"

"Lucille?"

"You got it right that time, buster."

Aaron tried a smile but couldn't quite make it. "I'm surprised."

"*You're* surprised. I spotted you during 'Comfort ye.' " I wet my panties and had to get rid of them just now. I have to sing without for the rest."

Lolly held out her hand. "Let me introduce myself. I'm his wife."

"Oh . . . You, too? Tell her, Aaron. I used to be your wife, didn't I?"

"Well, yes, I guess that was you."

Lolly held her hand in position, waiting. "I'm Lolly McCloud."

"What a funny name. Lolly. McCloud's okay, and boy was he ever named right. Once we got married he went into the clouds and never came out. But I guess you already know that."

Lolly lowered her hand. "No. Not really."

"Well, some people are luckier than others. I mean . . . I wish you all the happiness in the world."

"Thank you. But we have it already." Lolly put sufficient heat into her words to sound almost convincing.

"Well," said Lucille, her laugh close to giddy, "I got my wish. You're the luckier one."

"Apparently." Lolly not only smiled but bowed as well.

"Isn't it time," Aaron said to Lucille, "to be getting back?"

"It's okay. They give us a long break to rest our voices. And I want you to pay special attention to my husband's solo after 'I Know My Redeemer': 'The Trumpet Shall Sound.'

He's the bass you already heard, but that's his big number. It'll tell you in the program. Stanislaus Glyzinski."

"Glyzinski?" Aaron was genuinely surprised. "I thought your husband's name was Aldershot. Jack Aldershot."

"Oh, no, not Jack. How could I stay married to him? He played me the same trick you did."

"Me?"

"You. If your name's Aaron McCloud. That's who. When Jack and I met at St. Joseph and he was a baritone, he did the same thing to me you did."

"Oh?" Lolly let her mouth stay open, as if the response would enter there instead of her ear.

Lucille decided to address the current Mrs. McCloud rather than the man to whom she was now the former Mrs. McCloud. "He did. Just like Aaron here, when he wanted me to fall in love with him, he did all these beautiful things. He was so thoughtful, so kind. Just like Aaron, he took a real interest in my voice, in my singing. At least it seemed real, the same as it did with Aaron. I even sang 'The Last Rose of Summer' for Jack more times than Aaron had me sing it for him. And when I just hinted I liked a man who opened doors, he began opening doors. Like Aaron did. And I couldn't sneeze or he'd worry, or I couldn't clear my throat or he'd be concerned was I all right. He cared. All the time, he couldn't care enough. And when he wasn't kissing and hugging, he was always polite. A real gentleman. But you probably know all this. Right?"

"Our circumstances," said Lolly, "were somewhat different."

"Well, that was when your luck started. But then I got married, first to Aaron, then to Jack. And know what it all turned out to be?"

"You'll tell me, I'm sure."

"They weren't 'courting' me, as some people would put it. They were giving me lessons. They were instructing me. What they were really saying all along was 'This is the way I expect *you* to treat *me* after we're married. Pay close attention. This is how thoughtful you're supposed to be. This is how seriously you should take my work'—for Aaron, his writing, for Jack, his accounting. Can you believe it? Words from one, numbers from the other. And I'm supposed to care like all get-out. And be kind and generous and cheerful and uncomplaining? All that. That's what I was supposed to do. That's who I was supposed to be. Hadn't I been taught properly? Hadn't I been given a good example? I'd been taught by the best teachers, shown how by men who knew what marriage was all about! With Aaron it was sort of okay because I was inexperienced. But when it happened all over again with Jack, I said forget it. It's men. And there's no hope for us women. Then I met Stan. He told me right out I couldn't sing worth diddly-screw and please not to do it except when there are enough other voices to drown me out. He never bothered to be polite, not particularly. No presents, not even an engagement ring. For our wedding I had to use the one Aaron gave me. And I knew then that all men are *not* alike. They're not all just instructors of how to act once you're married. I was thrilled. I started out with Aaron, a tenor. Sort of. Then Jack, a baritone. Now I know where I'm supposed to be. Stan. A bass. And you're going to hear him. And he's really great. Someone to love at last. A man who knows how to really get himself a good woman. I hope, Lolly—that funny, funny name—I hope Aaron has become a Stan and isn't the same old Aaron."

Before Lolly could say the least little word, a low, hoarse

voice—quite the opposite of Lucille's—said, "Hello, Lolly McKeever."

The voice came from somewhere near the tombstones. With the same girlish laugh that had animated her before, Lucille called out, "McCloud, dummy. She's Lolly McCloud. Can you believe it?"

A man came close to where they were standing. He was wearing rumpled woolen pants, a well-worn coat, and muddied boots.

Lolly grabbed Aaron's upper arm and squeezed it hard enough to stop the flow of blood. "Declan," she said, attempting to sound pleased and surprised.

The man joined them. "I saw you at the castle, but you ran away. Am I interrupting?"

"No. Not a bit. No." Lolly's attempt was becoming a bit less successful. "We're just standing here. Talking."

For whatever reason, Lucille seemed to find this amusing. "Not that we're saying much." She held out her hand toward Declan. "I'm Lucille. A friend, I guess, of Aaron's."

Declan looked at the hand and drew back. Like Lolly earlier, he seemed reluctant to encourage intimacy. To Aaron he said, "Then you're Aaron."

"Aaron McCloud. I was at the castle, too." He indicated, more than achieved, a bow, not wanting to risk an unaccepted hand.

"Kitty's cousin?"

"Nephew."

"Well, why not."

Lucille, fully aware by now of Declan's avoidance, began to pull back the outheld hand. Aaron had a momentary fear she was going to make the sign of the cross, but was relieved to see her scratch her scalp. As she was enjoying this displacement of her hair, Lucille said, "I used to be his wife. Lucille McCloud. Now I'm Lucille Glyzinski. And *she's* Lolly McCloud. I mean, they're married to each other."

After Declan had stared a long moment, as if trying to determine what sort of creature it was confronting him, he looked again at Aaron. "You're married to her, then?"

"That I am."

Declan turned to Lolly. "And you're married to him?"

"It would seem so." Then she added, "Yes, yes, we're married. Over a year now."

Declan was looking at the ground. Very thoughtfully, as if his mind were slowly working its way through the words that had been spoken, he quietly said, "I remember now. At the castle. I heard something like that, but I wasn't sure what it meant. It seemed so . . . well, . . . so, never mind. I should have paid better attention."

Aaron wasn't ready to let it drop. "Seemed so what?"

It was Lolly who answered. "Wonderful?"

Lucille let out a whoop, then instantly covered her mouth.

Declan, as if not having heard the sound, said, still thoughtful, "And Kitty McCloud is married to Kieran Sweeney. A Sweeney married to a McCloud. It's been a bit busy the while I was gone."

Aaron wasted no time. "To say the least."

Declan hadn't bothered to hear. He was looking directly at Lolly, into her eyes. "I didn't expect everything to be so different."

Lolly shrugged. Lucille decided it was time to contribute to the conversation once again. To Declan she said, "You think it's funny she's married to him? How about what I said before? He used to be married to me. He does all right for himself, doesn't he?"

Again Declan could only stare, still trying to account for her presence in this place, at this time. Even the red choir robe seemed to offer no clue. To say something, *anything*, Lolly, as if expressing approval of the most exciting news heard in a long time, said, "And, Declan, you're to do thatching at the castle. Is that true?"

Genuinely perplexed, Lucille intervened. "Castle? What's this I hear about a castle?"

Aaron and Lolly shuffled their feet, but no one bothered to answer.

It took Declan a few moments to take in what Lolly had said. After seeming to consider a series of possible responses he, too, shrugged. "The castle thatching was always done by a man of my family. From the day the first stone was raised." He continued to look into her eyes. "It's the one thing that will never change. Everything else can change. Never that. I'll be faithful to what was meant to be."

Lucille had begun to shift from one foot to the other, suggesting she was about to wet herself again. "I hope you'll excuse me. I have to get back." To Declan she said, "I'm singing. But I guess you could tell with me all done up like this. Well, it's been real. We don't get to talk to the Irish much, so I'm especially honored, I guess. It's certainly interesting, and I love the way you people say things. I could listen to the way you talk for days, no matter if it makes sense or not. But you have to excuse me . . ."

To divest Lucille of any expectation that they'd wait after the performance to see her again, Aaron managed to say, "We probably won't be seeing you later, so I congratulate you now. It will be wonderful. It already is. And my regards to your . . . to your husband. The current one."

Lucille, not unmoved by such uncharacteristic courtesy from the man to whom she had been married, drew both her clasped hands to her throat and shook her head. "What a terrific surprise this has been. For all of us." She touched Lolly's shoulder. "Especially for you, huh? And it's been a pleasure to meet you. Truly." She then grabbed Declan's hand. He gasped. "And you, too, whatever your name turns out to be." She vigorously shook the hand she held, then released it. She started to turn away, but stopped. "And don't forget. My husband, the one I have now, he has his big number this next part. 'The Trumpet Shall Sound'. Be sure you listen. He'll appreciate it." Creating a swirl in the skirt of her robe, she started down the pathway, an "Excuse me, excuse me" offered to each person she managed to nudge aside until she left the path itself, moved onto the grass, and made her way along the side of the church, hurrying toward the glory awaiting in the great choruses yet to come. Aaron and Lolly watched, wanting to make certain she was truly gone.

"Should we go home now?" This time it was Lolly who asked.

Aaron sighed. "I think we could use more Handel. I can't just walk away."

When they turned to see what Declan had decided, they saw that he was gone. They looked around. They looked among the tombstones. They searched the crowd returning to the church. He was nowhere.

Aaron took Lolly's arm. "Come. Handel will help."

"What makes you think I need help?"

Aaron didn't answer. Lolly let herself be led back inside. Lucille was already in place, sans panties, fifth from the left, second tier.

•

For the rest of the oratorio, Aaron and Lolly sat there transfixed. When they dutifully stood for the "Alleluia," they held themselves as straight as statues and let the music assault their all-too-corporeal selves. After "I Know That My Redeemer Liveth," Lucille's current husband, Stanislaus Glyzinski, began his number, "The Trumpet Shall Sound." Only too meaningful did the words seem: "And the dead shall be raised incorruptible."

During the first repeat of the aria, there was a stirring off to their right, a few pews ahead. A man was stumbling his way out into the aisle. He fell more than genuflected on his right knee, then stood unsteadily and started toward the high portals at the back of the church. His pants were rumpled, his coat well worn, his boots muddy and too heavy on the marble floor. His head was bowed, his right hand clamped over his mouth as if struggling to stifle a sound he couldn't permit.

As he passed Aaron and Lolly, it could be seen that tears were welling from his squinted eyes, running down over the back of his hand. "And the dead shall be raised incorruptible . . ." Again the trumpet made its proclamation, the clarion sound echoing throughout the great spaces, soaring to the arches high above the nave. Onward the man lurched. As he passed the pew where Aaron and Lolly were seated, Lolly was heard to whisper in a voice given over to heartbreak, "Declan."

The man stumbled on.

7

It was decided. Kitty would e-mail the young professor at the college in Cork and tell her she'd changed her mind. She would be most honored to preside, along with the teacher herself—a Ms. Eileen Mulligan—over a special late summer seminar that would compare Kitty's "corrections" to the canonical novels that had been their inspiration. With students selected by Ms. Mulligan and approved by Kitty after scanning their applications, there would be readings given, discussions held, and papers presented. There would be disagreements; there would be arguments. There would be denunciations and accusations, insults and dismissals, passionate defenses and equally passionate condemnations. For Kitty, all of this was not without appeal: She had a congenital love of contention. The seminar would nourish and perhaps satisfy her need for controversy. She slavered at the thought of it.

And then to make the offer even more attractive, Ms. Mulligan confessed that no remuneration would be offered. Kitty would be working for nothing. No budgetary allowance could be made, and Ms. Mulligan, turning this to her advantage, had told Kitty that her presence and participation were beyond price; any amount, no matter how munificent, would have been insulting, and she, Associate Professor Eileen Mulligan, would never be party to such a travesty. Kitty was priceless—a claim Kitty was not inclined to refute.

It was also pointed out that colleges and universities all over Ireland could boast the employ of writers of great eminence and celebrated reputation. Surely in Ireland there was no lack. An actual surfeit was only too evident. But name the institution that had persuaded an acknowledged hack willing to brave the ready scorn, to say nothing of the perverse advocacy of admirers she would no doubt excite. This was Kitty McCloud, ceaselessly reviled but prodigiously paid, the Ms. McCloud who had dared to claim that she, and she alone, had been called by the muse that dispenses writerly gifts to fulfill the original inspirations so stupidly compromised by earlier literary icons who should have known better.

Well, Ms. McCloud did know better and didn't hesitate to let the world know it. With what could be called unmitigated nerve (but should probably be called unmitigated gall), she went beyond a critic's competence and had charitably set about identifying truths ignored, to say nothing of redeeming the writers who had lacked the guts to risk ridicule in the cause of providing a more honest ending to novels she had deemed worthy of her attention. And now she had been asked to "compare and contrast"—as the alliteration goes—her desecrations of the sacred texts she had so ruthlessly, so charitably corrected.

The lure was obvious from the beginning. The opportunity to stand up for hacks was irresistible, especially when it occurred to her that she would not return scorn for scorn, but error with pity. She would be patience itself. Here was a chance to practice one of the spiritual works of mercy she'd been taught by the nuns: 'To instruct the ignorant.' She would thereby earn a fair dose of heavenly approval, which might come in handy should her pity threaten to reveal itself as pride or her wrath become aroused when confronted with certitudes equal to her own.

She had told Professor Mulligan, when the offer was first made, that she'd think about it—and think about it she did. Among the concerns to be considered, there was her husband. Separation would be intolerable. Also, a distraction from her present project, *The House of Mirth*, now titled *The House of Fenimore Blythe*—a reconsideration of the name given by Mrs. Wharton's Lily Bart, now transformed as the novel itself was sure to be. Also, her vegetable garden was already beginning to yield. That, too, weighed heavily upon her. Beyond this, how would Brid and Taddy and, yes, the pig, how would they fare when she would no longer be observing their sorrows and bewilderments? Add to that the share of those sufferings she had taken to herself at the sight of them. What would her days be without them? She must refuse. Reluctantly. *Very* reluctantly.

That decision was made, however, before she had had the good sense—to say nothing of the conjugal obligation—to consult with her husband, informing him first of the offer, then of her refusal and the reasons supporting her final decision.

They were in the garden, harvesting green beans. There would be ham hocks and green beans for supper, one of Kitty's several specialties brought back from the Bronx (one of the greater benefits dating back to her years at Fordham University). Kieran seemed distracted. To Kieran, Kitty seemed distracted. The task at hand usually inspired an enthusiastic delight prompted by a disbelief that their labors seemed somewhat minimal in comparison to the real work done by the soil itself. Nature had played a joke and their response would surely gratify the Gods of Plenty whose contribution had easily surpassed their own.

In an attempt to distract Kieran from his distraction, Kitty said, "The college in Cork wanted me to be part of a seminar based on my novels. I told them no."

Kieran, suddenly no longer distracted, said, "So Miss Mulligan told me."

"What?"

"Miss Mulligan. From Cork. She told me you said no."

"Why would she tell you anything?"

"Because you said no and she wants very much for you to say yes."

"But why you? What business is it of—"

"Of mine?"

"Well, yes. What right had she to—"

"None, I suppose. But the young woman seemed not to be overly concerned about right or wrong. She wants you. Desperately."

"I know that. And I took it under consideration."

"She wants you to reconsider."

"But I went over all this. Over and over . . ."

"Then you're practiced enough to go over it one more time."

"Kieran, I am not going to go shuttling back and forth to and from the city of Cork—"

"Don't shuttle. Go there and stay there."

"Go . . . ? What are you saying?"

"Why waste time coming and going? Cork is a reasonably interesting sort of town. Always has been."

"I should go there? And stay there? How can you—"

"Why can't we stay with my brother's family outside Blarney, which means we could take the cows?"

"And what would your brother and his wife and his family think of—"

"They like the idea. I asked them. They're delighted."

"But . . . but I'm not a teacher."

"Oh? Think of all the things you've taught me."

"Are you talking dirty?"

"Kitty, my love, here's a chance to do what's long been needed to be done."

"And what might that be?"

"You know as well as I."

"Defend myself?"

"No. You need no defense."

"Then what? Tell me."

"You could correct *them*. Isn't correction your prime purpose is life?"

"No. You're my prime purpose in life."

"Then make teaching a secondary purpose. They'd say what they have to say. And you'd correct them. Isn't that one of your more than several gifts?"

And so it went. But not for long. By the time they had plundered the bean patch, Kitty had promised to e-mail Ms. Mulligan. And Kieran would phone his brother to tell him that he and his wife, Kitty, would be coming to stay with him and his family. He'd bring the herd; Kitty would bring her computer. Brid and Taddy, Kieran told his wife, had survived without them for over two hundred years. A few months would hardly matter. As for the pig—well, as Kieran was wont to say on special occasions, "Who gives a shit?"

•

That evening, gorging themselves on ham hocks and beans, Kitty reconciled her husband to the idea that Declan would be thatching the sheds. When they had first come to the castle, Kieran had advocated slate—which, in turn, had activated Kitty's contrarian nature. She immediately opted for thatch. The impasse had caused the cows to be housed in the great hall from the first days of their tenancy. The cows' characteristic scent had, from that time forward, permeated the castle, reaching even to the widened second landing of the turret stair where Kitty plied her computer-driven wares.

She'd made the agreement with Declan the day he'd delivered the sea-soaked copy of *The House of Mirth*, but Kieran had yet to suspend his preference for slate. Kitty mentioned that Declan had been their friend and fellow Kerryman all their lives. Kieran, reckless beyond rationality, laughed and said, "Friends indeed, Miss Kitty McCloud. Have I not known you from the day of your birth? And haven't I known you from that time to this? And didn't I, sworn enemy that I was, of necessity keep myself aware of your comings and goings and all of your shenanigans between? And didn't I, along with everyone else, know that you, when still a girl, with Declan Tovey—"

Eyes ablaze, Kitty stopped him dead in his tracks. "What is it you're saying Kieran *Sweeney?*"

"Let me finish and then you'll know. Kitty *McCloud.*"

"Finish if you can."

"I'm only speaking of common knowledge known by one and all."

"And what might that knowledge be?"

"No need to say the words."

"Don't contradict yourself. That's my job. Finish the sentence you started. 'When I was still a girl—' Yes? Say the words so I can take them and do with them what deserves to be done. Such as shove them back down your throat. Say them. Say them!"

"Kitty dear—"

"Don't 'Kitty dear' me.. If it's slander you're going to speak, be a man and say it unafraid. Your *wife* is waiting."

"Kitty, it was a long time ago."

"Then why is it mentioned now?"

"Well . . ."

With growing intensity, Kitty said, "Is it because you want to deny me my way for the sake of denying me my way when I say thatch? And you'll do anything, say anything, to win out over me? Is that it? If so, then it's locked in mortal combat, are we?"

"To be locked with you in any way has always been my first hope in life. So let's not stop now."

"Then I'll say this. It's your wife you're slandering."

"Is the truth slander?"

With diminishing control, Kitty answered, "It is. It is. When it's said to hurt and to humiliate—"

"Not when it's said to make a legitimate point?"

"And what's the point, then?"

Kieran folded his arms across his chest. "The point is that it had to occur to me that your choice of thatch in the current circumstances, and the employment of Declan Tovey here at the castle day after day after day—"

"Are you saying that I . . . *I* . . . that I . . ."

"It had to occur to me. How could it not?"

"And if it did, had you not the good sense to know that it was a foolish thought being thought by a foolish man?"

He unfolded his arms and placed his fists on his hips. "What I thought *did* happen. When you were—"

Kitty's voice was lowered an octave. "All right, then. And while we're at it, let me present what else is common knowledge. I was a girl, you say. Well, you were a boy . . . and it involved a heifer. And who is there doesn't know it?"

"It was a dare! Conan Kennedy dared me!"

"And little resistance is what I heard. And I'm going to add this. You impute certain motives to me in wanting Declan near. Well, Kieran Sweeney, did I ever object to you sharing the same roof with a herd of cows and all number of heifers? Did I? Did I?"

Kieran had no choice. He began to laugh. "Well, maybe you should have."

Kitty's lips trembled, struggling to hold back the sounds about to erupt, but to no avail. With her head thrown back, a raucous howl came out of Kitty's mouth, a form of laughter usually let loose by the demented or the damned. On it went, and Kieran's laughter, too, until they had to throw themselves onto each other and, to rescue themselves from the pains of high hilarity, kissed and kissed again until only murmurs were heard.

They separated. Kitty touched her husband's left cheek, scratching the bristle of his tawny beard. "Yes, my darling," she said softly, "I went with Declan. But only because I knew I'd never marry—and I wanted to know what it would have been like. And he would let me know the glories I'd be missing."

"And why never marry?"

Kitty slowly shook her head. "You should be the first to know."

"I don't."

"I was brought up to see you as my eternal enemy. And

yet, from all the time I've ever lived, I wanted only you. But it was not only against my flesh; it was against my blood. And if I couldn't marry you, I'd marry none at all, glory or no glory. And I will tell you this: With you greater has been the glory—" She stopped. "I'll say no more."

And so it was decided. Declan Tovey the thatcher.

The reeds had not yet arrived, but Declan was there, readying the sheds, putting up supports, taking the measures, and staring, from time to time, at the places where the thatch would go. Then he would hold one of his tools and stare at that, as if trying to remember what it was and what it was for. When Kitty came out the doors of the great hall, trying not to spill the turnip soup she was carrying, she saw him, unmoving, his gaze fixed on what she recognized as his thatcher's leggett. It was similar to the one she had seen in the grave, beside the buried bones. She wondered if she should interrupt him. But the soup would get cold and, reheated, might lose some of the savory taste and sturdy scent Kieran had coaxed from something so negligible as a turnip.

Keeping her eyes on the soup to check any impulse it might have to spill over the side of the bowl, Kitty continued on. When she looked up to make sure she was on course, she noticed that the pig—or, rather, the ghost of the pig—was regarding the man intently. Declan turned slightly and looked at the pig. For a full minute he seemed to fix his gaze on the animal. Then, as if he had sufficiently acknowledged its presence, he returned his attention to the leggett in his hand.

Kitty waited. She knew from Maude why Declan could see Taddy and Brid. But why the pig as well? She continued to wait. She already knew Declan could see the pig. The ghost of the pig. And the pig, with its casual presence, seemed to have the same relationship to him as it had to Taddy and Brid. That phenomenon was understandable. Taddy and Brid and the pig inhabited the same realm. But Declan was not, like them, a ghost. And there was Declan, acknowledging it. And then going on about his business.

There was, of course, an added complexity. Kitty herself and Kieran, too, were not ghosts, yet they, like Declan, could see the pig. There was only one explanation that could encompass these shared sightings: the pig was—and would most likely remain—a mystery. As Kieran had once said, "Sometimes the unknown is better left unknown." To this, Kitty, uncharacteristically, had had no ready challenge.

She started again toward the thatcher, still careful not to spill the savory soup. Holding it out, she said, "Kieran wants you to try this."

Declan shifted his gaze from the pig to the bowl in Kitty's hands. He gave it the same concentrated stare he'd given the pig. No muscle in his face moved, no sign indicated recognition of what was being held out toward him. "Turnip," Kitty said, purposely avoiding the tone of encouragement one would use with an unconvinced child.

Declan lifted his stare and looked directly at Kitty. So pitiful did he seem that she almost took a step back, which would have spilled the soup and most likely sent the spoon down onto the ground. Without blinking or flinching, in a calm voice, Declan said, "I have some cheese and some bread and a bit of bacon and an oatcake from the Widow Quinn where I'm staying."

"But doesn't the house always—"

"Yes. I know. The house provides the food in the middle

of the day. But for me it's this way: the cheese, the bacon, the bread. But I thank you kindly."

"Well, maybe just this once since it's already here—"

"I have enough. And I do thank you. And Kieran, too."

"Well, if that's what you—"

"It is." He paused, then said, "But I do thank you." At that, he retreated to the farthest shed.

Without Kitty's having noticed, Peter McCloskey had come up to her side and was scratching with his shoe an itch near his left ankle. "I've come to ask did you ask him," he said.

"Peter, aren't you at school?"

This brought forth a giggle. "You don't know we've finished for the summer? But did you ask him?"

Holding the soup bowl more firmly, Kitty looked for a place to set it down and be rid of it. With no place available, she shoved it into Peter's hands. "Here. Eat this."

"But I'm to be back home to eat."

"Well, since you're here, this is a first course."

"You're giving it to me? And did you know I was coming?"

Kitty was tempted to remind him that *he* was the clairvoyant, not she, but she let it go. "Yes. I knew it. Now go sit over there on the stones and eat it."

"Mother said she knew you knew—"

"Never mind all that. Go eat it before it gets cold, like a good boy."

"And you haven't asked him?"

"I forgot. I'll do it now. Go. Eat."

Ever obedient, Peter went to the stone wall, got to the top without spilling a single drop, and settled down to have the first course of his midday meal. Kitty went to Declan. He was studying some structural work he'd done, not responding to the achievement much less anticipating the next phase of his assignment. "Peter McCloskey wants you to teach him how to thatch," she said. "I was supposed to ask you but forgot. He wants it terribly. It would be a sin to disappoint. He's a good boy, and you're going to need some help, I'm sure. He doesn't expect to be paid. And he'll go home to eat. Or he can always eat with Kieran and me."

Declan had been shaking his head, first slowly, then with increased urgency, until now the movement had become a furious wagging back and forth. His lips parted, his eyes those of a man terrified. "No! No!" the word was repeated, part growl, part plea that no more be said, as if Kitty had asked him to commit some vile crime.

She tried to continue. "But aren't you going to need—"

"No one! I need no one! Ever." His words seemed an even greater pleading than before, an entreaty that he be released from whatever was tormenting him.

Peter, who seemed to have heard none of this, called from where he sat, "Mrs. Sweeney, is there any bread for the soup?"

Distracted, Kitty repeated the word, befuddled, as if it were foreign to her vocabulary. "Bread?"

Peter came toward her, toward Declan, the soup still filling more than half the bowl. "Yes, please. I think the soup wants some bread."

"Oh. Bread. You want some bread."

"It's for the soup." To prove his point, he held out the bowl as if the soup could speak for itself.

"Yes. Bread. I should have thought of it. I'll get you some. Wait here."

After a glance at Declan, an unspoken request that he, like Peter, stay where he was, she hurried toward the great hall.

Peter looked down at the bowl, then held it out to Declan. "Would you like some?"

"No," he whispered. "But I thank you."

"Did Mrs. Sweeney ask you about me? About me being a thatcher?" Without waiting for an answer, he continued, "If she did, I hope you said yes. My mother hopes so, too. She said at first she was worried it was becoming a lost art with everyone so rich now. They say that thatch was considered a sign of the old poverty. Then, according to what my mother said, thatching will come back and not just like some imitation of the old ways. It'll come back because we'll all be poor again. We're going to be, she said, like the Americans, where all the money goes to just a few, the way it did here for so long a time, and the rest go without, like it was before. In America, she said, thousands and thousands of people are soupers in what they call soup kitchens spread out over the whole country, like here during the famine, only there you don't have to change your religion to get something to eat. It's been like that for a while, but it's getting worse and worse, the way fewer and fewer have more, as if they were lords and all the land was theirs and the little left is for everyone else. It's in America now and it's sure to come here. That's what my mother said. Then thatching is going to be needed again. And I'll have a skill so I can take care of my family. Being a thatcher. So I hope it's yes. My mother, she says you're the best that's ever been, only I shouldn't be the way you are, and no girl, no woman safe. So I won't be like that. I'll just be a thatcher. So I can take care of my family when we're all poor again and the rich have all the riches again. The way it was here in the days now gone."

Declan had been backing away from the boy little by little. He stopped when Peter stopped speaking. "I told her no,"

Declan said, first a whisper, then louder. "I work with no one. I want no one. I need no one. Go away. Don't come back. Find some other thatcher. Go find him. And go away from here. Do you hear me say it?"

"But Mrs. Sweeney is bringing me—"

With an arm flung out, Declan slammed the back of his hand up against the bottom of the bowl, sending the soup flying onto Peter's shirt and the bowl broken at his feet. Declan glared at the boy. Peter leaned down to collect the broken pieces. "No! Leave it. Go!"

Peter stood up, holding a small shard. After a puzzled search of the man's face, he turned and ran toward the courtyard road where he'd left his bicycle. He jumped on, but when he tried to reach for the pedal with his foot, it missed and the bicycle tipped, falling onto the gravel with Peter beneath it. He raised the bicycle and ran alongside before swinging himself up onto the seat and pedaling as fast as he could, still clutching the fragment of bowl in his fist. He sped toward the road that would take him home.

Kitty returned with a sizable chunk of Kieran's home-baked bread—one day old, but home-baked nonetheless. (Kieran baked every other day. Every *other* day, it was day-old bread, but there had been no complaints.) "Where'd Peter go off to?"

"Peter?"

"The boy who was here. Who asked for the bread. And what happened to the soup? Is that why he went off? Just because he dropped the bowl and it broke?"

"He's gone."

"Was he ashamed or what?"

"Yes. Yes. He—he was ashamed."

"Well, then you'll just have to eat it. The bread. I'm through running back and forth."

"All right then. Give it to me."

Kitty handed it over, then bent down and began slowly to pick up the shards.

"I'll do that. I was the one broke it. I'll be the one to collect it. Leave it. I'll do it."

"*You* broke it?"

"I broke it. I knocked it from his hand."

"You what? Whatever for?"

Declan shook his head. "No reason. No reason at all."

Kitty stood up and let the collected fragments fall back onto the gravel. When she turned to leave, she saw Peter, returned, dismounting his bicycle and taking a few cautious steps toward her and toward Declan. Kitty couldn't help hoping the boy hadn't come back to plead his cause himself. Declan was obviously in no mood.

Peter stopped a fair distance away, his left hand steering the bicycle at his side, the right hand closed in a fist held against his thigh. "I've come, Mr. Tovey, not to bother you again when I made so much trouble before."

Kitty glanced at Declan. His face was impassive, his stance indifferent.

"I only want you to know that it was all right you were so troubled and Mrs. Sweeney's bowl all broken with the soup spilled. You had your reason, so if you feel wrong about it—and you do—you shouldn't. It wasn't your fault. Nor was it mine."

Declan had stiffened, but lowered his eyes. He muttered in a voice hinting at a renewed fear. "What is he saying?"

"He says he doesn't blame you," said Kitty. "For breaking the bowl, for spilling the soup—and look, it's all over his
shirt."

Peter tugged his shirt forward and looked down at it. "It's
all right, it's all right," he said. "I won't let my mother see it."

"Maybe he doesn't blame you," Kitty said to Declan,
"but I—"

"No," said Peter. "You mustn't. I understand. I really do."

Declan, his fear grown to desperation, said, "Please. Send
him away."

"Why?" asked Kitty. "He's a harm to no one. He even
says he understands. What he understands, I don't know.
Ask him."

Without waiting for Declan to say anything, Peter continued. "If you're wondering how I know this, I don't know
myself. I did know, but I forgot. I sometimes know things
and then I forget them as soon as they come to me, and then
they're gone. It happened now, on my way home. I was that
surprised by what happened, with the bowl broken and all, so
I stopped for a bit. I leaned against the stones of the bridge
crossing the stream to wait until I wasn't so afraid. And I was
looking at this piece of the bowl. I still had it in my hand. If
you want it, Mrs. Sweeney, to mend it all back together—"

"No," Kitty said softly. "No. Let it be in bits. It's all right
now." She thought a moment, then said, "But give it to me
anyway, why not."

Peter opened his fist and regarded the fragment, then
came to Kitty, his hand held out. "There was something came
into my head—and I don't know what anymore—but I can
say now that I've understood. And it's all right. That I can't
remember doesn't matter, does it?"

"No," Kitty murmured. "It doesn't matter. Not any more. But if . . . if you do remember—"

"No," cried Declan. "He doesn't know. There is no reason. No one knows anything. Home to your mother now."

After Peter had studied the man's face again, he turned his bicycle around, swung himself up on the seat, and pedaled away, this time more slowly.

Kitty glanced down at the shard. "You needn't have been so harsh with the boy." She looked at the bits of broken pottery on the ground, then at Declan. He had turned and was walking back toward the sheds. Kitty watched, then followed slowly. "Why did you have to be so mean? Peter said he knew the reason. Do you? Do you know why you treated him so rudely? You a grown man and him only a boy—and a skinny one at that?" Declan continued walking. "You were never a harsh man, Declan. And just now, you were. Why is that? Do you have an answer?"

"There is no answer." He spoke quietly and continued on. Kitty waited and watched. An uncertain stride had replaced the swagger that had characterized his walk all his life. Now, preoccupied still, he was removing from the farthest shed the last remnants left behind by the young squatters who had commandeered the castle before Kitty had made her purchase. Instead of simply tossing the refuse out onto the gravel as it deserved, he was carrying it, no more than several pieces at a time, and placing everything in as ordered a heap as possible. Clothing and cushions stained past rescue, shoes and boots, odd technological contrivances long obsolete, along with a disassembled guitar, a red wig, and half-filled bottles of lotions and unguents meant to assure anyone susceptible to the illusion that youth could be made to last forever. Carefully each armful was added on, each given a consideration it hardly deserved.

The phantom pig had come to watch, the living pig asleep, content in its pen. Declan, carrying an armload of magazines, paused to acknowledge the ghostly pig's interest, deposited the tattered remains on top of the accumulating junk, and then returned to the shed for yet more of the abandoned leavings.

The pig had climbed to the top of the pile, and, without any effect, was rooting among the trash, as if the animal still possessed the means to disrupt any given accomplishment, even objects already declared worthless. Declan, carrying a mattress he was trying not to hold too close, stomped his foot in the vain hope of shooing the pig away. The phantom animal, unfazed, continued to stick its snout in among the objects it was sadly unable to move or shove in any direction whatsoever. Declan gave it a few more seconds, then simply threw the mattress onto the heap. Had the pig been corporeal, it would have suffered a considerable inconvenience. As it was, it simply reappeared at the foot of the pile and continued its observation.

Kitty had been looking with perplexed exasperation at the shard, wondering how Declan——Declan Tovey—could have done what he had done. She moved toward him and stood near, looking just past him, as if seeing nothing.

Declan paused at his labor. "What?"

Kitty looked again at the shard nested in the palm of her hand. She started to close her fist, but stopped and opened the hand completely. Again she tried to close it, but again could go no farther than halfway, as if the hand itself was resisting. Surrendering to the palm's resistance, she let it open completely. The hand twitched slightly, then held still. Staring down at the shard, her voice barely audible even to Kitty herself, she

said, "It's a boy was found in the grave, the skeleton dug up
by the pig. Or a young man it could be. He was an apprentice,
learning the thatcher's trade. He fell. His head. The cracked
skull. He died. *He* was buried in the garden, a cap to cover
his wound, a leggett in a sack at his side to honor his hopes
of becoming a master. It was meant to be only for a time. You
fled to the north, to find the family that would know him for
their own. And we found the bones and washed and clothed
them and gave a proper wake and dug a deeper grave.

"But then the sea took sight of him and saw him about to
be given back to the earth. A great rage came upon it. Too
fine a man he was, lovely and good, and the sea must have
him. The winds were summoned. The waves battered themselves near to death against the cliff. The winds howled the
sea's intent. And it was done. If the house, too, had to go, so
be it. It was the young man was wanted. And the sea must not
be blamed. So lovely and fine he was. And now he's there.
And we are here. And we wait and we search, but he'll never
come, not to the shore. Never."

Slowly she turned the shard over between her thumb and
forefinger, then closed her fist, covering the broken bit completely, pressing it into her palm.

With his voice even quieter than before, Declan said,
"How is it you know these things when there's none to have
told you except the one who will never speak of it?"

After a glance in his direction, Kitty pressed both hands
together, the shard held between her palms. When she
stopped and had returned it to the right hand and pressed it
into her flesh, she said, "Know what?"

"What you said."

"I said? I said? Said what? I said nothing."

"You told it as it should never be told."

"Told what?"

"His name was Michael—and will always be. The rest you know."

"I . . . I know nothing. What are you talking about?"

"Just now. You were looking down into your hand. At that bit of the bowl. And you saw there all that has happened. And all of it the truth."

"I . . . I . . ." Kitty looked down at her fist, then opened it. There was the fragment. She closed the fist, fast enough for the shard to cut into her palm. "I . . . I did what? I said what?"

"Everything."

"But I know nothing."

"You do. All of it. It was from a roof he fell and lived the rest of the day, and was just leaning against a stone wall and he . . . he . . ."

Kitty again opened the fist and again stared at what was in her hand. "No! I refuse! I saw nothing. I know nothing. I swear!"

"Maybe you know nothing now. But you knew it when you were speaking it."

"No. I refuse. Do you hear? I refuse."

"Refuse what?"

"To . . . to know anything . . . to see anything . . ."

"You saw a boy you said, a young man was in a grave and now he's in the sea."

"I said that? I couldn't have."

"But you did. You said it was an apprentice—"

"An apprentice? But that . . . oh that. That would make sense, then. I must have been referring to the way you treated Peter about being an apprentice. I could easily have—"

"And did you know I'd gone to the north to find the family? To bury him there so he wouldn't be where he was never known?"

"I . . . I . . ."

"And did either of us know it was the sea that had to have him—he was that fine?"

"I said that?"

"You did."

"Then I . . . I made it up. I must have. I . . . I'm a writer. I make things up all the time. I embellish. I make them as interesting as—"

" 'But then the sea took sight of him' "—he began repeating her words—" 'about to be given back into the earth. A great rage came upon it. Too fine a man he was, lovely and good, and the sea must have him. The winds were summoned . . . ' "

Kitty flung the shard onto the piled trash. "It was Maude McCloskey did this. She . . . she . . . Maude. It was Maude. And tell her for me I refuse! I will not be a Hag! It's a terrible thing she's done."

A coven of crows had been cackling overhead, mocking Kitty's protest, flying high over the castle turret, then swooping down over the heap, on the lookout for prey. Kitty started to raise a fist, to threaten them with some dire vengeance yet to be devised, but noticed that Declan had started to walk away. He was returning to the farthest shed, again his movements slow, again his head bowed.

Kitty knew now why he had become a man of sorrows. She herself had apparently, unknowing but all-seeing, spoken of the young man's death, of his master's search in the far north. And now not even his skeleton awaited Declan's return so it could be given the obsequies the thatcher had needed to perform.

He was lugging more from the shed and adding it to what he'd already brought. The crows settled along the newly raised roof beam of the far shed to watch. The pig, too, was still in attendance, its pig habits keeping it alert to the possibility that something of interest might appear. Kitty had the urge to go to Declan, to speak of the sorrow she, too, now felt herself. For him. For the young man dead. For Declan's loss that nothing could appease.

He had placed on the top of the pile a brightly colored sheet and a pillow leaking feathers. That seemed to be the last of it. He stood there, regarding his achievement.

A crow flapped down and perched on the discarded pillow, spreading its wings wide and taking possession in the name of the coven of all that was piled beneath it. The pig, meanwhile, taking advantage of its incorporeal status, disappeared into the mound about halfway up. It must have seen something discarded that appealed to its porcine aesthetic and decided it deserved one last snouted inspection.

Kitty believed it would be better if she went no nearer. She would respect Declan's solitude, allow him the grief upon which no one should trespass. Not daring to give voice to her sympathies or to her own newfound sorrows, she slowly turned away and went not back to the castle but off toward the rising slope of Crohan Mountain. She would wander quietly, slowly, among the ruminating cows. The walk would do her good. If good in this instance was possible. Including the threat that she was to become a Hag.

8

The obstreperous cross-eyed pig that Lolly and Aaron had given back to Kitty and Kieran—the one originally intended for the great feast—had, for whatever reason, calmed down during the days since its return to Castle Kissane. It had become docile and cooperative, which meant it ate and ate and ate and was now sufficiently fattened for advancement into the final phase of its prescribed destiny. It would now be surrendered to the butcher in Tralee. Both Kitty and Kieran had been given hints as to the source of the pig's serenity: the ghostly presence of the eaten pig.

As far as Kieran and Kitty could figure out, the living pig sensed rather than saw the phantom pig and the phantom had instilled a composure that bordered on joy. In an attempt to bring common sense—a contradictory phrase if ever there was one—to what they were witnessing, they decided that it was nothing less than true love, a love strong enough to defy death and find solace and even happiness in the sensed presence of the departed beloved. Had not the original pig, now the ghost of its former self, been given to Lolly because she was a committed swineherd? And was it not given back because it had lesbiotic leanings, the exercise of which had maddened the male swine, even though it had seemed not to have both-ered the sows chosen as the objects of its heartfelt affections? It was more than possible that during the time of their shared residency, that of the original pig and the one originally cho-sen for the feast (the one now at Castle Kissane), that a rela-tionship made in hog heaven had flourished, and when fate (also known as Kitty McCloud) had intervened, the surviving pig had been returned to its herd, where any sexually aroused shoat could intrude upon its bereavement with importunings that had cried out to that same heaven for rescue.

To some degree, answered prayers had sent the anguished animal back to the castle, there to be given the unseen com-pany of its beloved. The upshot, of course, was that the pig had grown obese with contentment, and the end of this par-ticular tale was now to be a lovers' parting.

Lolly swung the truck into the courtyard. The porked-up pig was slothfully sunning itself near the sheds where Declan was busy going about his thatching. She brought the truck to a sudden halt, got down from the cab, and regarded the fattened animal with satisfaction, ignorant that the courtyard was somewhat heavily populated. Brid and Taddy were solemnly watching Declan laying thatch on the second-farthest shed. The phantom pig was there as well, keeping faithful watch over its slumbering inamorata. Thinking she had Declan all to herself, Lolly strode toward him with a most unhesitant stride.

"Declan," she called out, her tone exuberant, without the least trace of the uncertainties that had characterized her behavior when she had seen him here in this very courtyard, before she had taken refuge in the scullery rather than confront him directly. Her step was purposeful, her attitude confident. It was as though a spell had been lifted, some evil enchant-ment exorcised. This was Lolly of old, the self-approving woman who had found amusement in adversity and an easy pleasure in companionship, be it human or porcine.

"Surely the work you're doing restores Kerry to itself. How handsome it's all going to look."

Declan nodded, his concentration not willing to accommodate interruption at this particular moment. Expertly he lay the reed in its course, careful not to show favoritism to one part of the roof over another, even more careful that the thatch be looser on the surface to ensure the rain's swift descent down the pitch of the roof. What could Lolly do but laugh at such determined indifference?

"No need to stop for me. I've not come to make a further spectacle of myself. You've been spared few things in your life, but let my foolishness be one of them. It was Lolly McCloud you were seeing those other times. And please, let's forget that unfortunate encounter in Caherciveen with that ridiculous woman." (Lolly had apparently decided to overlook her own strange behavior and Declan's as well, as if poor Lucille had been the sole cause of the event's bizarre exchanges. Anything that would make possible the return of the Lolly Declan had always known.)

"Now I'm Lolly McKeever again. Oh no, I haven't shed my husband whom I dearly love, but I've recovered my calling . . . and my sanity. I'd only pretended to be a McCloud, as if a name legally taken could make a writer of me. I even wrote a book. As stupid a bit of nonsense as was ever put to paper. Can you believe that a woman of my intelligence and good sense would write a novel about ghosts and people crazy enough to fall in love with them?"

This managed to be of interest to the thatcher. For a moment too brief to be noted, Declan glanced over at Brid and Taddy, who were also giving their attention to the woman holding forth just a few feet away. Their response seemed to be a deepening bewilderment. It was as if the woman, with her ridicule of ghosts and her scorn for those who might love them, was saying that these were happenings beyond comprehension, a form of conduct to which they had never been introduced.

Declan's attention returned to the task at hand. Lolly, unequipped to observe the ghosts' consternation, continued. "Well, that's what I did. That's what I wrote. And it gets even worse. I put the ghosts in a castle, sort of like this one. And I was trying to think of ways to get the ghosts out. And do you know what Kitty—or was it Kieran—what *they* suggested? Blow up the castle. That's what they said. Sky high. It was supposed to end the curse or whatever it was. Now I have nothing against special effects, but blow up a castle and that would get rid of the ghosts? Isn't that a bit too much? But they went right ahead and said it as if they were some kind of authorities on the subject. Can you believe it?"

Declan had become even more interested. Still, he pretended to continue his work, his ears attuned to what was being said. The ghosts, too, had become more observant.

"And then I'm stupid enough to ask how. How do you blow up a castle? Then it was Kieran—or was it Kitty—who said, 'There's gunpowder in the flagstones of the great hall.' How convenient, I thought. You need to blow up a castle and, who would have thought it, there's gunpowder right there all the time. Can you believe that someone would actually suggest such a thing? I'm new at the game—writing a book—but even *I* know you don't do a thing like that and expect readers to accept it. But I did it anyway. And I'm recovered now. No more ghosts. Madness it was. Part of the same madness that turned me from a keeper of pigs into a teller of tales. But

I've left behind my wayward ways and I'll never stray again, believe me."

Declan had stopped working. He turned to observe the speaker more closely. She was clothed in well-fitted jeans and a shirt, possibly her husband's, its blue deepening the blue of her eyes. And her auburn hair still caught and held the sun.

To rescue his concentration, he gave his attention to Brid and Taddy. It helped. Except that, to look at them, he could not avoid the old sadness. As a boy, it had been the same. After he was initiated into the family mysteries and introduced to ancient truths, he would come to the abandoned castle to find the pair roaming the rooms into which he would steal, the fields where he would walk, the turret landing where Brid would be at the loom, Taddy at the harp. And young Declan, still a child though considered a man, was there as well, their accepted if unacknowledged companion, himself awed by their beauty and made sorrowful by their exile. He would have done anything to complete their journey into glory.

But he had had no power of that kind. He had been given no knowledge of the rites that would speed them on their way. As a youth, he had pleaded with them to speak, to make some gesture that would hint at what might be required. But their powers, too, were limited. They had nothing to offer but their presence. At the age of fourteen, he decided never to come to the castle again. The sight of Brid had become more than his growing urges could bear. He would apprentice himself not to his father but to an itinerant thatcher. He would leave his village, his county; he would travel and only sometimes return, but never to the castle. Yet now, in his grief, he had come to seek solace among them—wanting, hoping, praying that they would be joined by his own dead, Michael taken by the sea, and the boy allowed to be their companion. Brid and Taddy, though, had no influence either. Shade could not call to shade, summoning those who, like themselves, were bereft of life but allowed to be company to the living. Emissaries of the divine they well might be, but their message was silence, and Declan must join his own to theirs.

From Lolly, however, he might have heard things of potential importance. Destruction of the castle would assure their release? It had been Kitty and Kieran who had told it to the woman standing there. Was it intimate knowledge or fanciful invention? If it was for them to know, it was for him to find out.

Lolly, with happy laughter, was poking and prodding the somnolent pig. An occasional grunt was all she received for her efforts. The ghostly companion was taking special note, lowering its massive head, readying itself for an assault—as if such an act were still possible. Which it wasn't, much to the woman's benefit.

Abandoning the less sensitive parts of the pig, Lolly, with an even more delighted laugh, struck a blow across the animal's snout. Screams not of pain but of indignity were sent forth. Encouraged, Lolly gave the snout another whack. This roused the pig to a standing position, the shrieks and squeals raised in both pitch and volume. It came out of the pen. The watchful companion, too, raised its own snout to the sky, though able to contribute no sound to the protest.

With skillfully applied encouragements, each thrust causing the pig to turn more toward the waiting truck, the animal was, in a vain attempt to avoid the humiliations, tricked into moving in a direction not of its choosing. With jabs and nudges of the most pitiless kind, Lolly sent the beast up the ramp and into the bed of the truck. The ramp was shoved on board and the tailgate secured. The pig continued its complaint as its beloved now braced its huge head and massive shoulders under the side of the truck, as if determined to upend it. Had the animal still been invested with its earthly bulk and strength, it might, in Declan's estimation, have been successful. But alas for the poor ghost, all effort, no matter how heartfelt, was in vain.

As if possible rescue had arrived, a cream-colored Bentley drove into the courtyard. Unmindful that it blocked the path in which the truck was aimed, the car stopped, its passenger side all but scraping itself against the trunk's bumper. Out of the Bentley stepped a man of slightly more than middle years, arrayed in linens and silks of muted colors except for the Hermès scarf tied ever so casually around the gentleman's neck, protecting it, no doubt, from the collar of the raw silk jacket that best conveyed the presence of money, rank, and privilege. So pleased with himself seemed the man that Declan had to make a special effort not to snort in the manner of the pig. With a condescending smile, the man advanced toward Lolly, who was now standing at the back of her truck. "I apologize for arriving unannounced," he said, "but I happened to be touring the countryside and thought I'd pay my respects to Mr. and Mrs. Sweeney, who, if I am not mistaken, still reside here in the castle."

"They're away" was all Lolly was inclined to say.

"Oh. How inconvenient. I suppose I should say it's my fault." With an almost undetectable bow, he said, "Lord Shaftoe."

Unbowed, Lolly responded, "Lolly McCloud, born McKeever."

"My pleasure, I'm sure."

"If you say so."

A twitch of a smile distorted the man's mouth into a tight-lipped grimace. "McCloud, you say. Then you are related to the tenants?"

"Owners."

"Of course." Another twitch, but the same grimace.

"I'm married to Kitty McCloud's nephew."

"Oh, then you are quite at home here."

"I live elsewhere."

"But your welcome is ever ready, am I correct?"

Lolly shrugged.

When Declan took his eyes off the man, he noticed that Brid and Taddy had vanished. As this was their sometime habit, it didn't particularly disturb him until the phantom pig's attention was drawn away from its beloved and given to the man now standing near the unimpressed Lolly. Declan, too, would be more attentive. This was hardly a casual visitor come calling.

"Would you mind?" Lolly was saying. "Your car is blocking my truck."

"Oh. Sorry. Thoughtless, of course. But first, may I ask, does my name—Shaftoe, as I said—Lord Shaftoe mean anything to you?"

"Shaftoe doesn't. And Lord certainly doesn't."

"Amusing, yes." Instead of twitching, the man tittered. "But I must confess my reasons for stopping by are, I'm afraid, sentimental to a shaming degree. You see, this was my ancestors' home, and there has been some misguided contention between the present tenants and myself, which has been resolved, I must admit, in their favor."

"So I've heard." Lolly was still unimpressed. "Aren't you supposed to be in prison?"

"For a time, I was. Yes, yes. A diversion really. An unlooked-for opportunity to develop a skill I hardly knew I had, for racquetball. Such are the punishments imposed by a civilized society. And after all, one is not a lord for nothing, even in these days of diminishing regard."

In contradiction to the man's words, there was, Declan noticed, an almost undetectable application of a flesh-colored cosmetic tinting his lordship's cheeks and forehead. The poor fellow was trying to cover over the pallor imposed upon those denied the sun. Racquetball, indeed. The man had languished in a cell—as befits a society given to lawful responsibility.

"I now take pleasure in the certainty that my ancestral home," his lordship was saying, "is in such capable, may I say, such *loving* hands."

"You may," said Lolly, "but your car is still blocking—"

Declan had come down from his perch, waiting to see if his intervention might be necessary.

"Yes, of course," his lordship said. "And I must move it immediately. But first, do you think it would be objection-able if I were to, shall we say, wander the grounds and indulge myself in reveries of what was never meant to be? I mean, of course, the return of the castle to its rightful . . . I mean, the fulfillment of my childhood hopes that I, as Lord Shaftoe, might walk again the halls and fields my ancestors graced in happier times?"

"I'm afraid it's a permission I have no right to give. Now if you'll just move your bloody—"

"Oh, yes. But wait. Here comes someone who might be more obliging." He raised a hand and called out, "Mr. Swee-ney! It's myself. I've . . . yes . . . I've come to thank you. I hope you don't mind."

Declan had already seen Kieran coming down Crohan

Mountain, then making a wide arc to avoid the mire at the foot of the hill. As he approached the courtyard, he acknowledged the intruder's call. "Mr. Shaftoe, is it?"

His lordship laughed a laugh that managed to be both a giggle and a cackle. "If you prefer. Surely I'm as much an egalitarian as the next fellow—depending, of course, on who the next fellow might be." He delivered himself of a congratulatory guffaw, undeterred by the want of amusement among those around him.

Kieran came closer. "Why aren't you in jail?"

"Well, one can't demand of the state unending keep, can one? Or, I should say, I can't. I accepted its hospitality for a sufficient time and must now become responsible for myself again. As would any self-respecting citizen."

"You've come with a purpose, I suppose."

"Mainly to thank you. I won't go into the details, as I'm sure you haven't forgotten your kindness. You did, after all, prevent me from committing an act inconsistent with my nature, to say nothing of my station in life. You, in effect as well as intention, saved my life. That day? On the tower? You *do* remember?"

"Vividly."

"Good. I, too, shall never forget. Nor will my gratitude be subject to the mutations of time. I am a man steadfast when it comes to a point of honor. And your action surely makes demands of me that are far beyond my powers to commensurately discharge."

"Very nice. Thank you."

"That said, I don't suppose . . . I mean, I'll soon be returning to Australia, but I was hoping that before I . . . I almost said *embark*, but one hardly embarks any more, does one? Then, before I take leave of this land of my ancestors, best exemplified by the castle here, I am hoping you'll allow me one final . . . well, perhaps a quick tour—"

"I think you have memories enough."

"Then perhaps you'll allow me to renew . . . to revitalize them before I—"

"I really don't think—"

"Surely you're more aware than any other mortal of what the castle means to me."

"Yes. Enough for you to try to steal it with forgeries and false oaths."

"But doesn't that all the more eloquently give measure to my affection? That I would so far forget myself as to descend into common criminality? That I would debase my name and resort to manipulations reserved for perjurers and scoundrels?"

"Very nice. Very nice indeed. But I still don't—"

"Let's compromise then. Forget the tour. Perhaps just a quick step inside. Into the great hall—for which I had such magnificent plans, none of them to be realized. Surely that much can be allowed."

"Well, if it will bring an end to this conversation—"

"Gracious as ever. And I thank you."

"You remember that it's little more than a barn at the moment."

"Of necessity I have long since schooled myself to ignore . . . nay, to be oblivious to that which offends, be it sight or scent. I am prepared, I assure you, to be selective in the experience you've so kindly agreed to."

"Okay. Come on. But be careful where you step."

After a dismissive guffaw, his lordship started toward the doors to the great hall, passing the truck with the now whimpering pig aboard. Kieran opened wide the imposing doors.

The reek easily reached both Declan and Lolly, but nei-

ther made the least response. To them it was a smell associ-
ated with cows, beasts of sweetness and docility. It improved
the air with the reminder that a being so comforting as a cow
was a castle resident, and Declan went so far as to feel a twinge
of regret that soon, thanks to his labors, the cows would be put
into the sheds, protected from the elements by his masterly
thatch. That they might miss the comparative opulence in
which they'd lived for more than a year was a possibility, but
Declan dismissed it, giving the animals credit for an adaptabil-
ity denied to most of the species that took such advantage of
their maternal generosity.

"I hope he goes down in dung," he heard Lolly mutter.
"And has to roll over in it to get himself up. Or maybe I'll go
in and give him a small shove."

Declan was about to return to his roofing of the second
shed when he saw his lordship emerge, his left arm firmly held
by Kieran's right hand. The man was limping and his shoe was
covered, it would seem, with a coating of fairly fresh manure.
Lolly was thrilled beyond speech. His lordship stomped his
foot, but to no effect. The dung refused to be dislodged. "I
didn't expect it to be quite *that* befouled."

Kieran was completely unable to suppress a gleeful smile.
"You can't say you weren't warned."

"No warning could possibly have been sufficient."

"You're safely out of it now—and let me say goodbye
before any more 'befoulings' come your way."

Kieran steered him toward the Bentley. He even opened
the driver's door himself. His lordship paused before crouch-
ing down to get himself inside. "I don't suppose I could take a
few steps over there, to the grass . . . to . . . well . . . as you can
see, there's a considerable deposit on my shoe—"

"That's not the grass. That's our garden. And it's been fer-
tilized enough, thank you."

"But surely one of you can do something for—"

"It's a service not included in my hospitality. Goodbye,
Mr. Shaftoe."

"Well. Really."

His lordship got inside the car, slammed the door, and
revved the engine, perhaps a bit more insistently than was
necessary. With a quick turn that spewed gravel, he was off.
Kieran brushed his pants, more to observe the departure of his
lordship than to rid himself of the dust and dirt deposited by
the speeding car.

After a nodded greeting to Declan and Lolly, Kieran went
over to the garden and began picking something or other, the
captive pig now bashing itself against the tailgate, screaming
and screeching as if its slaughter were already underway. Lolly
got into the truck and started it up the roadway. The phantom
lover galloped ahead and threw itself in front. But to no avail.
The truck continued on, the pig appeared again as whole as
only a ghost can be, solitary in the middle of the road, proof, if
proof were needed, that the spirit world cannot make good its
intents without the help of an earthly agency.

The phantom pig, head lowered, then lifted, looked for a
moment or two at the door left open by Kieran after he had
escorted his lordship out of the great hall. It entered. Although
Declan knew it hardly needed an open door to make its way
into the hall, he himself took advantage of the convenience:
he walked over and went inside.

There, for all to see, was the smeared manure to mark the
spot where his lordship had come to grief. There, too, was the
pig, staring upward. And there, hung by raw and rasping ropes

from the grand chandelier of a hundred candles, were the bodies of Brid and Taddy, circling in the mild breeze brought in through the open door. There were the black and swollen tongues, the bulging eyes.

Never before had Declan seen this. Never had he been warned of its possibility. He would have to cut them down. Quickly. But before he could reach the door to fetch the needed tools, he realized that even the ropes were ghostly, impervious to his intervention. He turned back to look again. Slowly they turned, first toward, then away from each other, their unseeing eyes unable to give the solace the sight one ghost might bring to the other.

Almost solemn in his movements, down into the heavily strewn straw, Declan Tovey knelt. Down into the reeking stench he put his forehead. Out from his sides he spread his arms and made his vow. They would be freed. They would be sent on their way. By whatever means, a means he would make it his cause to find.

He lifted himself and stood erect. They were gone. The pig, too, had vanished. He was in a great room given to shit and piss. This sacred place, defiled. Yes, he would thatch the sheds. They would be finished this day, this hour, the cows expelled, the air scented only by mists sent up from the sea. This he would accomplish—and consider his life fulfilled. For this he had descended from ancestors he would now honor. All would be achieved. All would be accomplished.

When he went out through the door, he passed Kieran carrying a bunch of something Declan took no time to name. He hurried past, not seeing the puzzled look on Kieran's face. Declan didn't doubt that the man had seen him covered with dung and smelling of piss. But what was that to him—or to anyone.

9

And so Declan had vowed the castle would be blown to dust and it would be his doing. The sight of Brid and Taddy hanging had given him more than the needed impetus. Long had he wished to be the instrument of their release—since the day of his tenth birthday, the day on which, by family custom, he was considered to be a man. In September, on the Feast of St. Michael, his father had taken him by the hand and led him to Castle Kissane, a good distance to go, but a long walk was required for his father to prepare him for the mysteries into which he was about to be initiated.

From Declan's first days on earth he had known of the ancient Tovey heroism, when his ancestors, aged as they were, had offered themselves to be hanged and the fine young Taddy and the fair young Brid set free to fulfill a destined happiness, and how they had been whipped for their attempt to thwart the greater pleasure his lordship would find in abbreviating the life of one so fine and one so fair. But now the time had come for ten-year-old Declan to be inducted into the more intimate mystery that attended it. "The first thing you must do," his father had said, "is swear an oath it would be your damnation to break. Are you the man for it?"

"Yes, Da."

"Then listen—and show no one except a child of your own what you'll be shown today. Do you understand?"

"Yes, Da."

"You're a good man, Declan, and your father's a proud father." And then the tale began.

Declan and his father arrived at the castle. "Say nothing and make no sound," his father said. After removing some stones at the base of the tower, his father pointed down into the blackness opened before them. "Follow me there. But take my hand, because only I know the way." Down some earthen steps his father went, into the dark, Declan behind him. Dank and rancid was the earthen floor, and no air to breathe. After a few panicked wavings of his hand, Declan hit his father's shoulder and quickly found the hand he was to hold. His father led him through the dungeon, up a rotting stair, and through a door flung wide leading to the main floor of the castle. Through rooms walled by stone, some covered with lime, his father took him to yet another stair, this one winding upward. They were in the castle tower, ascending.

They came to a wide but empty landing with a window high on the wall, but continued on until they came to a second landing. What Declan saw there disappointed him. All this solemnity—and it had taken them to nothing more than a young man sitting on a stool with an unstrung harp held against his chest, and him foolishly pretending to play. There, too, was a loom, ancient by the look of it, and a girl, perhaps a bit more than a girl according to the stirring that ten-year-old Declan felt at the sight of her, and she pretending to be weaving.

"Watch and say nothing," his father whispered.

Obedient, Declan watched. The young man ignored them as did the woman, each continuing their foolishness as if no one were there. Was it to see these obviously demented people who'd made their home in a castle ruin that his father had brought him all this distance? And then Declan saw their necks, raw from the rasp of a rope it seemed, the flesh scarred by the wounding. His father put his finger to his son's lips. The two of them continued to watch.

"This is Brid," his father finally said. "This is Taddy."

Declan's mouth fell open in awe. These were names he knew. Long did he watch, and his father, too. The harp silent though plucked, the loom moving noiselessly back and forth, though without a single thread to give it purpose.

And then the boy and his father silently left. On the way home, they were as soundless as the youths they'd seen. And his father no longer held his hand. Declan, now a man, was on his own from this day forward. The secret was now his; he was now the keeper of the mystery.

The sun, well toward setting when they had left the castle behind, was now gone below the mounded hill ahead. His father spoke. "We are the ones who can see them and no one other. The cause of it is known, the offer of themselves by our ancestors. How it is will be forever a strange and wonderful thing none of us can ever completely explain. All we know is they are there. And we, if we choose to share their sorrows and their suffering, and the sorrows and sufferings of those ancestors gone before us, we may return and Brid will be there, and Taddy, too. Somewhere. Other rooms, perhaps. Or in the fields I've seen them as well, and walking the orchard gone to a ruin. And now, you, too, may go. If it is your wish.

But you must always remember the oath. The Toveys would be thought mad—and mad we well may be. But it is a sacred madness. And ours alone. By blood. Ancestral blood, and may it never cease to flow. And Brid and Taddy never be forgotten or forsaken. Have you heard my words, son?"

"Yes, Da." And Declan took his father's hand, and his father did not refuse it.

With no one having told him anything directly, Declan had begun to piece together, bit by bit, evidence that Kitty and Kieran knew not only the necessary means to free the trapped spirits, but also how to implement their release. This he had deduced from Lolly's rantings about her scorned novel. There was a distinct possibility it was less a fiction than Lolly knew. Kitty and Kieran, Declan was inclined to believe, had spoken with considerable authority. The flagstones of the great hall could really be impacted with the needed gunpowder. And it might still be activated after all this time. But, then, Declan should keep in mind that Kitty McCloud was no slouch when it came to devising plots and bringing them to satisfying con-clusions. She could, in her wish to help her friend Lolly, sim-ply have rattled off the easiest way to relieve the woman's agony and bring her stupid novel to an extravagant ending. Just let the book be done and the poor "writer" be put out of her misery. Still, inventive as he knew Kitty to be, he was more than ready to accept what he had heard and deduced as possible clues.

Of course, he could try different ways of testing his knowledge—and, in the process, blow himself up, and Kitty, Kieran, and the cows as well. He considered asking Kitty outright, confronting her with his guesses, but he quickly realized that if she and Kieran *did* know how to blow up the castle but still hadn't done it, they had obviously resolved not to do so. If he were to ask questions that could be considered intimations of his own resolve, a resolve inconsistent with their own previous decision, they might try to thwart any and every attempt he might make to end the tragic hauntings of Castle Kissane. (Why Kitty and Kieran might have made such a curious decision would be none of his concern. He had made his own vow and nothing would effect its fulfillment.)

Immediately he also reminded himself of Kitty's weird vision not only of Michael's death but of Declan's own most secret feelings. But then, when the spell, or whatever it was, had ended, she remembered nothing of what she'd seen or said. Still, anyone endowed with powers that allowed the unseen to be seen and the unknown to be known could not be trusted to remain ignorant of his unstated plan. Considering this, he must not even *think* of any plottings in her presence.

As he applied another crook to attach the sways, the rods used to secure the reeds to the rafters, Declan saw from the corner of his eye Peter McCloskey standing shyly in the courtyard entrance, his bicycle leaned against the wall of the shed that would be the last to be thatched. Clutched in his left hand, held stiffly at his side, was a book. "I know you want no helper," the boy called out in his piping voice, "but I've come to ask may I watch? I'll say nothing and do nothing. Only watch. And that's my promise."

Declan looked at the fresh face, the floppy hair fallen over the hesitant eyes, the unmuscled flesh common to an eight-year-old. So controlled was the fear in his voice—*manly* was the only word for it—that Declan had to concentrate more completely on applying another crook. After this proved to be an impossibility, he muttered, without looking up, but loud enough for the boy to hear, "You'll say nothing? You'll do nothing?"

"It's my promise. You heard me say it. Will I say it again?"

"No need. I have ears." He nodded toward the heap of the squatters' discards piled nearby. "Over there."

Without hesitation, the boy climbed to the top of the trash as if he were ascending to the pinnacle of Skellig Michael itself. Smiling with unbounded gratitude, he settled, after a squirm or two, into the abandoned rejects, then nodded to let Declan know he was exactly where he wanted to be. And grateful beyond expression.

"I'll explain nothing," Declan said, resuming his task. "Is that understood?"

"Oh, you needn't explain. I know what it is being done." He proudly held up his book. "I've been studying, reading. About thatching. Like I know it's water reed you're using and those are crooks you're working with now. And there, the next shed down, there you've already made the construction you'll need, those slanting pieces are rafters, but the thinner wood above them are battens and those underneath are purlins. Am I right?"

"Is that what it says?"

"Here." Again he held up the book. "If you want to look."

"You think I have a need?"

"Oh, no. I wasn't thinking that at all."

"But it's there in a book? How to be a thatcher?"

"Not all. How could that be? One learns only by doing.

What's in the book doesn't even begin to teach what only a master himself knows. That's why I was hoping you'd at least let me watch. And I'll say nothing." With a light laugh, he added, "A promise I've broken already. I'm sorry. I hope you won't change your—"

"Stay there and all will be well."

"Thank you, sir."

"I am not a 'sir.' I have received nothing from a king or from a queen—and were they to put a sword to my neck, it would not be to make me a 'sir.' "

"Sorry, Mr. Tovey."

"That will do well enough." He grunted and, as best he could, tried to concentrate on his work. He regretted deeply having been so harsh with the boy that other day. The child was blameless. And skinny. And eager. Declan continued to do what he was supposed to be doing, trying not to be distracted, the boy so intent on his every move. He should tell him to leave. No. He must make sure he stayed.

After a time, Declan said, "We'll stop now. You'll eat a bit of something." It was more a command than an invitation.

Bewildered, the boy said, "What?"

"We'll have some food. It's time." He came down the ladder, wiped his hands, one palm against the other, and went to the leather sack tucked away one shed ahead. From it he took, wrapped in newspaper, the ingredients for a midday meal.

"Oh, but Mr. Tovey, I can't do that."

"Why not?"

"I should eat at home."

"If it's a thatcher you want to be, you eat wherever and whenever the hunger comes. And it's come. We'll sit there on the stones."

"But I only thought I'd watch—"

"And am I supposed to have you watch me eat?"

"I should go home. And, if you say, come back later. But whatever you tell me, I'll do it."

"I've already told you. We'll eat, and then you'll watch some more. And if you want, you can read more of your book while you have your food."

"I've already read it. Twice."

"Then you'll do nothing but eat. There, where I said. On the wall. On the stones."

They sat. They ate. Declan made the mistake of glancing to his side. The boy, staring straight ahead, was thoughtfully munching the bread and the bacon, crunching occasionally as his teeth cut through the crust. Declan should not have looked. He was recalled, but gently, to his grief. Even at the distance he could hear the sound of the sea. There would be waves assaulting the cliffs. Farther out, the waters swelling, then moving on, indifferent to what lay beneath.

Peter was given a leek. "And is there enough?" he asked.

"From the garden there. Plenty. I plundered it this morning. But it's by invitation only, so don't make too free."

Peter giggled.

Declan considered saying "You're a good man," but thought he had already, with those few words, said more than he wanted.

And besides, the boy was so intent on chomping the leek it was probably best not to interrupt. Until, that is, Declan found himself forced to say, "I was wrong to be so harsh the other day. And getting the soup splattered all over your shirt." He paused, not particularly eager to say what followed, but said it anyway. "I'm sorry. It was a wrong thing to do."

Peter chewed away at the leek. "But you had a reason."

"A reason is not reason enough for doing something like that."

For a long time neither spoke. Peter's chomping and chewing was all that could be heard. A thought then came to Declan. The boy, like his mother—and like Kitty, who had told of Michael—might see or have knowledge of Brid and Taddy, and of what could be done to free them. And of how it might be done. Hesitant, reluctant, Declan heard himself say the words. "Over there, on the side of the hill where the cows are, do you see anyone?"

"See anyone?"

"There." He pointed past the castle toward Crohan Mountain.

"But there's no one there."

"No one, you say."

"Yes. I see no one. Why do you ask?"

"You've heard of Brid and Taddy?"

"Brid? Taddy? Of course. Who hasn't? They say they're here in the castle, but I hope not.

"Oh?"

"I'd be afraid. They're dead, and they shouldn't be here."

"And if they are?"

"They should be sent away."

"Oh? And how?"

Peter laughed. "Just tell them to go."

"And if they can't?"

The boy shrugged and took another bite of the leek. "Ask them why not."

"What if they don't know?"

The boy considered this, then laughed again. "Then why don't *they* ask?"

"Ask who?"

"Someone who knows."

"And who might that be?"

Still chewing, Peter said, without any laugh, "I thought I wasn't supposed to talk."

Declan would say no more. He should not have introduced the subject. It did not concern the boy—and it should stay that way. As he was breaking the bran cake in two, Peter, with a depth of seriousness available only to the innocent, asked, "Do you see them? Brid and Taddy?"

Declan gave this a thought, then nodded toward the mountain. "They're there."

Peter swallowed, then parted his lips. "Is . . . is it because you're doing work here? And if I were doing it, would I see them?"

"No. It's none of that."

"But . . . but Mrs. and Mr. Sweeney . . . they . . . they see them. That much I seem to know."

"They told you that?"

Puzzled, the boy answered, "I don't remember. I don't think they told me."

"Did they tell you why they see them?"

"Oh, no. How could they? They didn't know themselves."

"But you did?"

"I did?"

"And do you know now?"

"I . . . I don't know if I do or if I don't."

"But you *do* know things."

"I . . . I guess so. Sometimes."

"Like when I was so harsh with you?"

"That? Oh yes. But then . . . I told you . . . I forgot."

"And you forgot what you told Mr. and Mrs. Sweeney?"

Peter blinked and looked down at the last bit of leek

held in his right hand, the leek from the garden planted by and cared for by Kitty and Kieran. "Did I? I mean . . . did I tell them it was because it was their ancestors . . . one of Mr. Sweeney's and one of Mrs. Sweeney's . . . ." He began to bring the last of the leek up to his mouth. Declan, gently, lowered it back toward the boy's knee. Peter looked at it as if wondering what it was and what it was doing in his hand. Then he said, "They were to be married. The ancestors. And so they went off to invite their cousins and their uncles and their aunts. All the way to Tralee they went, asking them to the wedding. And while they were gone—"

"Yes?"

Peter looked up and turned his head toward the mountain slope. "Are they still there?" he whispered.

"They're gone."

"To be hanged?"

"Yes, to be hanged." He, too, was whispering.

"But it was supposed to be . . . to be . . . ."

"The kin of Kitty McCloud and of Kieran Sweeney?"

"Is that it? Maybe. A McCloud? A Sweeney?" He licked his lips, still looking at the mountain.

"Yes? When?"

"When?"

"Do you remember when you told them all this?"

"It . . . it could be the time . . . with the burnt bit of the . . . of what? Yes . . . the burnt bit of the flagstone they'd put into the fire and it . . . what? It . . . it exploded. It blew up into little pieces. And I picked up a bit of it when it had cooled and I . . . I . . . I don't remember. They . . . Mr. and Mrs. Sweeney . . . they live in the castle now . . . ." He tried to say more but could only shake his head.

Declan gently took the piece of leek from Peter's hand.

The boy looked long at his empty palm. Declan reached over and closed the hand, then touched Peter's arm. "It's enough. It's enough. Let it go now. Let it go." He handed back the bit of leek.

Peter gave this some thought, then put the last of the leek into his mouth and began to chew. Slowly. After a respect-ful silence, Declan said, "We've still the bran cake. And then we're done."

10

The drive to Killarney was uneventful except for Aaron's guilt at having lied to his wife. Being Irish, his guilt went beyond simple accusation into unrelenting harassment. It gave him no peace. Three times he had been tempted to turn around, go back, and confess to Lolly that he was not going to Killarney to tour the restored Ross Castle, but to see Lucille. It was his plan to attend the afternoon performance of Messiah—the last before the singers returned to America, laden with praise. It was Aaron's expectation that Lucille would see him again as she had in Caherciveen and search him out during the intermission. His purpose, aside from tanking up on the spiritual fuel the oratorio unfailingly dispensed, would be, as conscience dictated, to perform the manly act of forgiving his errant wife for her transgression of their conjugal vows and for seeking connubial comforts in the arms—and wherever else—of another.

He could have told all this to Lolly. It was, after all, to his credit that he could find it in his wounded ego to forgo all the ill feelings justified by his first wife's defection. His magnanimity touched him deeply—just as it would Lucille. But had he mentioned the name Lucille to Lolly, it might have occasioned snide mockery he would rather avoid. Accusations would not have been made outright, but, in their place, there would have been not-so-subtle suggestions that more than forgiveness was on his mind.

Although his wife's insinuations would hardly prove fatal, he would just as soon do without them, as much for Lolly's sake as for his own. Why distress the good woman so? Why cause her unnecessary concern? With this thinking, Aaron was able, by the time he passed through Killorglin, to convince himself that, as regards his wife, his act was not one of hypocrisy but of loving-kindness. He would, he realized, enjoy the music very much. His conscience was clear. And his self-approval would soon increase with the absolution he would bestow on the undeserving Lucille.

The church in Killarney was not as imposing as the one in Caherciveen, although it rose from more impressive grounds, green lawns that could feed a fair-sized number of sheep for at least a week. The pews seemed a bit more severe, but nothing could stanch Aaron's growing euphoria.

Again, two tiers were ready to receive the chorus. Also, there were chairs for the soloists, the members of the orchestra, and a podium for the conductor. And there was the crowd, come in from the Sunday weather—a mist rather than a less ambiguous rain—willing to be uplifted, to be given sufficient respite from bearing fardels and grunting under their weary lives.

And there, soon enough, came Lucille, this time fourth in her tier, which suggested that some choir member had returned to America early or (if such were imaginable) had been given a better offer. Lucille was as aptly clothed as before, her scarlet robe lacking only a large letter A to make it even more appropriate. Still, she *was* pretty, in a clichéd sort of way: blond hair angelically curled and waved, down past her shoulders, eyes whose blue reached easily to where Aaron was seated in the fifth row, not much in the way of cheekbones, but the well-formed and generous lips more than compensating for the deprivation. The skin, however, was her real claim to beauty, a freshness that hinted of perfect health and well-being, of easy good cheer and amiable companion-ship. Perhaps it was Aaron's current life of rusticity that made him feel that the sum of all these parts added up to nothing more than a bovine placidity, an appraisal that ignored a tem-perament adventurous enough to send her off with a baritone. Aaron decided on the spot to forgive her not only for her adulterous behavior but for her more general inadequacies as well. The cup of his magnanimity threatened to overflow.

The oratorio began. Lucille seemed to be working harder than the others, but, then, that could be because she had to, given her limited equipment. Aaron made an effort to detect her inimitable voice from among all the rest, but the cho-rus was too well trained to allow for one singer—even with Lucille's distinctive pitch—to distinguish herself.

Part One ended to appreciative applause. Aaron, cer-tain that Lucille had spotted him (she seemed a bit rattled in "For Unto Us a Child," but had managed to recover by "All We Like Sheep"), hurried though the main portal out onto the walkway that divided the green acreage. This would pro-vide him with an appropriate stage on which to perform the inspired scene he had so touchingly scripted.

He waited. No Lucille presented herself. Perhaps she had

not seen him after all. Perhaps the peculiar behavior he had observed—a nervous tugging of her right earlobe, a repeated sniffing he was sure he'd heard—was just Lucille being Lucille. Maybe she'd wet herself again at the sight of him. He considered going around to the back of the church and asking whomever he found there to inform the soprano, second tier, fourth from the left, that an acquaintance from America wished to see her. (Even in anticipation, he was unable to say "Lucille Glyzinski," which would have simplified his request.) But before he could make his move, he heard the all-too-familiar voice. "This time I held it, so I had to go pee just now," it said. "And what are you doing here? It's raining. I looked for you in the narthex and then saw you—"

"In the what?"

"What do you mean, in the what?"

"That word you used. You looked in the what?"

"The narthex. What's wrong with that?"

"I never heard it before."

"It's the vestibule. You should go to church more often. And what are you doing here anyway? You already heard all this. And the rain can't be good for my voice."

"It's mist. And it's very good for the voice. Softens it."

"Where'd you hear that?"

"Lots of places."

"Name one."

"You sang very well."

"Thanks. How could you tell?"

"I know you. I could tell."

"You don't know me."

"We were married. Remember?"

"That's how I know you don't know me."

"Well, be that as it may—"

"I don't have all day. This is only an intermission. What are you doing here?"

"I came to hear Handel."

"Yeah. Sure. You—the great enthusiast of the baroque. Uh-huh."

"All right, then. I came to tell you . . . I mean, I want you to know that I . . . I . . . I . . ."

"Oh, spit it out for shit's sake."

"I forgive you."

"What?!"

"I forgive you."

"Oh? Really? Why? What'd I do this time?"

"I forgive you for leaving me."

"You what?"

"I forgive you for leaving me. There. I've said it. And I mean it. You're forgiven."

"*I'm* forgiven?"

"That's what I said."

"I heard you."

"So now you know. You're forgiven."

"Well, if that isn't the bee's knees."

"I beg your pardon?"

"As well you might."

"Lucille, we don't have time. I came to forgive you and I've done it. Now, if you have to go back—"

"Sure I have to go back, but all that can wait or they can go ahead without me. *I'm* the one should do the forgiving, not you. And I'm here to tell you I *don't* forgive you and I never will. You little twit."

"Lucille—"

"I know my name. You want to know what I don't forgive you for?"

Now, Lucille—"

"To you the name's Glyzinski. Mrs. Glyzinski. And I don't forgive you for making me believe you loved me."

"I did love you."

"Stop using words you don't know what they mean."

"I loved you."

"Stop or I'm going to pee again—from laughing."

"Believe me or don't believe me, but—"

"I don't believe you. I believed you then. I don't believe you now. What you thought was . . . that four-letter word again . . . was just you wanting someone who would make other men jealous, make them wonder how a jerk like you could get himself a gorgeous piece like me."

"That's not—"

"Shut up. I'm not finished. And what you wanted was someone you could lay any time you wanted—which, by the way, wasn't often enough as far as I'm concerned."

"There's more to being in love—"

"And someone to adore you and worship you like you were a god instead of a twit. To say nothing about you having a free char and a maid and a cook and . . . Oh, wait. All right. There is something you can forgive me for. I can't cook. I never could, and now I don't even try. You forgive me for that and I'll forgive you not just for being a lousy husband but for being a lousy writer."

"I am not a lousy writer."

"Oh for God's sake! Just for once, believe what you read in the papers. You're a lousy writer. And I forgive you for it. It's not any more your fault than it's mine I can't cook. So is it a deal? You want to talk forgiveness? I'll talk forgiveness. Come on. Talk."

"Lucille, I . . . I . . ."

"I . . . I . . . I . . . All the time I. Forget it. Now I've got to pee again. Thanks for coming. Enjoy the rest. And try to remember, it's not about you. It's about the Messiah. The *real* lover. Got it?"

"I never said . . . I never thought . . ."

"Sorry. Now I've *really* got to pee."

Aaron considered not returning for Part Two, perhaps going to Ross Castle after all, just to make an honest husband of himself. But before he knew it, he was seated and waiting. The chorus came into the sanctuary. Lucille was not in her appointed place. After the singers, except for the soloists, were completely assembled, on came Lucille, who, to get to the far side, had to walk past the entire chorus. Apparently, she *did* have to pee. Some of the audience took her for the first of the soloists and began to applaud. Lucille turned, bowed a little, then continued on to the second tier, forcing the singers assigned to her right and left to make room for their tardy colleague. The applause that had diminished once Lucille had moved beyond the chairs awaiting the true soloists began again when the soloists *did* appear. The clapping became even more enthusiastic when the conductor took his place.

Aaron looked and listened. There was Lucille, heeding him not at all. The music started. She sang and sang and sang, giving it all she had, negligible though that might be. She cared nothing for her inadequacy. To give her whole heart seemed enough. Passion was there in plenty. And a depth of feeling he had never noticed in her before. She was magnificent.

Not until now had he seen it. Not until now did he have the slightest idea of who and what she was, how gallant and unafraid, possessed of a sweetness of spirit of which he had been totally unaware. Now, too late, he adored her. He wanted to make her happiness his first and only purpose for living. He loved her.

The "Alleluia" was unbearable. "Worthy Is the Lamb" brought tears of both joy and despair. He made no effort to hold them back or to wipe them from his cheeks, his lips, his chin. Freely they dripped onto his only good tie.

After the last echo of the great "Amen" had faded to silence and the applause had exhausted itself, Aaron dashed from the church. By the time he had elbowed his way through the crowd massed ahead of him, since no one was particularly eager to step out into what had become a torrent of rain, she had apparently already boarded one of the buses lined up near the sacristy door, waiting to whisk them all to Shannon Airport in time for the evening flight to America. Unmindful of the rain, he moved alongside the buses, hoping for some last sight of her, but it was a hope never to be fulfilled. The buses pulled out, one after the other. She was gone. Gone with the husband who, during "The Trumpet Shall Sound," had gone flat, then flatter with each of the unending series of repeats Handel had demanded.

The last bus made its way down the street, disappearing at the first turn. Aaron, accustomed by this time to being bedraggled, went to his car, got in, and sat for a moment, wondering which direction he should take—to Shannon or to the pig farm? Actually, he had no choice. He started the motor, eased into traffic, and went home, where the pigs awaited. And his wife.

When he saw Lolly slopping swill down into the troughs, with the pigs screaming in anticipation of satiety—his wife, indifferent to the elements, a slouch hat pulled over the indestructible beauty of her auburn hair—he realized that this woman, too, he loved. And, as he paused to watch the swill falling into the troughs, he knew that he loved her even more than he loved Lucille. Yet he felt the final sight of his former wife singing the great "Amen" would remain a vision he would never banish. It would be with him, *she* would be with him, forever. As befits a man entangled in the mysteries of the land to which he had come, he had found his proper haunting, his very own version of Brid and Taddy, or of Declan—and his acceptance, like that of all the others, was total and absolute.

He went to his wife's side, a second bucket of swill in his hand, and took up his part of the evening task. Hearing the clamoring pigs, he had to reflect on the pig that, in its own way, had led him to this complexity, the one that had followed him to his aunt's house and dug into the cabbage patch. Should he curse the pig or bless it? For the moment, he'd do neither. He must concentrate on the bucket of swill and the pigs screaming for his attention.

While Aaron was having thoughts about the now deceased pig, the animal was very much within Declan's view as he, at the rain's insistence, was gathering his tools in the shelter of one of the completed sheds. The phantom pig had been particularly attentive to him these past few days, keeping watch as if it were an overseer intent on making sure he was performing according to specifications.

Declan had enjoyed the scrutiny, a mild distraction from his obsession with the castle, with Brid and Taddy—and the pig, too—with his determination to bring the castle to ruin and release Brid and Taddy from the curse's thrall.

He dropped his tools into his sack and drew the rawhide thong that closed the top. The pig, he noticed, unaffected as it was by the pelting rain, had been giving its attention to the debris that had yet to be removed from the castle courtyard. Then, as if it were a perfectly natural thing to do, the pig climbed the side of the unsightly mess and disappeared into the pile, snout first, as if, still alive, it was simply digging its way into available trash, intent on scattering its unsavory contents throughout the landscape. This, fortunately, was beyond its present competence. It would have to content itself with a ghostly exploration of the interior of the heap and emerge satisfied with the memory of times when it might have wreaked considerable havoc as in the days of old.

The pig did finally reappear, nothing having been disturbed by its intrusion. It found its way, without calamitous effect, down to the ground, then turned and stared at the point of entry, its snout lifted, its gaze intent.

Declan snorted his amusement and slung the sack over his shoulder. He took two steps toward his rattletrap truck. He stopped, waited, then turned. The pig remained transfixed, interested only in the site of its recent exploration. Inscrutable were the ways of a pig—and of this pig more than any other. Was Declan supposed to take up a similar interest? Was he expected to become engrossed—as if he, too, were a pig—in a pile of junk? He turned away, took a few more steps, then stopped again. He turned back. The pig hadn't moved. Its concentration was impervious to distraction. Warily, Declan moved closer. As he neared the animal, he sensed that something was expected of him. And it had to do with the heap that had so completely claimed the pig's attention.

He traced the trajectory between the pig's snout and the place where the animal was staring, then went closer and stood next to it. The stare remained fixed. Declan reached out and tugged at a plaid skirt bunched in among the other spurned artifacts. More was removed: what appeared to be part of a tent, a battered teakettle, a broken ping-pong paddle, and a moth-eaten brown sweater. So far, the junk above was still in place, but it would soon sink down, filling the tunnel he was making into the center of the mound.

He was considering starting at the top and dismantling the entire structure when he managed to pull out a small metal box with wires attached, probably a device of Kieran's invention, a timer perhaps, for use in his cooking and baking in the castle scullery. The pig continued to stare at the hole Declan had made. The thatcher reached in again, this time retrieving a soiled and well-thumbed book. Not a book, really; more of a catalog, the kind sent to clog the mails at Christmastime. He let it fall to his feet and put his hand—indeed almost his entire arm—back into the heap where he'd found the book. At this, the pig lowered its head, turned, and, trotted away on its silent phantom hooves. When it reached the third shed, it vanished altogether.

Declan withdrew his arm, then looked to see whether this might affect the pig's return. It didn't. The pig was no longer interested in what might still be done. Declan had been fool-

ish to think that what the pig did or didn't do had a particular meaning, that it had anything at all to do with him. He
allowed himself a short quick laugh. He had played the pig's
game and must pay a loser's penalty: the acceptance of the
humiliation imposed for having been duped by a pig—and the
ghost of a pig at that.

He began to collect the retrieved junk, his strict upbring-
ing requiring that he replace what he had disturbed. The pile
must be made whole again. The kettle, the skirt, the paddle
were returned. The book and the device, whatever it was,
were next. He would stuff them deep into the hole where
he'd found them, then jam in the sweater and whatever else
lay at his feet. He picked up the thumbed pages to give them
a glance before shoving them into place. It might tell him
something about what had interested the squatters. Perhaps
he would be given insights into their behavior, their motives,
their plans for the future. As if he cared.

He opened the catalog at random. He read what was there,
including some marginal notes written in pencil, accompanied
by a sketched diagram. He read further, but only a little, before
he slowly closed it. He picked up the metal box, the tangled
wires dangling down. He examined it more closely, then again
consulted the catalog.

He stood where he was. How long he remained without
moving, indifferent to the rain, he could not tell. His first
move was to open his shirt and shove the pages and the box
inside to protect them as much as possible. Quickly he went
to the sheltered shed and opened his sack. The catalog and
the box were thrust inside, then, with trembling hands, the
thong was drawn. Now they were safe from the torrent falling
all around.

Declan stumbled his first few steps, then forced himself to walk as steadily as the situation would allow. He paused when he reached the doors to the great hall. He used the key Kitty had given him should he want to avail himself of the "facilities." He went inside, closed the doors, and leaned against them, then opened the sack and drew forth the retrieved book. He opened it again, then closed it, having read nothing. He had no need. He knew what he held in his hand. It was not only a catalog outlining in detail the methods for detonating explosives, but, scrawled in its margins, it had notes and diagrams showing how to attach the wired metal box to the already planted gunpowder.

Declan looked up at the hundred-candled chandelier of beaten iron where he had seen the hanged bodies. He glanced down at his feet and, with his boot, scraped off to the side the flop in which he had stepped. He stared down at the flagstones, now visible. Again, he slowly knelt and placed his open palms on the gunpowdered flooring. Eyes shut, he blessed the pig.

11

I t was a day as fair as any Kitty had ever known. The sky had rid itself of clouds and presided without impediment over a sea content to raise only one unbroken swell after another, feeling no need to indulge itself in the turmoil that was its preferred occupation. The swells, by their nature, advanced inexorably to the cliffs, but on this fine day they seemed merely to lap and lick the rising rock face like a suppliant puppy. No vessel broke the horizon, not even a curragh taking advantage of the sea's agreeable disposition.

The grass through which she'd waded to come to the cliff's edge was still fresh with dew, and she'd noted that the purple-headed knapweed and thistle had begun to flourish in the untrod soil. Also, on such a day as this, even the irresistible smell of the sea could not compete with the scent of clover brought to her by the gentlest breeze coming from somewhere to the north. Even the cormorants soaring and plunging out over and into the water had muted their expectant cries, and the sandpipers on the beach below scurried toward, then away, from the surf, managing, as always, not to get their feet wet.

Kitty had to admit that her perceptions might well be influenced by the new knowledge that she was pregnant and had shared the news with Kieran at bedtime the night before. As if to remind her of his unceasing efforts to bring about this pleasant pass, he'd offered up not some tender or solicitous phrases, but the words "And about time if I say so myself"— accompanied by a pleased smirk.

When he had then fallen into Kitty's arms, she thought at first that he'd fainted, but his recovery was quick enough. He pulled himself away and clamped his huge hands on her shoulders. Speech was impossible. The sounds coming from his mouth, from his throat, and regions farther south were completely animal: growls and roars, high-pitched screeches, then throttled screams that only a renewed plunge between Kitty's breasts could still. He brought Kitty to such a pitch of joy that she feared she would be assumed heavenward before the great event could even take place, but was calmed somewhat when she felt the heaving of her husband's body against hers. Her thought then was that he was sobbing, but the good man withdrew himself again and she saw and heard raucous joyful laughter that had been smothered against her flesh, now free to shiver the rafters above and the flooring below. Suddenly the laughter ceased. Kieran was looking almost fearfully into his wife's eyes, reaching toward the deeper depths he reserved for moments of greatest tenderness. Slowly he enfolded his wife in his arms and rocked the two of them gently from side to side. Then he was crying, and Kitty, too.

Just before dawn, Kitty, still asleep, had moved her arm over toward her husband and was abruptly awakened when she failed to find him there. Her eyes opened immediately, and she raised her head from the pillow. There was Kieran, naked, at the window, his mouth half open, his brow furrowed, staring out into the growing light.

How could she not, even in her somnolent state, appreciate the splendors so readily apparent? Compared to her husband, with his rugged features and tawny beard, other men seemed over-evolved. They had gone too far beyond a previous perfection, leaving Kieran Sweeney as a reminder of what men once were and should be still. His wide-set eyes, a blazing blue, could penetrate stone, to say nothing of her own susceptible heart. His nose, somewhat oversized and leaning slightly to the left, was paired with a mouth extending beyond what lesser beings found sufficient to their needs. The chin, beneath the well-trimmed beard, could jut out farther, but had rejected the arrogance it might suggest. As for his form, it was shaped according to some lost design fashioned by gods more rugged and less fussy than their indulgent successors. The sight of his spine slanting down at an inward angle to give greater emphasis to his rock-hard buttocks was enough to forever undo her, forcing her to concentrate on his feet, which were, in mercy, not particularly interesting beyond being among the largest in the county.

Kitty, no less naked than he, slid her legs noiselessly over the edge of the bed, got up, and went to his side. Saying nothing, she, too, looked out. When he didn't acknowledge her presence in any way, she reached up and placed her hand on his shoulder blade. She waited. She would stay silent. She would wait forever if necessary.

After a time, Kieran, still not moving, said in a low voice, "And will our child, in its cradle, sleep under the gaze of ghosts?"

Kitty hadn't thought of that. Under circumstances of

lesser importance, her ready response would have been, "We'll jump off that bridge when we come to it." But this was a subject far too serious to be diminished by anything snide or silly. Since she was unable to respond, she uncharacteristically said nothing.

After a respectful pause, Kieran spoke again. "She . . . or he . . . our dear, dear child, *our* child . . . and because it *is* our child . . . will see them. Brid. Taddy." He paused again, then added, "Possibly even the pig. Do we want that?"

Again Kitty could offer nothing but silence.

After a lesser pause, Kieran went on. "What will it do to an infant to discover that the world at times exceeds its limits, that the boundaries of the real have been redrawn, that there are secrets that will make our child unlike any other, that this might force a bewildered girl or a befuddled boy into a solitude where every moment is shadowed, day and night? And we have to tell where all this began, and how and why. Born to a shame that can never be lifted. A *child*, to be burdened with *that*? And when should the tale be told? And when will it be explained? What comforts can we offer when we ourselves are descended, the same as the babe, from ancestors complicit in the hanging of Brid, the hanging of Taddy? They are ghosts, and their visitations will be perpetual reminders of an ancient wrong. And our children will be heirs to this remembrance, and their children after them. And do we say 'Live with this if you can'? 'Live with this as you must.' How, Kitty, how?"

Kitty went and sat on the edge of the bed. Without raising her head, without looking over at her husband, she said, "We go to your brother's soon. For my teaching. It was my plan to return here to the castle so the baby could be born in the place it would inherit in God's good time. I had thought of little else."

She waited for Kieran to say something, but he, too, had lowered his head, no longer wanting to look into the distance. Kitty's breathing was slow and steady. She had found a solution. She had made up her mind. "We will go to your brother's. We will never come back—not to the castle." Kieran said nothing. "This place will pass into other hands. To others unable to see them. To someone free of the curse that's put upon us."

"The curse? Or the honor?"

"Both."

Without allowing much of an interval, Kieran said, "Someone like Lord Shaftoe? And Brid and Taddy left to hang, the harp and the loom untouched? Is that what we're to do?"

After she'd waited for the inevitable image to pass through her mind, Kitty lifted her head. Kieran was searching the lightening sky. Kitty was tempted to go to him again, but she decided to keep some distance between them for what she had to say. "Then you know as well as I what we have to do. Am I to say the words or will you?"

No answer. Kitty remained quiet until she could wait no longer. "This castle, more my home than the house where I was born and raised, this witness to our great love, this inheritance I'd hoped to leave to our children and their children, it will come down at last. And that will be the end. There's no other way. We'll see to it together."

"We'll not do it." Kieran spoke quietly but firmly.

"Then I'm to do it myself?"

"No one will do it. It will never be done."

"But you yourself have been naming all thereasons—"

"Not reasons. Merely truths that have to be faced. But there are other truths."

"Oh?"

"And they show us another way."

"Oh?"

"The child is born. Here. In this castle. In this bed, if you will. And Brid will come to see the baby. And Taddy, too."

"No!"

"Yes. They will come. And the child will see them; we will see them. The child will see them looking down. The child will see them in the courtyard and on the mountain. The child will see them in the orchard and . . . oh, Kitty, Kitty, the child will see them at the loom and at the harp—"

"But—"

"No, wait. Wait. Let me finish."

"But you're—"

"Please, dear wife, please."

"Go on, then."

"When the time comes—and it will let itself be known—we'll tell who they are. We'll tell *why* they are. And the child will hear and the child will know. The whole story, everything. Your ancestor and mine, pledged to set off the gunpowder. The journey to Tralee. And the sweet and innocent hostages taken. The nooses prepared, and their fair bodies—"

"No . . . Please, no more. We can't tell a child—"

"We can. And we will."

"How?"

"With words."

"And who will say them?"

"I will. You will."

"I? Never."

"You will. And I will tell you why."

"No 'why' is possible."

"Listen. And then say that again if you can."

"I'll listen. And then I'll say what I said all over again."

Kieran shifted sideways to look directly at his wife. Kitty preferred to concentrate on the opposite wall. With quiet intensity, Kieran began. "Brid and Taddy, who they are and what happened to them, is our story as much as their own. And the story tells of our country and what it suffered and what was done to it. It's all going, Kitty. It's going. We are a different Ireland now. The country of Brid and Taddy is gone, and we give thanks for that at last, but it must never be forgotten. Isn't it possible that they're here, revealing themselves to us, not because they've been robbed of the eternal joy they deserve more than any, but because they want us to see them, to know their story and our story? They have died as you will die and I. We can be forgotten. But not Brid. Not Taddy. They must be remembered for all time to come, for as long as Irish blood flows through the human heart. Our child will know it. Our child will tell it—as we ourselves will have told it. And the castle stones will stand and be their earthly home. Please, Kitty, Brid and Taddy, we can't send them away. They have a tale to tell and it must be told. It must. And it will be, for as long as I have breath to say again and again what I've said to you now."

Unmoving, Kitty continued to regard the far wall. She let her breaths come and go, one after the other, neither shallow nor deep. Just the ordinary breaths that sustained her ordinary living. She got up and went to her side of the bed. She drew back the sheet and the blankets and plumped first Kieran's pillow, then her own. She reached out her hand. With a small, sad smile, she said, "Isn't it our time of morning? Or have you forgotten?"

•

Contrary to what could be common surmise, Kitty had come to the old familial ground not to wallow in sentimental communion with her forebears about her coming contribution to the future of the family line. Nor had she come to see Declan, who was known to visit the scene where—as Kitty now knew—he could try to either indulge or assuage his grief. If they should meet, she'd say but a few words if any, then do what she'd come to do and leave him to his solitary needs.

She had come to the cliff's edge, the copy of Mrs. Wharton's *The House of Mirth* in hand. When Declan had brought it to her, a remnant of her sunken house tossed onto the shore, she took it as a sign, an omen that it wanted her correction. She had, after all, kept it with that as a possibility, and its peculiar arrival could suggest that she accept the assignment. She had come to realize, however, as Teresa of Avila might once have said, "Sometimes a coincidence is just a coincidence." Or, at least, that was Kitty's chosen interpretation, which now spared her the admission that she was not up to the task. It would be with reluctant resignation, not wrathful vengeance, that as soon as the tide came to the foot of the cliff, she would toss the copy back into the waters from whence it came.

She could, of course, keep the book. It *had* been part of her lost library. But she feared she would see it, there in the tower landing where she fashioned her wonders, as a rebuke, a reminder that Lily Bart, the novel's ill-fated heroine, had successfully resisted her efforts at rescue, despite Kitty's having changed her name to Fenimore Blythe and the title of the book to *The House of Fenimore Blythe*.

The difficulty was that Lily/Fenimore was not as cooperative as Kitty had expected her to be. Given the woman's release from the coincidences that had thwarted her landing a man of sufficient wealth and pedigree to guarantee lifelong happiness, she remained, as in Mrs. Wharton's version, more than a little fussy about whom she would accept as consort.

Also, Kitty realized that the coincidences imposed by Madam Wharton, aka Pussy Jones, while distinctly unlikely, were not exactly impossible. Kitty's accusation that Lily was destroyed because it suited Mrs. Wharton's agenda that she should be destroyed still held. But it had to be admitted that the temper of the times in which she, Lily/Fenimore, had lived were equally responsible for her fate.

Kitty had tried making her a Wall Street whiz, a woman taking command of her diminishing stock portfolio and transforming it into a bulging bundle that not only shamed the men of her acquaintance but brought them stampeding to her door, newly aware of her charms. Who except an American or a Frenchman would want to write a novel about a stockbroker, though? Not Kitty McCloud.

Our author then granted Lily/Fenimore the advantage enjoyed by both herself and Mrs. Wharton: She would be artistically gifted. Not a writer, but, acting upon the original author's choice of a possible profession for her heroine, a milliner—with the difference that now Lily/Fenimore had a near magical propensity for creating hats that caused a sensation, with the women of her set now the ones clamoring at her threshold, pleading not only for her hand in marriage to their dreary sons, but for one of her rather vulgar creations, one suitable for next week at the opera.

Still, Kitty wasn't satisfied. A small voice was telling her something she had hoped to ignore, but couldn't: Edith

Wharton, had been telling truths that needed to be told; Kitty McCloud was not only obscuring but dismissing those truths. Lily's fate *had* been preordained. Also, if Mrs. Wharton had been overgenerous with her coincidences, Kitty was no less guilty with her own manipulations. She should be ashamed. And she was.

In one last effort to find a truth beyond what her predecessor had uncovered, Kitty could come up with only one inevitable but unacceptable ending. From the beginning she had rightly scorned Edith's closing scene: Lily's fantasy, in the last moments before her ambiguously induced death, of cradling a friend's baby in her arms. The yearning for a child had never been an important issue for Lily, and it was disgustingly sentimental to bring it into play in Lily's most vulnerable moment.

So what would Kitty do? Kitty came up with only one answer, the one that prompted her to shut down her computer and leave her desk. For her Fenimore there was but one honest ending. Kitty would give her the only job available to a woman in her situation—at the Triangle Shirtwaist factory in New York in the year 1911—then let the absence of workable fire codes do the rest. Like all those other young women at the factory who had failed to find a rich and pedigreed man, she would meet her ordained doom, at first being trapped, then jumping to her death from the tenth floor to escape the flames.

A container ship had appeared and a single cloud had come from the north, bringing with it an even more intensified smell of clover. Gulls had joined the cormorants out over the sea, and behind her Kitty could hear ring plovers distressing the high grass. Below her she saw that the tide was coming in, the water still licking and lapping the foot of the cliff. She'd wait for the waves to rise higher before returning Edith's book, neither omen nor sign, to the element from which coincidence had sent it. More aggressive waves would be needed for the undertow to bear Lily back to the drowned house and the deeply mourned bones.

She heard a car stop on the road. She turned, assuming it was a longtime acquaintance who had stopped to give her a quick greeting and exchange gossip about the tumbled house. But it was Lolly she saw, cutting off her motor. Lolly glanced over and looked at Kitty looking at her. She immediately switched the ignition back on, ready to drive off. After a light push on the accelerator, she lifted her foot. The motor slowed, then stopped. She turned off the ignition a second time, waited, then got out and came toward her best friend, Kitty.

"You're here," she called out, even though she wasn't that far away.

"So it would seem." Kitty considered getting up from the cliff's edge, but didn't feel like accommodating the intrusion. What Lolly's purpose might be she had no ready idea, unless—and this was a thought she'd prefer not to entertain—it was the hope or expectation of meeting Declan. If so, Kitty preferred to hear that news sitting down.

Lolly, in a more conversational tone, said, "You've come to look for Declan?" From the sound of her voice, Kitty could tell she was more than a few paces behind her.

"Why would I come here to see Declan? I see him most days, doing the thatching."

Oh. Well. Of course. But . . . is he here?"

"I've not the least notion. So it's he you've come to find?"

"Well, yes. But he's not here, I guess. I've something to

tell him, but maybe it's not that important." That Lolly had some reason to be either reticent or apologetic about being there was apparent from the way she was speaking.

"Did you try the castle? He could be there by now."

"I thought I'd come here first. It's said in the village he comes here often—early in the morning or late in the day. The men working on the road, they see him often."

"They don't think it strange?"

"Well, it *is* strange. To them."

"But not to us?"

"To us nothing Declan does is strange. Or, rather, all of it is. We're used to it."

"And that's the end of it?"

"If he wants anyone to know his reasons, he'll tell them, is how I see it. Otherwise, nothing."

"Well, come to think of it, don't try the castle till later. He may be down at the bog cutting sedge so it'll dry by the time he ridges the thatch."

"Oh. Thanks. I can always find him another time." Kitty waited to hear more. It finally came. "And you," Lolly said, "are you looking to see if the old house is going to show itself or what?"

"No. I've let it go. It can show itself or not show itself. I have a better home by far. And what is it that's maybe not important if I may be so bold as to ask?"

"Oh, nothing. Not really."

"Now it's beginning to sound important after all."

"All right, then. I'll tell you and you can decide for yourself." Lolly sat next to Kitty on the cliff's edge. With the heel of her shoe she gave a light touch to the cliff-side below, a lifelong reflex to make sure something was there to support her.

Kitty could see she was wearing a dress, hardly her usual

daytime attire, her bright blue one at that, linen, and newly ironed by the smell of it, the one whose blue deepened the color of her eyes—which, by common consent, heightened her allure. Whatever that might be.

"There's a thatcher wanted in the north past Connemara, putting up holiday houses. Aaron came across it on the Internet and I made a printout to give Declan. They plan to make them cottages and the roofs thatched so those who come can feel themselves living like long ago. I don't see any work for him around here, now that the thatching you've given him to do is all but done."

Kitty looked sideways. Lolly had cocked her head, waiting for Kitty to say something. Kitty felt no need to say anything. She was content to give her full regard to the blue dress and the intensified eyes.

Assuming an attitude of lofty indifference, Lolly, still looking directly at Kitty, said, "After all, I *am* an old friend of his. Surely, I'd do something that might help a man destroyed as he is these days."

Kitty turned her face again to the sea. Her voice was quiet. "You are a good friend of Declan's, Lolly, that you worry about him having work to do. And I hope the man knows it."

Less loftily, Lolly said, "Well, there's nothing here for him. Nothing to keep him. There'd be no purpose to it, him not going off the way he always does. Why would he want to be here? He'll find something worthwhile a distance away. As he always does. I have to laugh to think about it." To reinforce her words, she let out a laugh that sounded reasonably like the real thing.

Kitty considered changing the subject, but Lolly went on. "How foolish we all were. But we were young then. Younger than young. And just the sight of him. The great dark hero come from another world." Again the laugh, but less convincing. "Nothing on his mind it seemed but . . . well, you know what. And even our guardian angel's sheltering wings no protection we'd know. But it wasn't just 'you know what' he was after, but the offering of himself as if he were the Eden apple itself, daring you to come to the feast. Oh the life of it . . . the . . ."

She stopped and brushed her hand across her forehead. Softly she said, "And we believed we'd known the last of him and him gone into the sea, never to come again. But the sea couldn't keep him. He's come up out of the waves, Kitty. How could waters wide as the world hold him forever? It could never be. Not for him. He's come again—"

"From the north, where he'd gone."

"I know. I know. But isn't it allowed that sometimes the old madness comes over you—"

"Not over me. You, maybe. But not me."

"Ah, of course. Not you." Again a small laugh, this one unforced, but not without its sorrows. "And not over me, either. It's not permitted. It must never come, the madness. And we must make sure it never does."

The full tide had come in, the waves now battering away as if enraged by the cliff's earlier indifference to its lapping and licking. Kitty shifted Mrs. Wharton's book from her left hand to her right. The moment was near. She must toss it, not merely drop it as if it were a thing to be rid of. She must cast it out as far as she could, in tribute to her sister writer for whose flaws she had nothing but respect.

Again Lolly interrupted. "You were reading. I didn't realize. You probably never noticed, but I can be thoughtless at times."

"No, I never noticed." Without previous consultation, they giggled together. Lolly began to draw her right leg up from the cliff's edge, but stopped, then lowered it again. After an interval sufficient to let Kitty know she had more to say, Lolly smoothed the bright blue dress covering her lap and began what seemed a soliloquy, even though the words were obviously meant for Kitty as well.

"It's the bones of a boy out there beneath the waves. Declan told me and said how it happened. You know it all as well, he said, but according to him you needed no telling. He said all this to me when he was showing me the way up the secret stairs. Did you know he found them? They're still there, where the priests escaped and where we hid the skeleton when the gardaí, Tom and Jim, came looking for a man escaped."

"I knew," said Kitty, "but never went up them or down. They were a part of the house. They should have gone with it."

"But they didn't. It was dark even with Declan's flashlight, but I wasn't afraid. Not with Declan there. Halfway up . . . Oh, but I guess I should tell you. I came looking for him after I'd made such a fool of myself telling him about my book, trying to convince him I wasn't the crazy lady he'd seen when Aaron and I went to Caherciveen to hear the *Messiah*. And he offered to show me the stairs. Halfway up he stopped on a landing, the damp stones all around and the smell still there from the years gone rotten so long ago. The flashlight he kept aimed toward the steps above and he spoke to me. About the boy's fall and the dying. And him buried in Declan's own coat because the ground was so cold, he said. And with the thatcher's tools and other things besides from Declan's life put into the old sack so the boy wouldn't be left without things he'd known in the world and that Declan had known, too. And then the search to the north and no one to claim the boy. Now the coming here, and it's all gone away, given by the wind and taken by the sea. And the grief was upon him, telling me all, and nothing to be done." She paused, then added more quietly, "Well, almost nothing." She paused again. "I'll say no more."

Kitty let the book fall.

Lolly shifted back from the cliff. She stood up, then paid the sea some final obeisance: a prolonged gaze. She started toward her car. After a few steps, she stopped. Kitty waited, hoping she'd continue on. She'd wait until Lolly was gone, then get up, her task completed, and go back to whatever work she could find for herself to do. When Lolly began to speak again, Kitty simply sat and listened, looking up at the cloud from the north.

"It was to me Declan came the night he buried the boy in the garden—though I didn't know that at the time, until he told me that day on the secret stair. That a change had come over him that night I knew, and him with more of a need of me than ever before, and I all gone wild to give. Let me say it and I'll go. We were together through the whole night, until he let me sleep just before morning. I had no dreams, but the sun woke me before too long went by. He was gone. That part hadn't changed. He was gone and the sun up full. But it was to me he had come that night and no one else besides. Only to me."

Kitty waited to hear more, but there was no sound until the motor started and the car drove off. The cloud from the north changed course and headed out to sea.

12

Declan saw the infamous Bentley come into the court-yard, purring like a cat much too pleased with itself. With no other vehicle to inconvenience, it made a turn and came to a halt alongside the shed where he was working. Through a window opened to the country air, the man called out, "Hard at it, eh? And it's a great work you're doing." He stepped out of the car and, with a ruthlessness that seemed central to his nature, slammed the door.

Again he was wearing his linens and silks, the only variant being the scarf, which this time had been dispensed with, the better to display an Adam's apple that seemed more a knot of words trapped in the man's throat to keep him from afflicting the earth with yet more pollutants.

Declan considered it best to simply continue his task and pay the least attention possible to the visitor. In an attempt to end the man's stay before it could begin, he muttered, "There's no one here. They're off."

"So I understand." The man spoke with a cheerfulness that revealed his preference for their absence. "Mrs. Sweeney to Dublin where she's to read from her most recent triumph, the title of which escapes me. And himself to somewhere below Blarney to see his brother on some business of which I'm ignorant."

Declan was tempted to mutter, "To see a fine lady upon a white horse", but he wanted as little conversation with this man as possible. He said nothing.

Undeterred, his lordship continued. "I regret the mishap that brought my recent visit to such an unhappy end. But that's hardly your concern. You are an artist and therefore exempt from the least regard for the woes of common mortals. But allow me to say your artistry shows an uncommon skill."

The man waited for a response. When none seemed forthcoming, he plunged into what was obviously a well-prepared speech meant specifically for Declan's benefit. "The true reason I've come is to see again, as I did before, the masterly work you're doing here. As I'm sure you're aware, my family were once protectors of all these lands, including, of course, the castle. And I lack the words to tell you how deeply pleased I am to see the courtyard restored to its earlier perfection. What you're doing is the practice of a craft long in decline, allowing me the privilege—nay, the honor—of seeing the castle as my illustrious ancestors so happily beheld it."

By a force of will not congenital to his character, Declan managed to control himself. The man paused, expecting, hoping, for some expression of gratitude for his fulsomeness. Puzzled by the lack of appreciation, but as determined as ever to complete his speech, he went on. "I'm told your name is Tovey. Fine name, too. I've already used the world *illustrious*, so I'm forced to say merely that it is a name distinguished by English gentlemen and scholars down through the ages. Is it possible that you're related to Sir Donald Francis Tovey, the great musicologist?"

Declan managed a look of utter incomprehension. His

lordship chose to ignore the thatcher's lack of response. "He's a man who's added so much knowledge and enlightenment to our appreciation of the great composers and their noble works. You yourself are, from what I observe here, also a singular con-tributor to your own noble traditions. Hardly a surprise con-sidering you're obviously descended from a familial line that continues to bring distinction to our English heritage."

Declan was sore tempted to inform the man that "Tovey" was a corruption of the good name "Tuohy" imposed upon his family by authorities inclined to record names more congenial to their own spelling than the names spoken in a language they were determined to render extinct. Rather than reclaim their original identity at a later date, his family had decided to retain the imposition lest they forget the corruptions thrust upon them, determined that the name be a perpetual reminder of perfidies practiced during the centuries of imperial intru-sion. Let his lordship rattle on. He obviously had some insidi-ous intent, and perhaps, before long, he would indict himself completely.

Which he did. Forthwith. "As you may have overheard during my recent visit, my attempt to claim my birthright—the castle and all these grounds—were diverted by some legal misunderstandings. I am sure you appreciate my determina-tion to take up again my obligations to my forebears, and it occurred to me that I might enlist your own good offices. That a generous remuneration is involved goes without saying. And since we obviously share a common past, it came to me as in a dream, that the fates had put me into the company of one who might lend his support to a plan that should restore these lands and the castle itself to their legitimate owner. Myself, of course. No, you need say nothing now."

In a hushed voice meant to suggest confidentiality and the

need for secrecy, with the unsubtle hint that the conspiracy admitted only the most privileged into its company, he said, "I will expand on this at some near date. There's a boy over there, reading, who might overhear, much to our disadvantage. You understand."

That a boy was there, reading, Declan had understood from the beginning, but he also understood that the man was plotting some mischief that could not possibly be to the benefit of his Kerry compatriots. Rather than become enraged, he immediately decided that feigned complicity was the better course. There was more to be revealed. And here was a God-given opportunity to become a recipient of these revelations. In the mutter he knew the man had come to expect, he said, without interrupting his work, "I might possibly be the one you're looking for. But I'll need to know more."

"And you shall. You shall. Soon enough. Meanwhile, make no mention of today's visit. And instruct the boy to forget that I stopped by. As for you, Mr. Tovey—as for *us* I should say—we shall meet again and all will be put before you. We needn't make a gesture of our pledge, with the boy in attendance. But I consider this visit most successful. And I don't doubt that, in time, you will come to a similar conclusion. Let us content ourselves with my goodbye. And my promise to return—at an even more propitious time. *Au revoir*, my countryman." His slight bow, his smile, captured so accurately the oily farewells of so many villains in so many ill-acted films that Declan managed to stifle a hiss only by reminding himself that there existed a plot against his friends, and that he, Declan Tovey—of Tuohy descent—had been appointed by heaven itself to frustrate it in the making.

After the Bentley had made its self-satisfied departure,

Peter came to where Declan was working. "That was Mr. Shaftoe. Mr. Sweeney saved his life. He was going to jump from the top of the tower because he wanted the castle and it wasn't to be allowed. But Mr. Sweeney wouldn't let him. Jump, I mean. Did he come to try it again, do you know?"

"I know nothing. And there's nothing I need to know. Keep watch at what I'm doing. And let our agreement be enforced. No talking."

"Yes, sir. I mean, yes, Mr. Tovey."

"Tuohy if you want."

"I beg your pardon."

"Never mind. Just remember. No talking."

The boy stood where he was, watching, the book held against his side. Declan Tovey—Tuohy of old—went on with his work.

Lord Shaftoe, to continue the work to which he was now so completely committed, went to his London tailor to have himself outfitted in the eighteenth-century clothing worn by his ancestor, the gentleman threatened by the Irish rabble with a gunpowder plot that would surpass the perfidy of Guy Fawkes and all the papist traitors conspiring against a Crown and a Parliament committed to the cause of supremacy and to the preservation of privilege. Not for his lordship the musty threads still reeking with the sweat of actors or the perfumes of masqueraders. Not for him the mothy leavings of the long-gone dead. Nothing but the new and the unique would do. He alone would wear these garments; he alone would reserve to himself the right to future vestings. (His one concession to inauthenticity was his decision to wear, instead of the joined cotton tubings that served as undergarments in his ancestor's time, his own silk boxer shorts, secure in the knowledge that no incident would expose, as it were, his inconsistency.)

His lordship had taken his presumed compatriot, Declan Tovey, into his confidence as to the reasons for this extravagance. Since Mr. Tovey's cooperation seemed assured to get him into the castle at the chosen time—when Mr. and Mrs. Sweeney would not be present but would return sometime after dark, dark being an integral element to carrying out his plot successfully—he had now moved on to the next phase of his plan.

At a date not that distant from his first interview with the estimable Mr. Tovey, he returned now to confide in him, spelling out in gleeful detail his brilliant scheme. "I will be dressed in a somewhat peculiar manner, but give it no heed. It will replicate the clothing worn by my illustrious ancestor, one of the more than several who legitimize my claim to the castle. I'll not go into the details of that, but suffice it to say that the present occupants are trespassers and must be dealt with as such."

Mr. Tovey had offered no reaction, but had simply stood and waited to hear what would follow. To interrupt with responses would only delay the denouement of the tale being told. "I shall," his lordship continued, "conceal myself in some out-of-the-way place in the castle, unseen. Then, when I feel the appropriate time has come, I shall emerge and present myself—a figure in shadow but discernable by the light of a flickering candle." He leaned closer and, his tone still confidential, whispered, "Wonderfully imaginative, don't you think? The flickering candle?"

Reverting to his more normal speech, he continued the narrative, his reptilian pleasure intensifying with each word. It was quite possible that this intensity would lead him into an ecstasy where speech would no longer be possible, but, unheeding, he went on. "There, by candlelight, I will appear, moving slowly as befits a ghost wandering through the castle wrongfully denied his descendant, the current Lord Shaftoe, I myself, no less. Mr. and Mrs. Sweeney will know at once that they are living among the restless dead, subject to a haunting that must, by its nature, stop the blood and halt the breath. They will be terrified. After all, the last thing they expect to see is a ghost. Am I not right?"

Mr. Tovey took this into consideration, then nodded his understanding of the horror to which the trespassers would be subjected.

"They will cry out! They will beg at the sight of me for relief from this shattering vision. I shall move through the room, slowly, not hearing their plaintive pleadings. They will cling to each other, so appalled by the knowledge that the castle they have appropriated will, from this time forward, offer them no peace. Their lives will be subject to disruption at the pleasure of a phantom, a phenomenon to which they could never adjust, as could no one in his right mind.

"The triumph will be mine. They will flee the castle, most likely that very night, and seek refuge in the first wayside cottage that will admit them. They will be distraught and wild, unable to explain their random arrival, with speech no longer available to them, so affrighted will they be by the presence of the very person they were convinced had no such powers to come among them at will, a person indifferent to their fears, scornful of their entreaties.

"You yourself, Mr. Tovey, can readily appreciate their consternation. Here you are, a man of considerable intelligence, not accustomed to seeing apparitions, until one appears, as if alive, there—there—there! See how he moves! He has come to bear you away to torments not yet imagined by the human mind. Oh, delicious, delicious! That there will be soilings I am quite sure. I mean, they *are* seeing a ghost. And the one they dread most: Lord Shaftoe himself, come from those celestial regions his nobility had guaranteed. But here's the rub. He *will* return—and claim again the domain given him by a monarch himself invested with divinity and thereby having acted with godly assent.

"Oh, how I wish you could be there, Mr. Tovey! Except you would howl with laughter at their inability to deal with the horror—and that would, of course, disrupt the scene. So you must, under no circumstances, intrude. Do you promise me that?"

For the first time, Declan spoke. "You have my promise. I will be nowhere near."

"Ah, the promise of a gentleman. One can't ask for better than that, eh, Tovey?"

Mr. Tovey, in his wisdom, realized no response was necessary. His lordship, in the throes of a helpless euphoria, climaxed and concluded his narrative. "The vacated, abandoned castle will then become mine. And there will be no ghosts to disturb the joy that will reign supreme. Of that I can assure you. Would it be convenient if we set a date for Saturday week?"

Mr. Tovey seemed to give this some thought. He furrowed his brow, then said, "That should do quite well. Every Saturday Mrs. Sweeney helps bring in the cows from the far side of the mountain there. Sort of a tradition they started when they married. Come then, just before sundown, and the doors will be unlocked. Go in and find a place to hide yourself—an unused closet between the bathroom and the master bedroom . . ."

Convinced that the man was unhinged, possibly by his prison stay or, more likely, by a lifetime obsession he could no longer contain, Declan began and continued to unscroll invention upon invention, giving no hint that his cooperation in the plot was being manufactured spontaneously, fashioned to oblige his lordship's needs as soon as they had been made manifest. Nor did he show any pleased surprise that the date recommended by his lordship coincided perfectly with the date set for the departure of the "trespassers" to move their cows to a place down from Blarney in preparation for Kitty's teaching assignment in Cork. By sundown they would already be on their way.

"Ah, yes. The bedroom," his lordship was saying, all the while rubbing his hands together in unrestrained glee. "That will be ideal for my brilliant presentation. Except that the wait will be rather prolonged—"

"No, no. There you're in luck again. After the cows (milked in no time by the two of them, it's another tradition), before even thinking about their evening meal, they retire to the bedroom—but not, I suspect, for sleep . . ."

"Say no more! Surely the gods themselves are in attendance! All is perfection. Absolute perfection. I shall enter. The candle will flicker. There will be ghostly shadows and I . . . and I . . ."

Overcome, he could go no further.

Declan, to give the man time to recover, said, "A week from Saturday, then? If that's your pleasure."

Breathing heavily, his lordship managed to say, "Pleasure

is hardly the word. I would act more quickly, but, as you can imagine, I am very much in demand in London and prefer not to disappoint. Saturday week will be excellent. Excellent. Agreed then, Tovey?"

"I'll do my best."

"Than which there is no better. Eh, Tovey?" His lordship chose to laugh.

Declan wasted no time giving him reply. "Saturday after this it will be. At your service. Honored to oblige."

Another laugh burst forth, this time more from the man's lordly nose than from this lordly mouth. "And if you see me, attired as I'll be, you must not believe you're seeing a ghost. Your good offices will exempt you from the horror. I will be very much who I am, prepared at last to receive what is rightfully mine."

"As you say." Declan made the slight bow the occasion demanded, and the interview was over.

The final fitting of the spectral raiments was being completed. For the outer coat, the justaucorps, a wine-colored velvet had been selected, not exactly a neutral color, the wine of choice being not a watery Burgundy but a virile Tuscan vintage known only to the most discriminating. A more insistent hue had been considered, but the tailor opined that this outer coat must not compete with the splendors decided upon for the inner coat, the one that buttoned only at the waist to give some prominence to the lace jabot, the frilled scarf worn at the neck of the silken shirt. Rich brocades shot through with crimson and gold, intricate embroideries not seen since the period being emulated—all were brought together in a cun-

ning design of the tailor's own invention, providing a climax
to the man's long and distinguished career, so that anyone
privileged enough to behold so magnificent a spectacle would
know immediately that he or she was in the presence of an
individual they were not worthy to look upon.

The cuffs protruding from the sleeves of the outer coat,
if less imposing, still had enough frilling to give them a distinction that competed with the jabot as to which was the
more decorative. (The jabot was, but the cuffs came in a
not-too-distant second.)

The outer coat, of course, flared below the waist, and its
front displayed buttons that added to the desired impression
of extravagance. The knee-length britches were allowed to be
rather plain (no need for distraction), and the white stockings
surrendered completely to the sartorial magnificence above.
(The stockings had been procured from a bystreet shop dealing mostly in medical uniforms for women.) The shoes, however, were another matter, having been made by a shoemaker
who boasted not only a crest but an elaborately printed state-
ment on his card that he was, by appointment, shoemaker if
not to Her Majesty, then at least to many of the courtiers who
waited upon her. The shoes' modesty was rewarded by golden
buckles, each easily worth the ransom of any of the courtiers
mentioned above.

The wig was then put in place, the hair a bit darker and
more profuse than the strands cross-combed over his lordship's
balding pate. This was, after all, a disguise. His lordship had
felt from the first that he was a faithful reincarnation of the
long-ago Lord Shaftoe immortalized in the portrait painted
by a close competitor of Gainsborough. If, as seemed likely
in the painting, a wig was worn, then he, too, must sport a

replica. (It had occurred to his lordship, on the previous day, that the wig did somewhat become him, and he briefly considered making it—or some portion thereof—a part of his daily attire. He'd have to think it over. Some might suspect it was not his God-given locks and be less than charitable in their response. Still, what did he care what others thought? Or said. Was he not Lord etc. etc. etc.? The decision was postponed, but he seemed inclined in favor of an even darker, thicker possibility.)

As his lordship was preening in front of the three-paneled mirror, his tailor, a man whose pretensions were even grander than any mere lord could hope to accumulate, said, "I assume your lordship is pleased."

His lordship fluffed the jabot, trying to determine how it could cover as much of his wattled neck as possible and create the illusion that his chin was not as recessive as the one bequeathed by those illustrious ancestors already mentioned. "It will do. It will do."

"And you feel it will influence others invited to the same event in . . . is it Dublin?"

"A bit outside, where there are more stately houses able to accommodate a ball so grand in scope and discriminating in its assemblage. They will be more than impressed, I have no doubt."

The change in his lordship's tone from reluctant approval to enthusiastic endorsement was made necessary by the arrangement he had suggested to the tailor: in lieu of vulgar payment, his lordship, at a date sufficiently in advance of the great event, would display the tailor's masterpiece—which in turn would occasion a crowding of his shop, each suppliant begging for similar treatment. The tailor had raised not one but two excited eyebrows and quickly acceded to the suggestion. He had long wished for a clientele throughout the entire kingdom, which (to him as to his lordship) included a temporarily misguided but soon to be repentant Ireland, reunited to its northern counties and received again into the forgiving bosom of the Mother Country, a prodigal come home. If no fatted calf were to be slain, at least a thin-lipped welcome would be offered.

The vestments being too valuable to be trusted to a delivery service, and the apparel too unwieldy when boxed, it was decided that the tailor's assistant, himself schooled in all the courtesies needed for waiting upon someone of his lordship's prominence, would accompany the gentleman to his hotel, bring the clothing safely to his room, all the time in the company of his lordship himself, who would oversee a proper handling. The assistant would then hang the outer coat, the inner coat, the silken shirt, and the breeches in an accommodating closet, reverently fold the jabot and the stockings into a well-designed bureau, place the shoes in the closet after having brushed them with his very own sleeve. His lordship felt no need to surrender his silk boxers for similar treatment.

Viewing it all once the assistant had taken his leave at the hotel, the man barely having disguised his resentment that no monetary recognition had been made for his professionalism, his lordship was mightily pleased and had only to worry how he could possibly wait for what lay ahead Saturday week.

13

Little by little, undeniable changes began to take place in the relationship of Peter the patient, silent observer and Declan the concentrated, efficient laborer. There was still the shared meal when, sitting side by side on the rock wall, Declan would force yet another chunk of bread on the shy but eager boy, or would insist that he eat his share of the oatcake baked by the Widow Quinn. The bacon or bits of cold pork chop or chicken leg were pressed upon him, along with produce from the castle garden—leeks, green beans, turnips, and tomatoes for the taking, especially after Mrs. Sweeney or Miss McCloud or whoever she was had commanded them to help themselves under pain of her displeasure. They greedily obliged. The leeks, threatened with decimation, were rescued just in time by the ripening tomatoes, which were surely the most succulent either of them had ever eaten.

But there was still little or no talk beyond Declan's gruff but quiet complaint that Peter would never grow to be a thatcher if he didn't eat more than what would keep a pipit alive. Then there arrived the day when Declan began to explain his actions: the use of the tarred twine and the various implements, the names of which Peter already knew from his book.

"And if you see any of this done any other way, it's wrong. I know only the right way and I'm telling it to you now. So you'll have it right for all time to come."

"Yes, Mr. Tovey. And thank you—"

"That's enough. I know you're a good and grateful boy. No need to keep saying the words."

"Yes, Mr. . . . I mean, I've heard and I won't forget."

Declan made some primitive sound that Peter accepted as approval.

Then the time for their parting had come. His work finished for the day, Declan was already throwing his sack onto the seat of his truck when Peter came into the courtyard, the wheels of his bicycle grinding the gravel. He dismounted and, letting the bicycle fall to the ground, called out, "Oh, Mr. Tovey, I was so worried you'd be gone. But you're here."

"And gone in less than a minute."

"I've come to say goodbye, and I hope I'm allowed now to say my thanks."

"They've been said more than enough. But why goodbye? You've given up thatching then?"

No, not at all. I'll never do a thing like that. But it's my da off in Tipperary."

"He's not well?"

"Oh, no, he's in the best. But he's sent for me to come there. I'm to work with the horses. In Ballysheen. He has it in his mind I'm to become a jockey because I'm skinny and small."

"That could change with the years."

"It will. I'm sure of that. But my da, he has it in his mind, and there's nothing to be done except for me to go to him. To Ballysheen. To the horses."

"You might like it."

"Oh, I will. I know I will. How could I not, and me riding into the wind? But I'm still a thatcher. Or I will be. That much I know. If I didn't know it the first time I came here, I know it now after all I've seen and all you've said."

"It will be finished here when you're back for school."

"First thing, I'll come look." Thrilled to be talking serious things with a master thatcher, Peter smiled and wondered if he could be so bold as to hold out his hand for a farewell shake. Mr. Tovey had moved away as if anticipating—and avoiding—any show of familiarity. He went to the large stone that marked the entryway to the courtyard, sat down, and tugged off the boot from his right foot. He wiggled the big toe poking through a hole in the thick woolen sock, almost approving its insolence in choosing this moment to put in an appearance. When he reached inside the boot, it became obvious that a stone had lodged itself, and the time had come to return it to the pebbled ground.

Peter watched as the master scraped around inside, then finally found the offending object and brought it out. Small wonder it wasn't that easy to find, a flat stone not much bigger than the protruding toenail. It was set down next to Mr. Tovey. Peter thought of asking for it, perfect as it was for being skipped across the water of the lake one valley over.

With a satisfied grunt, the master tugged the boot back on, took the stone in his hand, and stood up. For whatever reason, he rubbed it against his coat. A glint of sun caught its surface, but only for a moment. He held it out to Peter.

Peter shied back. How did Mr. Tovey know he wanted it? Now it was being rubbed between the man's thumb and forefinger. Peter had never noticed before how hard was the skin of the hand and how strong the fingers. The man stopped his rubbing and held out the stone again. "You're to have this."

"I?" He tried not to sound too excited, but wasn't as successful as he'd hoped.

"Isn't that what I've said? Take it."

"I'm allowed?"

Taking Peter's hand and placing the stone onto his palm, Declan said, "You're allowed."

His manner was as gruff as it had been when Peter had first come, begging to be permitted to watch the workings of a master, pledging himself to become one himself someday. "And you needn't say thank you," Declan added. "You've only to take it and keep it."

Peter looked down. Slowly he, too, rubbed the stone, then stared at it. Bewildered, he said quietly, "But this isn't a stone. It's a coin. It's money."

"And you'll keep it. And give it to the next thatcher you, as a master, might train—or to a son that might come to you someday."

"It . . . It's mine?"

"It's yours."

"But I can't—"

"You can. And you will."

Peter squinted and gave the coin another slow rub. "Seventeen hundred eighty-five." He raised his head. "That's a bit of a while ago," he said softly.

"It's been long in my family, come down from father to son."

"But then shouldn't you—"

"No. A Tovey soon won't be needing it anymore."

"But . . . but it's . . . it's money."

"Given to right a terrible wrong. But soon the wrong will be made right enough and the story finished. I'll no longer have need to be reminded of the tale it told. It will be ended soon, and happily, too. Then I'll want it no more." He was looking off to the west, but his eyes were searching a distance even farther away. His voice no longer gruff, he said, "I should have given it before this. To someone who, like you, wanted to be—" He stopped and jerked his head as if to bring his gaze back from where it seemed to have been searching. His voice gruff again, he said, "That's enough. Just take it."

"I don't understand."

"Good. No need to. You'll accept it—"

"I . . . I . . . I . . ."

"It's settled then."

With one swift move, Declan jumped into the cab of the truck, taking the sack with him. He pulled the door toward him. It closed with a loud rattle. The engine started. A quick turn was made, barely avoiding Peter's bicycle. The truck clattered down the road, away from the castle. Peter ran after, calling out, "But . . . but . . . but . . ."

The truck was gone.

He stared at the coin in his open hand. There was nothing to be done but put it into his pocket and take it home to his mother. She could certainly use some money—if the coin was still worth anything after so many years (he remained unaware that its value had grown with its age). He began to fold his fingers around it, but stopped, continuing to stare. Slowly his mouth opened; slowly it closed. With the coin clasped tight in his fist, he ran out of the courtyard entrance and started again down the road. "Come back! Come back! You mustn't do this. I . . . I can't. I can't have it. No one can have it. Come back.

You have to! It isn't for me. It isn't for anyone. For no one! Ever!"

He stopped running but kept looking into the distance. There was the castle road, then the road home, up the hill, then down, then up again. No cars came. No truck. No one. Nothing.

Stumbling on stones, he went back into the courtyard. Without realizing what he was doing, he almost brought the fist-held coin up to his chin, but caught himself in time to pull it away.

He made a fierce dash toward the doors to the great hall and barely managed to get them open so he wouldn't crash into them. He had to find Mrs. Sweeney. He must give her the coin. Get rid of it. Anything. Avoiding the flops, he kicked his way through the great clumps of straw, the bedding for the cows, untangling himself when they slowed his pace.

As if to confirm one more time the truth of what he had seen, he paused and looked down at the coin. A ray of light from the windows along the gallery struck the metal, a glint catching the profile of the monarch pressed into the gold. Before he could close his hand, he felt more than actually saw a movement over his left shoulder. He turned and looked.

Dangling from the great chandelier were mud-caked unshod feet slowly twisting away, then toward him again. He let out an unsounded cry, his lungs unable to find the needed air. He wanted to look up, but he'd seen all he could bear to see. He made a rush to the doors leading to the courtyard, this time crashing full speed against the solid wood, the rebound giving him enough space to reach out and lift the latch, the coin digging deep into his palm.

In the courtyard he stood and looked at the thatched roofs

of the sheds. The work was almost done. And beautiful it was, the work of a master's hand. But the master had given him a coin. He had it in his hand. He must be rid of it, and no one must ever hold it again.

He went to the far end of the courtyard, away from the doors of the great hall, away from the thatched sheds. He moved in among the brush. He reached down and wrapped his left hand around the spiky thorns of the furze growing there. With all his might he tugged, but the roots went too deep. He went back, closer to the edge of the courtyard where the soil was softer from the rains. With his fingers he dug down. Then, with his thorn-chewed hand, he scooped up the earth. He dropped the coin into the ground and shoved the soil back in place. He stood. While he was pressing down with his shoe, he heard a voice behind him.

"Peter? Whatever are you . . ."

He stopped, then slowly lowered his shoe and let it rest on the newly tamped earth. Kitty was standing there, amused, curious, eyes wide and mouth open. "Mrs. Sweeney . . . I mean Miss Mc—"

"Don't worry, Peter. Sweeney's all right if that's what comes to mind. It's a name I'll never be ashamed to answer to. But what are you—"

"I . . . I . . . my shoe. I . . . I stepped in a nuisance, and I'm just trying to . . . you know." He wagged the sole of his shoe back and forth on the turned earth. "There. I'm . . . I'm all right now. I didn't want to . . . you know . . . the pedal of my bicycle. It's all right now." He made a show of checking. The sole was clean. He quickly lowered his foot before Kitty could see it.

She laughed. "Good riddance they say."

He started toward his bicycle, keeping himself as far from Kitty as he could. To keep her from asking more questions, he offered what he hoped would be a change of subject. "Did you hear? I'm off to Ballysheen. The horses. My da. My mother, did she tell you? I . . . I . . . I . . ." He righted the bicycle and got on.

"But Declan is gone?"

"Yes. Gone."

"For the day?"

"Yes. For the day."

"And I have something for him. Well, another time."

"Yes. Another time." He grabbed hold of the handlebars. "Well, it's goodbye, then. And Mr. Tovey . . . Ballysheen . . . Goodbye, Miss Mc—Mrs. Sweeney . . ." When he raised a hand to wave it, he almost lost the balance of the bicycle, but was quick enough to make a few turns of the front wheel and head out onto the road.

Puzzled at the boy's peculiar behavior, Kitty watched as he rode off, then looked one more time around the courtyard as if still hoping Declan was there. He decidedly was not. She was mildly disappointed. She had something to give him—something he might accept or refuse, she couldn't be sure. It was Michael's knucklebone. What they had thought at the time was Declan's skeleton had been hidden on the secret stairs the fugitive priests had used to make their escape from the henchmen of the Crown in days gone by. As heaven would have it, two gardaí, Tom and Jim, had inadvertently discovered the stairs while searching for an escaped prisoner. To further call into question heaven's wisdom, Tom found the skeleton's missing knucklebone. Not without reason, he was immediately convinced it was the holy relic of a martyred

Jesuit and had hung it from the rearview mirror of the gardaí car he shared with Jim. It would protect them from all evil and shield them from all harm.

Kitty had stolen it when the car had been left untended. Tom, aghast at the theft, had immediately condemned the deed as sacrilege. He begged the villagers for its return. When the malefactor proved beyond the reach of his plaintive cries, he went to the local priest, Father Colavin. Surely the man would sympathize with his plight and make it his cause to effect the knucklebone's return. Thunderbolts must be dispatched from the pulpit. Anathemas hurled, excommunications threatened.

Father Colavin had listened, letting Garda Tom exhaust himself. To revive him, he gave him a fair shot of Jameson and promised he'd do what he could. He made this pledge in all honesty, knowing full well that little or nothing could be done. As Tom was slugging down the whiskey, the good priest suggested that it should be Tom's prayer that sufficient grace emanate from the knucklebone that the evildoer would repent and return the sacred relic. This was, Tom had to admit, contrary to the curse he'd already called down, but he'd give it a try—a promise he warily made after a second shot of Jameson had followed down the path of the first.

Kitty's purpose had not been to rob Tom of this source of blessing, but to give Declan this least remnant of his lost apprentice. A sentimental gesture, true, but the man was obviously desperate for some token toward which he might direct his grief. How he would react, what he would do, was anyone's guess, and Kitty denied herself the agitation any speculation would bring.

Declan was gone now, but he would be back tomorrow.

She'd complete the transaction then. Before going inside, Kitty decided to see which vegetable from the garden would be suitable for supper. She passed the spot where Peter had been cleaning his shoe. Amused, she shook her head. What could he have stepped in? No manure that she could see. And the dog, Sly, was with the cows all day on the far slope of Crohan Mountain. She had no chickens, no geese. The pig was gone. There'd been no fox, no wolf. Why would Peter lie?—Which is what he'd obviously done. Without taking time to make any surmise, with the toe of her shoe, she began shoving away the dirt that seemed to cover a hole. The boy had not dug down all that deep. She leaned toward where she was digging, then knelt and brought up with her hands more of the soil the boy had so strangely disturbed.

Her car passed Peter on the second hill. She pulled over and stopped, angling the car against the ditch to keep the bicycle from going further. Kitty got out and came toward him, holding up the coin so he would know why she had blocked his progress. Peter began to turn the bicycle around, to go in the opposite direction, but Kitty was close enough to stand in his way.

"Peter! What is it? What's this all about?" She continued to hold up the coin.

"Oh, Mrs. Sweeney, don't! Let it go. Don't hold it up like that. Don't touch it. Please. Please."

Kitty lowered the coin. "What is this? Where did it come from? Why are you so afraid—"

"I . . . I don't know. I did know, but all I can remember is that no one must touch it. Or even see it."

She looked down into her hand. She knew the coin was ancient, its gold not completely dulled by the years. She checked the date. 1785. She took note of the profile. George III. "I see nothing—"

"Then keep it. No, don't. You don't want it. No one wants it. No one *could* want it."

"But why?"

"I . . . I told you. I don't remember why. I really don't. I did . . . and that was enough. But now I—"

"But where did you get it? Did you find it? Where?"

"Mr. Tovey. But, please, don't ask me any more. I have to be home. I'm late. My mother—"

"And did he give it to you?"

"He said . . . and he . . . Ballysheen. The horses. My da. And he . . . and he . . . I . . . Even if . . . Please take it back to him. Make him take it back. He . . . he meant me no harm. Please. I have to be home."

"Oh Peter, Peter, Peter. You'll be all right. Some times I wish the gods would keep their gifts to themselves. But can't you tell me what you saw?"

"I can't."

"But what is it about the coin that—"

"Please. I don't remember. I don't *want* to remember."

Kitty touched his shoulder. "All right, then," she said gently. "You looked at the coin he'd given you. You saw something?"

"Yes."

"Something that frightened you?"

"Yes . . . and then when I went into the castle . . . the coin . . . it . . . it . . ."

"Yes?"

"When I was holding it in my open hand, then . . . then . . ."

"Then?"

"Their feet, up past my shoulder. All muddy and no shoes to wear, and they—"

"You saw—"

"Just the feet. I couldn't—"

"And it was the coin—"

"It . . . it must have been. Nothing was there before. I . . ."

"All right. All right. Don't say anything more. I shouldn't have kept at you like this. I'm sorry."

"But why . . . why?"

"You knew. And now you don't know. It's been that way before . . . when you told my husband and me about our seeing—"

"Brid and Taddy? Was that . . . was that their . . . their feet . . . and no one to wash them?"

"Yes."

"And there's no help for them?"

Again Kitty gently touched his shoulder. "Come. I'll park the car and walk with you until you're home."

"No . . . no . . ."

"It's the least I can do after what I just—"

"Please. I . . . I don't want to be near to what . . . what you have in your hand." He nodded sideways, in the direction of the held coin.

"I understand. Or rather, no, I don't understand. But I accept it . . . that you can't be anywhere near it."

Peter nodded his head in thanks. Kitty lightly touched his cheek, then started toward her car. Before she had gone no more than three steps, she heard Peter say, "I'm going soon to

Ballysheen. The horses. My da. Until I'm back here for school. But I told you about that already. I . . . I'm sorry."

Kitty didn't turn around. "You'll like it there?"

"It's horses. How could I not? Maybe I'm to be a jockey my da thinks."

"You'd like that?"

"Liking it won't be enough. I'm going to be a thatcher. At least that's what I . . . until I . . . the coin . . ."

"So now you're not so sure . . . after the coin. From Declan?"

"Yes," he whispered. "It's from Mr. Tovey. The thatcher."

Kitty nodded to let him know she would question him no more. She continued toward the car.

"Mrs. Sweeney?"

"Yes?"

"You . . . you want to know, don't you? What it was that—"

"Yes. But it doesn't—"

"It does. Maybe it's something you should hear."

"It's too late now. You've forgotten. And that's for the best."

"I . . . I could look again."

Kitty turned back. Peter's head was lowered, his hands at his sides, the toe of his shoe nudging a small stone away from the road. Kitty slowly shook her head. "I don't think you should—"

"But then you'd know. And you want to know."

"Peter, don't do anything that—"

"You'll be here with me. I was alone before. But now you're here."

"You'd really . . ."

He lifted his head and held out his hand. Kitty came to him. She looked into his eyes. How soft they were, their quiet brown. He reached his hand out farther. Kitty gently put the coin into his palm. Peter drew back his hand. He waited a moment. He swallowed. Kitty didn't move. He looked down.

After another moment, without raising his head, he spoke in a low uninflected voice. "They were hanged. His name was Taddy. Her name was Brid. And they the fairest of all the county around. They'd done no wrong. They'd planned no mischief. But they were hanged there in the castle and no one to wash their muddied feet. And the hangman, and there was a woman, too, they were given payment, a coin all gold with a golden king to reward them for their deed. But a shame came over them. They whipped each other with reeds from a thorn bush, but it wasn't enough. So they whipped each other again until the blood came through what they were wearing. They kept the coin hidden between two stones at the side of the hearth, and explained to their children it was a kindly merchant gave it for the offering of themselves and the whipping his lordship had decreed. Because they confessed to their priest and did terrible penance for the rest of their lives, the youthful ghosts do not appear to their descendants as hanged, but as the wandering shades they had become, the same as they present themselves to the descendants of the Sweeneys and the McClouds because they knew nothing of Lord Shaftoe's decree and they were, in the end, innocent even if they were part of the cause of their deaths. But the coin was passed from generation to generation, never spent, so it could be seen how brave the beaten ancestors had been. But it was for the hanging it had been given."

Transfixed, Peter continued to stare, unable to free himself of the vision. Kitty waited, fearful of breaking into his trance. Finally Peter looked up. "Mrs. Sweeney? You're here?"

She answered quietly, "Yes. I'm here."

He blinked, then looked down into his open hand. "No! No! It isn't mine!"

Her voice still quiet, Kitty asked, "May I take it?"

"No. No one should take it. No one should have it. It should belong to no one. Ever. But, yes, take it. Take it away so I won't ever see . . . even . . ."

Careful to touch with only the tips of her fingers the soft flesh of the boy's hand, hoping to show some gentleness, Kitty lifted the coin and drew it away. Slowly she closed it into her fist.

Peter waited, then looked down into his empty hand. He, too, folded his fingers into his palm, then opened them. Assured that he held nothing, he raised his head. "I told you, didn't I?"

"Yes."

"And you haven't forgotten?"

"No, I haven't forgotten."

"Do you want to?"

"No, I don't want to."

"I've forgotten. I forgot already."

"Good."

"But you remember."

"Yes, I remember."

"Maybe I shouldn't have told you."

Kitty shook her head. "You should have told me."

"And I can go home now?"

"You can go home."

"Yes. I'm going home now."

"Will I walk with you?"

"I have my bicycle. It will be enough."

He took the bicycle away from the stone wall where he'd leaned it, got on, and with neither a word nor a glance back, circled the car in the roadway and went up the second of the three hills that would take him home.

Kitty would not rebury the coin. She slipped it into the pocket of her slacks, then patted her thigh to make sure it was safely stowed. She would return it to Declan. Perhaps he already knew the truth. If he didn't, he would know it now. Just as she and Kieran had accepted the burden of shame passed on to them by their ancestors, Declan, too, must bear whatever the truth would lay upon him. It was not impossible he would dismiss it as being nothing of interest to him. He was not famed for the easy activation of his sense of shame. But at least he would know as she already knew, and as Kieran knew, that the consequences of ancestral deeds do not end with the final breath of the departed. They live on. And Declan must make of it what he will. Kitty would do her part.

Again she pressed her hand against her thigh. The coin was there, and the knucklebone as well. It was the coin that would be given.

14

Declan had finished ridging the peaked roofs of the sheds, having felt beneath him the firm cushioning of at least a foot of thatch where the two sides of the roof's pitch met, now capped with the dried sedge he himself had cut from the nearby bog. The sun was already lowering behind Crohan Mountain. He would do the edging of the gables tomorrow and then the work would be done, the castle reasonably restored to its modest but hardly negligible beginnings. It gave him an easy satisfaction that what he was seeing might be close to what his forebears had seen all those centuries past. And it almost saddened him to note that those same ancestors had been denied the sight of the red spikes and white flowers of St. Patrick's cabbage, an outcropping between the castle stones, attesting to its age and its endurance. To him they were celebratory proclamations of the castle's hard-won venerability.

A deeper sadness came over him. Soon all this would be no more. His labors had become a final tribute, an insistence that, at the end, at the moment of its going, the castle would never have been more itself: the crude repository of battles lost and won, of bitter struggles and great rejoicings, of hor-

ror beyond imagining, of sorrows and splendors that told the
tale of his countrymen's glory. He thought it better not to
dwell on the subject for too long, nor to allow himself some
farewell gaze that might challenge his firm resolve. Not only
would Brid and Taddy be released into bliss, but the man who
dared to call himself Lord of the Castle would be dispatched,
his howlings lost in the explosive sounds not heard since cre-
ation itself was unleashed into infinite space, never to find
rest, never to know peace, a fiery hurtling without end. He,
Declan, would see to it.

He saw Kitty standing on the tower ramparts. Thoughts
of her he added to all the others that crowded his mind.
Among his early conquests, she alone had pleaded no unending repetition of the initial event. Although this had been his
usual preference, a quick finish and a final farewell, a preference often enforced with ruthless cruelty, he was unnerved
when the preference was hers, not his own. This was not as
it was supposed to be. She had come to him with no importunings, no pleas, no offers of undying devotion, no threats of
self-immolation. To sustain his self-regard, he had, not quite
convincingly, decided that he had induced a satiety so sufficient that it needed no sustaining reenactments. From this
had come a sense of incompletion, an uneasy feeling that their
relationship remained unresolved. That Kitty herself seemed
to experience no such unease, that she had no further need
of him, was a notion he found impossible to entertain. The
thought did intrude from time to time, forcing him to shake
it off with the ruthlessness heretofore reserved mostly for
the termagants who made it necessary for him to seek refuge
for extended periods in distant places where he would initi-
ate anew the process that would keep him constantly on the
move.

Seeing Kitty now, he quickly suppressed the knowledge that she would be unhoused, that she would leave to teach in Cork this very Saturday, Kieran and the cows accompanying her, computer in tow, never to return to these austere and ghosted halls. Still, he had thatched the sheds. She could see her domain fully restored. And she must have some sense of satisfaction, temporary though it would prove to be.

Whether out of guilt or pity, he most definitely had the urge to go to her now, to experience at her side some final sharing of the castle, of the strange mysteries that, he realized, had bound them together in ways no mere sexual conquest ever could. Brid and Taddy, neither flesh nor blood, had achieved what no seduction, no yielding could accomplish: a common sympathy, a knowledge of the world in all its peculiarity, in all its unsuspected possibilities. Ghost-ridden, he and Kitty were, both of them, bound to this world and to the next. And bound, as well, to each other.

On the first wide landing of the winding stair, he passed through Kitty's work space, her computer and its components already cleared away, and all evidence of a manuscript as well. On the next landing were the loom and the harp, soon to be needed no more. As he was emerging onto the turret platform, he considered going no further. There was Kitty, seemingly caught in some reverie inspired by the late-afternoon light, the grazing cows, and, higher up the mountainside, Taddy with the ghostly pig and Brid down among the cows. Kitty, chatelaine of Castle Kissane, should be allowed some time alone, to see what she was seeing, to muse on what she was musing. Opportunities like this, as he well knew, were severely limited.

When he put his right foot back down onto the step below, he heard Kitty say, "Come, Declan. Please. There's glory enough for more than one."

He climbed the top step. "How did you know I was here? I thought I was making no noise." He had come to her side; he, too, looking out at the nearby slope of Crohan Mountain, the westward sun casting the lengthening shadows of the cows on the grass where they fed. Brid and Taddy and the pig cast no shadows, for they were already shadows themselves. No sun, rising or setting, would ever give them reassuring proof of their existence thrown against a well or stretched out upon the mountain green.

Although Kitty didn't bother to turn toward him when she spoke, he could see, at the periphery of his vision, a faint smile hovering. "Name the woman who's unaware of you, Declan Tovey, and you no more than a few steps away." She faced him directly, "You've been up here before?" The words were only part query, but the rest was said with a certainty that made the questioning intonation irrelevant.

"Often. But a long time ago."

"And you'd see Taddy and Brid."

The words failed to surprise him. Surely the time had come for the two of them to acknowledge openly their shared gift. And the pig, too. Setting his eyes on the mounded top of the mountain, he nodded, then said, "And you, too. Were they the reason you bought the castle?"

"No. I didn't know they were here, nor did Kieran, until I saw them on our wedding day, at the feast in the great hall. I thought they were the last of the squatters who'd been staying here and the two of them dressed as peasants to mock my pretensions in buying a castle. I learned different. And Kieran, too. And then we learned the why of it."

"I always supposed it was the same for you as for me. That somewhere in the past a kindness had been done to them."

"A kindness done? Not a bit of it I'm afraid."

"Oh?"

Taddy and the pig had been joined by Brid, and they were slowly moving toward the top of the hill. Kitty watched, and Declan, too. "It was a McCloud and a Sweeney were to carry out the plot to keep the Lord Shaftoe of that time from living in the county. It would mean the castle destroyed and him, the lord himself, his body sent skyward toward heaven, his soul pitched down to where he was already well known. But they'd gone away, and the two young people taken, then hanged." She brushed a strand of hair fallen to her forehead. "The rest you must know. And maybe what I've already said as well."

"I do."

"How?"

"It doesn't matter, not really."

Kitty considered this, then shrugged her acceptance of the evasion. It was hardly a story she enjoyed telling.

Declan raised an arm and pointed to where Brid and Taddy were making their slow ascent up the mountainside. "See them now. Is it the sunset they want to watch, do you think?"

"Not the sunset itself," Kitty said, "but the sign given that she go to her loom and he to his harp. It's always been so. At sunset, they are there. He to pluck the harp, she to put her foot to the treadle of the loom."

Declan was tempted to say, "That much I know. I've found the book, the catalog, and the notes and diagrams. According to your plan, Taddy would pick up the harp or Brid press down on the treadle, and the flagstones would do their work. But I've improved on that. His lordship will lift the latch to the door to the master bedroom—but you'll be on your way, and his lordship, in the lifting, be sent away as well, but not to

Cork." He said instead, "They come to us because of what was done long before we ever were."

Kitty nodded. "It's a great guilt and a shame that gives them to me and to Kieran."

"I'm sorry for your shame, but it wasn't you and Kieran had done it. Nor your ancestors from cowardice."

"It was a McCloud did it. It was a Sweeney did it. Or failed to do it I should say. The hanging. And you, Declan Tovey?" In a gesture Declan didn't understand, she gripped her thigh as if to reassure herself that something tucked into her pocket was still there, or, more likely she'd felt there a sudden twitch she wanted to calm. With a slow shake of his head, Declan turned his gaze from Kitty out toward the mountain. Brid and Taddy and the pig, too—they were gone. "Are they there now?" he asked. "Brid at the loom? Taddy at the harp?"

"Soon. Wait for the sun to lower a bit."

"And this every day?"

"It would seem so."

"And is it there they spend the night, not needing the sun?"

"I don't know. And I'll do nothing to find out." A lock of hair had fallen to her forehead. With impatience, she brushed it away. "But I asked you a question. And you, you have no guilt? You have no shame?"

"You don't know our story?"

"Rumors are what one hears. But the true story, can you tell it? I'd like to hear."

Declan was confused as to why the woman sounded almost severe. What had he done? What had he said? But he was immediately given the reason: of course she would resent a family history very much the opposite of her own, the hero-ism of his ancestors as opposed to the shame inherited by the

Sweeneys and the McClouds. However, if she insisted, the intensity of her shame would hardly be his fault. His story had hardly been a secret. All through the village, it had been passed on from generation to generation. She must know it already. Of course it made her angry. Now he understood as well the pressure she kept supplying to her thigh. It was to control a rising resentment.

So he began his tale, hesitant, reluctant, the ancestral offer, the scornful refusal. The whipping. And Brid and Taddy hanged for all their want to save them.

When he finished, Kitty's response was close to what he expected, the words clipped, the tone bitter. "And that's the way it happened? That's the true tale?"

He wanted to say something conciliatory, but he could think of nothing. He continued to search the place where only moments before young Brid and Taddy had been. "They're gone," he said quietly. "Why, in their place—or even there beside them—can't there be some vision of young Michael as well? He was even younger, and surely as fair." Slowly he shook his head. "Had I known the boy's fate, would I have cried out my ancestral cry: 'Let me fall and the stone be where I'll lay my head! I will fall. I will die and be taken by the sea'?" Even more slowly his head went from side to side. "I could never have said those words. Descended from heroes, I am a coward. Let it be Michael who dies. I'll not give myself instead. To the boy's fate I give assent. For me it can be no other way. And I'll say no more."

Kitty had taken her hand away from her thigh and placed it, almost tenderly, on the parapet stone. "You have no Michael," she said. "But we'll always have Taddy. We'll always have Brid. And let that be enough." Declan said nothing. Kitty continued. "We will have them all our lives, and no matter what the cause. You have told your family's tale. Now let it go. And we have ours. And that is how it will always be. For us and for them."

The time had come for Declan to go. If he stayed he might let Kitty know how wrong her words had been. Soon Taddy and Brid would be gone forever. The sun was on its way to the Western Sea. Soon Kieran would climb the hill and fetch the cows. Still, Declan felt something that could be said had been left unsaid. And so he said it. "Is it true what's been told? That to free them from the castle, to end what's happening to them, keeping them here, the gunpowder must be found and set off at last?"

Kitty didn't answer. She lifted her hand from the battlement stone, held it there, then slowly rested it where it had been. "How diminished our world would be without them" is all she said.

"But—"

"Yes. I know. We see their sorrow and how bewildered they are. Could they have given their assent to this? Did they want to be here with us and with those who will come after? That they not be forgotten? That what was done to them should never be lost to those who've been given eyes to see? Do we know for certain? Can we be sure of anything? Yes, it's right that we should want to send them to the reward their martyred bodies have earned with all that horror. But is there more to it than that? It's foolish, I know, to even think it. But can't we be forgiven if we want them here? Selfish? Yes. Most likely. Still, all is speculation in the end. But can't it be simply that our pride insists all mysteries must be resolved? And always, according to our interpretations, to justify our own speculations? To be honest, I don't know. Except I would be bereft without them."

"What you say makes no sense."

"Don't I know that? But what sense does it make they're here in the first place? Yes, we want everything to make sense, to be 'understood.' And who would blame us for that? We are born into chaos. We are visited by confusions. Surely we can be forgiven if we misjudge what was intended. If someone who comes after, even if it's kin of mine, and brings all of this to rubble, and Taddy and Brid, they have no earthly home and are gone to a great joy, I'll have no blame to rightly lay on them. Nor should they blame me for not having done what they—our children, or our children's children—decided should be done. And there's the end of it."

Declan, too, lay his hands on the battlement stones. "I'll go now," he said.

Kitty nodded, then, searching the mountainside, perhaps for the vanished ghosts, she said, "I'll stay."

No more was spoken.

When he reached the landing below, Declan paused on the lowest stair. Brid was at the loom. Taddy, the harp held against his chest, was strumming the long-gone strings. Declan crossed the landing, his step hurried, almost desperate.

Kitty looked down and watched the thatcher, once the scourge of the countryside, now mournful as he made his way to his time-battered truck. Never would she confront this man with the coin and thrust at him the truth of what it had revealed. There had been a moment when she'd felt obliged to carry out the pledge she'd made after Peter's harrowing revelation.

So incensed had she been by the boy's distress that only the infliction of the savage facts could begin to compensate for what the coin had done to him.

But Declan had been wounded enough. He had his sorrows, some known, some never to be known. She would become his protector—to the degree that protection was possible. Further woundings might await, but they would not be inflicted by the hand of Kitty McCloud. Not even the knucklebone would she give, a reminder of his loss. It would be returned to the sea, to the one to whom it rightly belonged.

As for the coin, she would see that it was delivered anonymously to his lordship. Not for a moment did she doubt that he would accept it, slavering at its worth, certain that it had come from some secret admirer, grateful for the honor of his acknowledgment on some occasion he felt no need to remember. If the coin carried a curse . . . well, she would not dwell on that.

Declan had arrived at the truck and was hoisting himself up. The door was closed, then the truck started out of the courtyard and up the castle road. When she shifted her gaze back to the mountain, with Taddy gone and Brid as well, and no Michael to take their place, it came to her that Declan, too, was a wandering shade, for all his fleshly presence. What he had considered pursuit was flight. What occasioned this, she would never know—no more than he. But his doom had come down, and release was nowhere to be found. Kitty spoke the words aloud: "Come back again, dear Declan. Here will be the waiting ghosts, I promise you. It may well be that the day will come when they'll be all you have."

The truck made the turn off the castle road and disappeared.

15

Kitty regretted that she'd called Lolly and told her to come collect her pigs, which, by whatever means, seemed to have strayed onto the slope of Crohan Mountain. She should have known they couldn't be Lolly's. The distance was too great from there to here. When the first one had appeared, Kitty surmised that the animal, calmed and fattened under the influence of the sensed presence of its ghostly love, had escaped the butcher's blow and found its way back to the place of its contentment.

But then another pig arrived, and then two more before the morning was done. Annoyed, she phoned Lolly. Lolly, equally annoyed at the absurdity of what she was being told, said she'd check her herd and call back.

She checked her herd. She called back. All her pigs were accounted for. Kitty did not believe this for a moment. Lolly—and only Lolly—in all of Ireland was obstinate enough to continue raising pigs when every other swineherd in the country had surrendered their animals to "intensive." Lolly must come and cart off her beasts without delay. They were not grazing animals, and before too long they would have uprooted the entire mountainside, denuding it of the heather and gorse, robbing Kitty's cows of their next meal. If Lolly weren't there by sundown, Kitty herself would round them up, take them to the slaughterhouse, and pocket the profits.

Kitty had acted precipitously. The next time she checked the mountain, she counted seven pigs. Her exasperation increased. Then, as she was watching from the gallery window of the great hall on the way to her turret study, she saw Taddy and Brid moving among the herd. And, if Kitty was not mistaken, they had been joined by Kitty's own pig, the ghostly one, snuffling with the rest of them, then raising a snout to take in the mountain air. The animal seemed to consider itself in familiar company. Also, none of the pigs was damaging the least bit of turf. They were not being pig-like.

It was when yet another animal appeared (yes, "appeared") in their midst that Kitty stopped breathing. The newly arrived animal had not come up the mountain slope. It was simply there. Kitty exhaled. By her accounting, eight pigs, as ghostly as her own, were gathering on the mountain. This could not be. It must not be.

Unmindful of the thickly strewn straw that tangled her feet, she fought her way across the great hall and out the door to the courtyard. There on the mountain Taddy and Brid seemed to be herding the pigs closer to the top of the hill. With uncommon acquiescence, flicked by no switch, with no hams slapped in encouragement or shins nipped by an officious dog, they slowly moved to higher ground.

They were ghosts come to keep the company of Taddy and Brid. To what purpose she had not the least idea. In her increased exasperation she decided to put the blame on herself. Accept one phantom pig on the premises and before you know it, the place would be overrun—as was happening now. Unchecked, they would claim the entire eastern slope, or more—one massive huddle of swine-backs and hog-hams crowding against each other, obliterating the mountain green. Lolly had better get a move on before Kitty's exasperation exploded into expletives not fit for a castle chatelaine.

Lolly was a pig person. She'd know what to do. But what could that possibly be? Totally inexperienced in the ways of a ghost (except for her recent ill-fated novel), she would be of no help whatsoever. Typical Lolly. Here Kitty was, Lolly's best friend, and what use would Lolly be in this moment of pig crisis? None. None at all. It had been so all their lives, and nothing would change. Ever.

It then occurred to Kitty that she must rescind her demand that the pigs be collected. Should Lolly arrive, no pigs would she see. And, not without cause, she would consider Kitty deranged. Kitty would be ridiculed. As eager as Kitty considered herself for Lolly's happiness, this particular form of enjoyment, her ridicule, was not within the prescribed limits.

As she started for the phone, she realized that it was to her benefit that Aaron was not coming instead of his wife. A McCloud like herself, he'd see the phantom pigs. He'd be amused. He'd return to his wife and—

A sudden realization entered Kitty's mind, scattering all other concerns beyond the farthest reaches of the four winds, and appropriating to itself every mental faculty and more than several of her emotional ones. It caused her jaw to drop and her eyes to widen into an unblinking stare. Her nephew Aaron was not her nephew. Far, far worse: he wasn't even a McCloud. It had come to her like a blow struck by an uncaring fist.

Aaron had not seen her own phantom pig. Nor had he

ever seen Brid or Taddy when they were manifestly present to any McCloud with eyes to see. Her oldest brother, in America, was vindicated. He had claimed years ago, at the time of his divorce, that his wife, herself a Kerry woman, had sullied her heritage, to say nothing of her marriage, by a susceptibility to a man emigrated to America from County Cavan, a susceptibility she chose not to resist.

Kitty's mother had been resolutely contemptuous of her son's insistence. No daughter of Kerry would degrade herself to such a depth as to consort with a Cavan man. Kitty had seen no reason to contest her mother's responses. She subscribed to it with an ease reserved exclusively for any and all denigrations particular to her brothers.

This, in turn, had allowed her, from the first, to welcome the gawky and bewildered boy—her presumed American nephew Aaron—and do what she could to remake him, during their childhood summers together at her ancestral home, in her own image: a transformation not spectacularly successful, but sufficient for her to invest in him a durable affection and an amused indulgence for his considerable shortcomings.

Slowly Kitty closed her mouth. Deliberately she blinked her eyes. Her spine stiffened; her mind was calmed. The new knowledge was still there, but her resolve was more than a match for its invasive presence. Never would she permit this revelation to reach her onetime nephew. More than sufficient was her old affection that she would, under all circumstances, spare him the devastation that would attend his being told he was not a McCloud. For her to rob a man of what was obviously his most valued possession would make mandatory her own damnation. The archangel's Edenic expulsion of Adam and Eve would become, by comparison, a casual inconvenience.

Love, born of pity, flooded her entire being. For the first time she cared deeply, very deeply for this man, now cast out, bereft of a lineage that had been blessed by the gods going back to the Druid days of yore. His secret was safe. He would never know of his newly revealed nullity. His no-longer-aunt Kitty McCloud would see to that. If she could extend a dispensation from unwelcome knowledge to Declan Tovey, she could do no less for her hapless ex-nephew.

Kitty's follow-up phone call was too late. Aaron informed her that Lolly was on her way. He added that his wife considered the trip a fool's errand and that Kitty should be prepared to be labeled the fool. As much as she resented the obvious pleasure he took in her imminent humiliation, it saddened her to hear his cheerful voice. Little did he know she possessed the means to wipe this and any future smile from his slaphappy face. And even less did he know she would never be so cruel as to use the deadly weapon so recently placed at her disposal.

The truck drove into the courtyard before Kitty had time to hang up.

Lolly greeted her friend with an enthusiasm that boded no good. Lolly was apparently anticipating an easy triumph. To respond in kind, Kitty waved with no less enthusiasm. She called out Lolly's name. She let out a trilling laugh that sickened her, so blatantly false was it, so obviously fake. "It's all right," Kitty yelled. "It's been taken care of."

Lolly slammed the door of the truck. "What's all right? What's been taken care of? I didn't come here to make sure everything was 'all right.' Where are these crazy pigs so I can prove they're not mine?"

"Oh, Lolly. Dear Lolly. You're in luck. The pigs. They've wandered off. Where they've gone, I haven't the slightest. Maybe an accident on the road and the poor darlings all scattered, like when . . . well, you remember. When Aaron first came and your truck tipped into the ditch and all the pigs . . . Well, something like that must have happened. And just like you then, whoever they belonged to found them and drove them back to where they'd come from." Her voice slowed, try as she might to sustain the pitch needed for her disingenuous explanation—during which time five more pigs appeared. Recovered, Kitty continued as best she could. "And took them away. From here. From the mountain. Where they . . . where they were when I phoned you."

"Oh?"

"Look. Look there. The mountain. You can see. They're not there. Where they were. Do you see any pigs?"

There were now twenty-two by Kitty's count. A nervous laugh tickled her throat. All she needed was for Lolly to actually see the pigs. To assuage her fear, she repeated herself. "Any pigs? Do you see any? Any pigs?"

"It's slop time at home and I'm here and Aaron has to do the slopping all by himself. Lucky he knows what to do. From when I was . . . you know. When I was writing my . . . well, you know."

"Then you . . . you don't see any pigs? Am I right?"

"I see Kitty McCloud, who should rightly be called Sweeney, trying to convince me I shouldn't be annoyed coming all this way for nothing. And Aaron having to do everything."

Kitty had every right to inform her friend that she should no longer rightfully be called McCloud, but the time had come for Kitty to test her restraint. With effort, she passed the test and simply said, "Tell him I apologize. And I apologize to you, too. I'm the last person to cause anyone an inconvenience."

"Oh? And when did that cosmic change come about? Must be within the last three minutes."

"I don't blame you—"

"Thanks."

Kitty decided she'd had enough of Lolly's sass. "Oh, Lolly, let it go. So Aaron gets to empty the swill buckets into the trough. There are enough tragedies in the world. This needn't be added. Heavens to Betsy—as they definitely did *not* say in the Bronx—what would you like me to do? Lick your face all over?"

"Please!" Lolly looked as if she might throw up.

"Please lick it? Is that what you're saying? 'Kitty, love, lick my face all over'?" Relieved by the image she'd summoned, Kitty laughed a genuine laugh.

"Kitty—don't. Now you're going to make *me* laugh. And I'm in no mood—"

"And isn't a laugh better than a lick?"

"Stop! I can't!" Lolly laughed.

And Kitty laughed as well.

When the sounds subsided, Kitty, her normal voice restored, said, "We go away two days from today. You'll come to supper tomorrow? To make up for driving all this way. If compensation is possible after all your trouble. A grand farewell, even if we're not gone for that long."

"I'll give it some thought."

To Kitty's surprise, she sounded somewhat tentative. "You have other plans?"

"Plans?" Lolly hesitated, then continued, her tone even less assured. "No, of course not. What other plans could I possibly have? You know my . . . I mean our . . . our routine seldom varies. Sometimes Aaron goes off to Dockery's pub, and I . . . well, I find ways to . . . to amuse myself. So, yes, yes. Delighted. Of course we'll come. Since you'll be going away . . . even if it's not for that long."

Kitty didn't like what she was hearing, her friend uncertain as she had been when she'd been practicing the art of fiction. Lolly seemed thrown off course by the simple invitation. It wasn't that extraordinary. They came to supper not infrequently, Kieran reluctant as he was to limit the achievements of his culinary gifts to his wife alone. Why the hesitation now?

An unwelcome thought came into her head. It was prompted not only by Lolly's present conduct but by what Lolly had said that day at the cliff. How eager she seemed to have Declan away. And then, talking of his grief for the boy buried in the garden, she'd said nothing would be of help. Then she'd added, "*Almost* nothing." Kitty had sometimes wondered what "almost" meant. Several interpretations offered themselves, one so absurd it made Kitty a bit ashamed to have thought of it. But it kept recurring from time to time. Kitty did all she could to dismiss it, but with limited success. Lolly's marriage to Aaron seemed happy enough. He'd even taken an interest in her pigs. And Lolly had appreciated his indulgence during the dread days when she'd taken on the joys of being a writer.

That Lolly had residual feelings for Declan was understandable. But was she doing anything to stir up the residue? What exactly might be going on? Kitty's immediate response to this kind of thinking was a fear for Aaron. With her new-found sympathy came a determination that no harm come to her non-nephew. Kitty would never allow him to be met with any untoward difficulties. He had been sufficiently deprived to exempt him from any further deprivations. Lolly must never be, like Aaron's Kerry-born mother, "a woman of susceptibilities."

Now a somewhat more appealing thought took precedence over all others. Maybe she could trick Lolly into revealing more than she might want—more, surely, than the mild suspicion that had already been aroused. Now could be a time of testing. It would be an unfair and despicable thing to do to her best friend—which meant that Kitty hesitated not at all and proceeded forthwith.

"And Kieran thinks Declan should be invited as well." (Kieran had thought nothing of the kind.)

"Declan?"

"Our thanks for the thatching. It seems the least we can do. Since he's refused all payment, not even the cost of the reed."

"Invite Declan?" Lolly seemed not to understand what Kitty was saying.

"Fine work, don't you think? And the courtyard restored to the way it's meant to be."

"Yes. Very fine. Very."

"Say what you will about Declan Tovey, he's a master at whatever he does, don't you agree? And now the sheds are done and he's the one did it. How can we not be grateful? Before he leaves again for who knows where or for how long, we should surely offer him a hearty meal to speed him on his way. You agree?"

"Well—"

"Oh, so we both have a history with Declan, but we've changed so much since those days. And nights. Even I. And you, too, what with Aaron your husband and all."

"Yes, of course, but—"

"You have an objection?"

"I did presume it was to be just family . . . and you and Kieran going away, and the cows, too . . ."

"Lolly, if it embarrasses you to have him and Aaron here at the same time—"

"Oh, no, not that. Why . . . why would I be embarrassed when . . . when—"

"When it all happened so long ago and we can hardly remember?"

"Well, yes, that of course—"

"And to think how intimate we were with what we thought were his bones. Washing them and sticking them back inside his clothes, using the same hands that . . . well, I needn't remind *you* of all people. But you prefer I don't ask him?"

"Not if you want to. But . . . but . . ."

"Yes?"

After she'd taken a deep breath, Lolly, resigned and impatient, said, "Oh Kitty, you needn't invite even us—and you getting ready for your time away—packing, making arrangements, probably preparing for those classes, and the cows besides . . ."

Kitty was not quite ready to let the testing end. "Let me hear none of that. Of course it's a sacrifice. But consider for whom it's being made. Do you forget that you're the wife of Aaron, my favorite nephew? It will be a feasting none of us will ever forget. Never mind sacrifice. Remember who you are. You're Lolly McCloud."

"I . . . I'll mention it to Aaron. We do have chores of our own, don't forget."

To show her acceptance of this generous consideration,

Kitty, with a muted chuckle, reached out and touched Lolly's cheek.

Lolly, in reflex, as if avoiding a contagion, withdrew, then quickly leaned forward to accept the gesture. Taking advantage of the intimacy, Kitty, her voice low to indicate confidentiality, said, "Lolly, you're not doing anything foolish these days, are you?"

Lolly slowly pulled away. "Kitty, whatever are you talking about?"

Immediately Kitty repented. She'd been too explicit. "Nothing. Really. Nothing at all."

"Oh? It didn't sound like nothing to me. Out with it Caitlin Sweeney." Her voice firm, she continued. "I'm standing here, waiting to learn your very own definition of 'nothing.' "

Dipping quickly and deeply into resources that, on more than one occasion, had rescued her from herself, Kitty, as dismissively as possible, said, "I mean . . . well . . . and you'll have to forgive me . . . I meant you're not writing another novel, are you? I mean . . . see what a foolish thing I had in mind?"

"And why on earth would I—would anyone—want to write a novel?"

"Because . . . because that's what one is born to do. I mean, I write a book because that's what I was born to do." Kitty realized that now *she* was the defensive one. She had no choice but to go on. "Just as you were born to be a swineherd. Which means you don't have to write a book. You get to raise pigs. Because that's what you were born to do. And I . . . I withdraw the question."

Looking directly into Kitty's eyes, Lolly, in tones that managed to sound both indifferent and menacing, said, "You can invite Declan if you want. If that would please you. I'll be there, and Aaron, too." After holding her gaze fast for three seconds more, she turned and went to her truck, got inside, and closed the door with no more than a barely audible click. Through the open window she called out, "And I've never done a foolish thing in my entire life!" She revved the motor three times, then added, "Not like some I could name!"

She drove off.

After the truck had made the turn off the castle road, Kitty said quietly, but aloud, "I wronged her." Silently, to herself, she continued the thought. It could very well be that Lolly, determined to send Declan off to a thatching job near Connemara, was desperate to rid herself of a temptation that was threatening to grow beyond the strength of her endurance. *That* was why she had come to the cliff, to the sea, to find him. Kitty, aloud, repeated the words, "I wronged her."

The pigs were still on the mountain. There were now more than thirty of them.

16

The day of departure had arrived. Kitty and Kieran, with a questionable assist from their dog Sly, had started the cows down the far side of Crohan Mountain. The truck was parked on the road below, ready and waiting for the journey to Kieran's brother's place, south of Blarney, not far from Cork. The sun still shone on the top of the hill but would soon begin its descent down the western slope and into the sea. Kieran was anxious to get the cows away and settled in their new quarters. They had yet to be milked.

The meal the evening before, with no Declan in evidence, had been a mixed success. Kitty had phoned Lolly and apologized for her mention of Lolly doing anything foolish. It was, Kitty admitted, she who had been the fool, and Lolly must forgive her. Kitty refrained from adding "just as I've forgiven you more times than even God remembers." Because this last was left unsaid, Lolly not only forgave but brought to the table an inordinate amount of good cheer and warm humor. Kitty at one point had begun to wonder if her leaving was the source of all this fond fellowship, but, in the interest of keeping the event celebratory, she decided not to pursue that line of thinking.

In deference to Aaron, Kieran had prepared an American meal: corned beef and cabbage, but with an Irish element— potatoes—added for local color.

Not long into the conversation, after they had given most of their talk to Kitty's coming defense of her writings in the guise of teaching, Lolly herself cheerfully introduced the subject of Declan's supposed burial and the new knowledge about the substitute skeleton put into the cabbage patch. There was, in Lolly's manner, not the least hint that talk of Declan was anything to be avoided; nor did it seem that she'd introduced it as a pretext for giving him a presence at the feast. Kitty had indeed wronged her friend. She had spoken the truth when she'd named herself the fool. The conversation proceeded with easy amusement and communal good cheer.

Soon enough they were speaking of the confessions each had made, since it had been assumed that Declan Tovey was not only dead but murdered. Each now explained the motive for his (Kieran's) and her (Kitty's and Lolly's) claim to be the perpetrator.

Because Kitty had been the first to confess on the night of the wake, she admitted she was protecting Lolly, who, she had most fervently believed, had done the deed in vengeance for Declan's earlier seduction of her, Kitty's, chaste self, a sisterly act deserving a no less sisterly sacrifice.

Kieran confessed that, in truth, it was not because Declan had called Kitty a cow-face, but that he had believed either Lolly or Kitty had committed the murder, since each was jealous of the other and more than capable and competent to perform the act. As a gentleman, he could hardly allow either of them to be called to account. They were women, and he, a man, could do no less than take it all upon himself.

Lolly, in gratitude, kissed his cheek. Kitty seemed not quite so taken with his gallantry. To ease his wife's disappointment that she alone was not the motive, he added, as something of a footnote, that he had indeed been tempted to murder the man—for the very reason given as he'd stood at the side of the coffin. Declan, he had been told, *had* called Kitty a cow-face. It was only through the direct intervention of Kieran's sainted mother in heaven that he had resisted the murderous impulses and let the man continue to live.

For whatever reason, this seemed not to improve Kitty's mood. She continued to give Kieran a sideways stare that could easily be the envy of the basilisk itself. Lolly chose to be unaware of her friend's discontent and gleefully told those assembled that she had confessed to protect her friend Kitty. After all, it seemed only right that Kitty had done it. Hadn't Declan moved on to herself, Lolly McKeever, once he'd found Kitty McCloud not that much to his liking? Small wonder that Kitty had done what she'd done and Lolly, as her best friend, had no choice but to confess in her stead.

Before Kitty could do anything she might regret, Kieran called out, "Apple Brown Betty anyone? Kitty herself made it, a recipe all the way from the Bronx in the United States of America." Kitty, to avoid being the cause of Lolly's extinction, then and there added, in tones lofty and agreeable, that the Brown Betty was consistent with the American theme established by the corned beef and cabbage. This was, after all, just one more occasion when she'd had to deflect the entice- ment to murder Ms. McKeever and mar the occasion with her blood. This was one of her much practiced social graces, and she put it into effect with what's called aplomb. The evening, sustained by a steady flow of stout and Tullamore Dew, ended with farewells characterized by hugs and kisses that managed not to deteriorate into tears.

•

The greatest challenge on the mountainside was to keep the cows moving, discouraging them from grazing along the way. The phantom pigs congregating on the other side of the hill—their number now beyond counting—had been avoided by skirting the lower slope and making the ascent that morning on this farther side. Neither the cows nor the dog seemed disconcerted by the pigs' presence, proof of what Kitty and Kieran assumed: their animals saw and sensed nothing out of the ordinary. Wordlessly, they gave thanks.

Sly trotted through the herd, barking and nipping, but to little effect. It would be up to Kieran and Kitty to do a dog's work and get the cows to the bottom of the mountain before the sun had set and the moon risen high.

Assured by Declan Tovey that the castle "tenants" were off rounding up their cows and would not return until near sundown, George Noel Gordon Lord Shaftoe, costumed in the manner of his ancestor, pulled the Bentley off the road and brought it to a stop in a copse a fair distance from the castle. He slipped into a Burberry trench coat, carefully placed the tricorn hat on his abundant wig, and began the trek across the darkening field.

His plot, well laid, was about to fulfill itself, his apparitional appearance certain to affright the usurpers to the point of madness, thereby making their abandonment of the castle an absolute certainty. The vision of a ghost, dimly lit by a single candle, would without doubt send them fleeing, never to return. To rescue their sanity and cut their losses, they would respond favorably to an offer made through an intermediary that would transfer the castle into his lordship's possession. How could they refuse? The offered sum would be most generous, considering that he was taking on property inhabitable only by one not susceptible to the terrors induced by a spectral presence. Surely his plan was a work of genius. Who but himself could have conceived of such an inspired solution to his difficulty? A ghost of all things!

As he crossed the field, the intensity of his self-regard threatened to explode his swelling breast. He must temper his expectations for the time being. The moment of triumph was at hand, and he must forbid himself all satisfactions until, candle aloft, he would make his lordly progress through the then vacated rooms and halls, taking full possession from the defected pretenders who, by then, would be far off, babbling incoherent prayers to all the appropriate saints who cluttered their abominable religion.

Then, and only then, would he declare himself Lord of Castle Kissane, faithful descendant, fearless heir, scion of Shaftoe, most worthy of that name.

After he had surveyed the courtyard, making certain he was alone, his lordship crossed to the portals leading into the great hall. As Mr. Tovey had promised, the door was unlocked. (He must increase his countryman's reward, munificent as it already was.)

Inside, the animal stench almost felled him, unaccustomed as he was to the unmediated smells of nature. With considerable resolve, he kicked his way through the repellant mounds of straw, then divested himself of the Burberry and touched the tricorn hat to make sure it was in place. Arrayed to the full, his justaucorps unbuttoned to give proper display to the heavily embroidered under-jacket, to say nothing of the lace-trimmed scarf that concealed the wattles dangling from his neck, he was forced to ward off again the thrills that imperiled the health of his throbbing heart.

He reached down and from the Burberry pocket extracted the assigned candle. A cigarette lighter did the honors, then was extinguished and tucked into the pocket of his under-jacket. It was there that he felt the single artifact that would unimpeachably declare the authenticity of his presentation. He withdrew the gold coin that had been mysteriously— nay, miraculously—delivered into his hands no doubt from some shy admirer, its kingly imprint more than suggesting that his deed had been approved, even blessed, by powers devoted to the rights of those who could justifiably reclaim what had been royally given.

He held the coin near the candle's glow. Glints of gold flickered from its surface, assurance that greater riches lay beneath. Higher he held it in an outstretched hand, his gaze transfixed by all it proclaimed.

A great cry came from his stopped throat. The coin, the candle, fell. For one paralyzed moment, he stared up toward the iron chandelier. There, before his lordly eyes, a young woman, perhaps still a girl, and a young man, perhaps still a boy, were hanging by thick raw nooses, their eyes about to spring from their sockets, their tongues disgorged through their swollen lips.

He stumbled away. The fallen candle had lighted the straw, the coin nowhere to be seen. Another cry, meant to be the terrifying word *fire*, came out but was unable to form itself. Twice he stomped on the blaze, but the flames were spreading. Too fast, too fast, their light was thrown toward the slowly turning bodies. The straw, as he forced his way through, caught at his buckled shoes. Twice he slipped, barely managing to right himself as he lunged toward the doors. His first try at the latch was unsuccessful. He banged on the wood, then tried the latch again. The door swung open. Out he stumbled, into the courtyard. Without a backward glance he ran to the castle road, bounded over a stone wall, then ran through the field the way he'd come.

He stopped where he'd left the car and looked back toward the castle. Lightning seemed to strike and thunder to crack, coming not from the sky but from the earth itself. The castle, astonished at this unexpected marvel, lighted up all its windows with more candle power than it had ever known. The walls stiffened, the stones held alert in this dumbfounding moment, surprised that the end had been announced. Then, released, they were sent up, up, until they reached a height beyond which they had been forbidden to go. Briefly they held themselves, unmoving, as if in disbelief that their seemingly limitless rise was subject to restriction. Then, in surrender to forces they had failed to conquer, they plummeted down, down in an angry roar, a storm of broken stones, bringing with them in their return the fragmented frame of a silenced harp and the dismembered remnants of an unthreaded loom. The tower, the austere rooms, the limed walls became a tumbling of debris, heaping itself in a growing mound that spread into the courtyard, collapsing the sheds, undoing the thatch.

Rising from it all, a massive cloud of ashes and of dust obscured in mercy the rubbled ruin that marked the ancient site where Castle Kissane had stood in modest majesty.

His lordship, without waiting for the dust to settle, began to whimper.

•

When the rumbling roar came from the other side of the mountain, both Kitty and Kieran were nearing the bottom of the slope, the cows lumbering ahead toward the waiting truck. They stopped: cows, Kitty, and Kieran. The cows then continued on, but Kitty and Kieran looked directly at each other. Neither moved. Then Kieran began to run up the hill but went no further than a thick growth of furze. Kitty was soon at his side. "Declan! No!" she cried.

Kieran had to shout to be heard. "Declan? Why Declan?"

"He did this. I know he did. He—"

Admitting the futility of words, she stopped. And Kieran himself could say nothing more. Nothing had been seen; everything heard. Then all sound ceased, even the clattering of the last few sifting stones, pebbles they must be, sounding like rain on a state roof. A cloud of dust was taking possession of the early evening air. Kitty had clapped her hand over her mouth. Kieran reached across her shoulders and drew her close.

There, toward the top of the hill where the dust cloud had yet to reach, the sun catching them in the last rays before its western descent, were Taddy and Brid, moving slowly, hesitantly, as if in response to a confused summons they were not sure they should follow. Taddy was slightly ahead.

Kitty called out, "No! Don't! Don't leave!"

After Brid and Taddy had gone a few more steps, Brid turned and looked toward where the dust of the fallen castle was rising. She reached out her hand as if in anguished farewell to the place where she had endured her exile. Taddy touched her shoulder. Her head bowed low, she turned away. On they went, no longer slow. Taddy held high his head with a newfound dignity. As they approached the waiting sun, Taddy stopped, then Brid. Again she turned. This time she was looking directly down at Kitty and at Kieran, an acknowledgement of their presence never given before. With her right hand she lightly touched the raw rope that collared her slender and youthful throat. Taddy, too, turned to look at them. He raised his arm, his hand palm outward, a farewell salute to Kitty and to Kieran, but also a resigned gesture to the place of his bewildered sorrows.

"No!" Kieran's voice was hoarse, pleading. "Taddy! Brid! No!"

"Let them go," Kitty said softly.

The fine young man, the fair young maid, lowered their heads as they turned away one final time and began again their fated ascent up the hill. Their drab clothing began to take on a radiance, as if some luminous threads had been woven into the coarse cloth. The raw ropes around their necks, caught in the last rays of the lowering sun, began sprouting delicate leaves of greenest laurel, sweet and soothing, an economical equivalent of a martyr's golden crown. And then, as Kitty and Kieran watched, the sun's radiance received into itself the radiance of the man so fine and the maid so fair.

"Remember us," Kitty whispered.

Aaron heard a distant sound and felt a slight rumbling of the kitchen floor beneath his feet. He attributed the phenomenon to the words he was reading, scrawled on the opposite side of a printout he'd made that morning from the third chapter of a new novel concerning a man who forgives his errant and unworthy wife for running off with a baritone she had met in a church choir. Aaron had difficulty focusing on the exact words, but there was little need. The message was clear. His wife, Lolly, had gone off with Declan Tovey. He, Aaron, was to make sure the pigs were slopped on schedule, since they had been bequeathed to him in perpetuity. Stupefied as he was, he felt some slight sense of relief. No more would he have to be a writer. He was given at last a less solitary calling. And he would be faithful—to his pigs.

When the dark had come down, Tom and Jim, the local gardaí, were keeping watch over the ruins. The dust had settled and a cold wind had brought a mist in off the sea that had found its way to the last of Castle Kissane. There was a full moon that could shed but a dim and shrouded light onto the broken stones and the fallen beams.

Nothing stirred. Then, in a slight lifting of the mist, Tom and Jim saw him there among the few stones standing where the tower had been. It was none other than the ghost they should have expected. He was in all his finest raiments, Lord Shaftoe himself from centuries long past, the gold and crimson embroidering of his inner coat catching the glancing of the moon. Glistening in the mist and in the dark were the buckles of gold that graced his fine-tooled shoes. On his head a tricorn hat was placed on his artfully arranged tresses.

He had come at last to take possession of Castle Kissane, the castle he had fled to escape the explosives that had now fulfilled their appointed task. From side to side he slowly cast his gaze over the mounded rubble, the settled dust, lord indeed of all he surveyed. The castle now was his, and no one, least of all Tom and Jim, must challenge his return. Too terrified to cry out, the men simply opened their mouths and let the mist seep in.

The soiling prophesied by his lordship was awarded to Tom.

•

The final words would be Kitty's. The cows were safely aboard the truck. Convinced that nothing was salvageable, Kitty and Kieran had agreed that others would be assigned to deal with the ruin. They never wanted to see it again. Before getting inside for the stunned and grieving ride, they became aware of unfamiliar sounds. They looked behind them and saw nothing but the darkening mountain. Then Kitty noticed, on the ground about ten feet up the hill, a snout ring that could have come only from a pig. She went and picked it up. It had been broken, the circle interrupted by a jagged opening as if the metal had been fiercely hit against a stone. It was not unlike the ring found near the breached wall the day the pig, still corporeal, had hinted at where the gunpowder plans were buried near the castle orchard.

She turned it over in her hand. It could not be the same ring; all its characteristics suggested the opposite. Just as she was about to fling the ring even farther up the hill, Kieran said, again in a whisper, "Kitty, look."

Kitty turned and saw where the unfamiliar sounds were coming from. There, out on the sea, was a massive herd of swine stepping easily on the bars of lingering light that crested the waves. In the lead was a particular pig well-known to the observers. It seemed to be showing those that followed the way that they must go. At first, the sound was the usual clamor expected from a gathering of pigs, screams and squeals, snorts and screeches that had always sent heavenward their least complaint. But soon the cacophony became transposed and transformed into what could only be termed a celestial anthem, a towering chorale of highest praise. Their wailings and torments now become harmonies and chords of surpassing beauty, as if their suffering had been exalted into a hymn of highest glory, lifted above the waves into a receptive sky.

Kitty, Kieran at her side, looked down at the snout ring in her hand. She felt, across her shoulders, the lightest touch, no more than a passing breeze that had chosen to go no further, as if a weightless mantle had descended upon her. She made no move to shrug it off.

Her voice, uninflected but firm, said, "There was a runt pig given by the Widow Colville to a youth named Taddy who had cut her winter turf. Faithfully the piglet was nurtured, fed with food meant for the young man himself. It grew healthier by the hour under his tender care. A secret gift known to no one but himself, it was to be given to a fair young maid named Brid, then given back to him at their marriage, the dowry her family could never afford. But the two were hanged, and on that day, at that moment, the pig disappeared into the wild. From then on, its descendants, now ghosts themselves, like the fine youth and the fair maid for whom the nurtured pig had been intended, whenever there was a confluence of the full moon and the ancient celebration of Lughnassadh, the Festival of Bread, would appear on the western slope of Crohan Mountain, a sign to Brid and Taddy that they, too, were waiting for the distant day when they would all be freed from the ghostly bondage decreed by the ghastly hanging. That day has come. They'll come no more: not Brid, not Taddy, and never more the pig."

Kitty fell silent, keeping within her heart another bit of revealed truth. From the angle and the direction of the march the exultant pigs were taking, it was apparent that they were headed, as had been so many other Irish before them, for a city in the United States of America called Boston.

Acknowledgments

With this publication of the third book of my trilogy, I want to take particular note of Delphinium Books and its publishers, Cecile Engel and Lori Milken, and of their marketing director, Carl Lennertz. In contrast to the innumerable corporate houses that rejected these books with their honest admission that they "didn't know how to market them," Ms. Engel, Ms. Milken, and Mr. Lennertz took on the risks that had so affrighted their craven competitors and made possible the book you hold in your hand. To them, many thanks—which I hope is commensurate with their self-assured audacity. Also, and not for the first time, I express my gratitude to Noelle Campbell-Sharpe and her Cill Rialaig Project in County Kerry, Ireland, where I was given hospice and experienced a sustained inspiration. Similar privileges and sustenance were provided by Yaddo and the MacDowell Colony. My gratitude gives a measure to infinity. My agent, Wendy Weil, and her incomparable associates, Emily Forland, Emma Peterson, and Ann Torrago, define the words *tenacious, faithful,* and *encouraging.* My appreciation is as unbounded as is their continuing dedication. Help and encouragement also came from friends: Van Varner, Daniel D'Arezzo, David Barbour, and Candace Wait. The librarians of the Saratoga Springs Public Library and the Peterborough Free Library gave eager and generous assistance. Then there is Christopher Lehmann-Haupt, whose depth of involvement as editor was as rare as it was welcome. As the beneficiary of all this needed help, I consider myself the most fortunate writer I know.